D.M. MARLOWE

EYE
OF THE
NINJA

Eye of the Ninja Chronicles

This is a work of fiction. Characters and events portrayed in this book are fictitious and not to be construed as real. Any similarity to actual events or persons, living or dead is entirely coincidental and not intended by the author.

Eye of the Ninja
Copyright 2015 by D. M. Marlowe
Cover Design by Claudia McKinney

For more information:
www.dmmarlowe.com

For my Youngest: For being my first reader, Mei's first fan and my all-around, head-banging, car-singing counterpart.

To Lindsey

YA Dictionary Player

Extraordinaire!

Enjoy RT!

D.M. Marlowe

Watch for the next exciting installment of the Eye of the Ninja Chronicles:

Obsidian's Eye

Coming December 2015

Table of Contents

Chapter One

Knees pumping, I run straight toward the wall. *Almost*. At the last possible second I breathe deep and give a little hop. One foot hits the low ledge on the perpendicular wall and I push off hard, launching straight up.

There. My fingers just caught the highest rail atop the wall. Easy enough to pull myself up and over, after that.

Whistles and clapping echoed up from below. "Nice, Mei!"

I grin, careful to keep my gaze lowered. Nodding a quick acknowledgement of the praise, I move away so the next freerunner could take a stab at this particular obstacle.

"Not bad for a girl!" someone called, teasing.

I pull my cap low and flip a casually insulting gesture in their general direction. The late afternoon sun beat down and I took refuge in a shaded corner, crouching down to watch the ever-shifting group below. My family was gone now. Close friends were not really an option. But these free-spirited parkour dudes? They might possibly be overly dedicated to the art of motion and a few of them were definitely far gone in love with their oversized sweatpants—but still, as friends went . . . well, they came as close as I could allow.

Once everyone who was interested had taken a stab at the wall, we moved on, ranging over the university campus. I vaulted over a low wall, shook my head over Ben's tumble pass between buildings, and managed a halfway decent copy of Alan's wall spin. It felt good to move, to train. I'd been more tense than usual lately. On edge. Fighting to not look over my shoulder. But the first rule, when you are being hunted, is not to look like prey. So I carry on with my usual routine. And now I allow myself to relax, just the smallest bit. No judgment here, no prying, insistent curiosity. I let the tightness in my chest ease and tried to remember what it felt like to be at ease and happy instead of wary, bitter and sad.

The group spread out when we hit the Stoneyard. I took up a position on the edge and watched a kid named Chris make a complicated, spinning double cork look easy.

"You've got to teach me how to do that," I breathed.

It looks like a nice way to dodge an arrow, or a thrown dart.

I froze. Though the thought had been my own, I'd heard it in my father's distinctive accent and thoughtful tone.

I clenched my fist hard, welcomed the bite of nails into the flesh of my palm. That is not the thought of a normal teenaged girl.

I was in no way a normal teenaged girl—but I had to appear as one. At all costs.

Chris just grinned. "You've already got your cheat gainer. All you need to do is tighten up and get some more pull."

We worked on it a bit.

"Do you want to try it without the extra weight?" He gestured toward my backpack.

I shook my head. I always kept my pack close.

He shrugged and didn't seem to mind the normal stance I took when I was in contact with people; cap pulled low and tight, eyes down, but ear cocked to show I was paying attention. I knew the guys wondered about me. I'd once heard someone speculate that I was vision impaired, but had highly developed other senses, like a real life comic book character. I didn't think that any of them had guessed the truth—that I was a real life freak.

Over and over, I crouched low and threw myself into the air. One benefit to a lifetime of training—I usually pick up new stuff quickly. After a few tries and a couple of pointers I was managing a credible cork, if not the graceful double that Chris was throwing.

"Let's finish over at Centenary," someone suggested. "At the bridge."

A chorus of agreement rang out. We set off, flowing across campus like water. We got some attention from other students, catcalls and taunts along with cheers and whistles whenever someone broke out a flip, trick or vault. At one point we pass by a group of protesters, all wearing the designer masks that were so widespread just a few short years ago.

The Filters are a Lie! Their signs shout it. **Protect Yourself from the Poison in the Air!**

I duck my head and settle my cap low and firm over my brow. It's surprisingly easy to go through life without meeting anyone's direct gaze. I live on the fringes, barely seen, hardly noticed. I am a creature of the shadows. It's only with these guys that I take the risk of discovery—and it's worth it. It feels so good to be part of a group, to be easily accepted into the larger dynamic, even though I don't say much. To train and run and sweat and work with people who understand the joy of it. My movement speaks for me, in this group.

"The filters are a fraud. The filters are a fraud." The group chants now. One girl steps forward, her passion ringing clear in the air. "Don't let the government trick you into birthing mutant babies!" she shrieks.

I keep to the middle of the pack, blending in until we rolled down into a grassy valley and approached the bridge. I hold back at that point. That sucker is high—tree top high. And I'm short. *Vertically challenged*, these guys called it.

A handful of guys try to get up the smooth-faced pillars supporting the bridge. A couple of them make it. Watching closely, I saw the secret. There were a few tiny hand and foot holds worn out of the stone, but the kicker was a crack or a ledge pretty far up. Too high for me to reach, even with a good vault.

"You should try it."

I glance sideways, under the safety of my hat brim. Ken Sato is Asian, like me. It had been a couple of months, hadn't it, since he'd hooked up with the group? I'd seen him a couple of times, and then suddenly he was a regular. I'd watched him a bit, noticed his unusual green eyes, his square jaw, the hard muscles that adorned his rangy frame, and most especially, the unusual grace with which he moved. I thought I could count on one hand the number of times I'd heard him speak out loud.

"Have you made it?" I hoped I didn't sound defensive.

He nodded. "With help." I quickly look away as he gives me a once over. I knew what he was seeing—half-Asian girl in casual student grunge, long ponytail of thick dark hair emerging from beneath a broad brimmed cap. He didn't wait for me to look up and meet his eyes as most people did. Instead I felt him focus on my flexible Feiyue shoes. "I could show you."

I hesitated. I shouldn't, really. But Ken had become a staple of the group, a calm influence. He was easily one of the most skilled freerunners, but he didn't showboat. I'd seen him helping others before, in his quiet way.

I wanted to trust him. That's what scared me the most.

"Sure," I said abruptly, standing up. "Let's do it."

I felt the weight of his gaze upon me again, but I stepped out ahead of him and focused on the bridge. The wind picked up, I could feel it against the nape of my neck, rustling my ponytail.

"You've noticed the ledge? On the left most pillar?"

I nodded. "All I need to do is get high enough to reach it, then I can foot match my grip and stand tall enough to make it to the top."

"I can get you up there. Using the *futari jinba*. Do you know it?"

I shook my head. I knew a bit of Japanese, but the phrase was not familiar. My mother had been my only link to my Asian heritage, and she'd died when I was young.

"It's easy enough. I'll crouch down at the base. You run for me, hit my cupped hands, and I stand quickly, using my momentum and yours to launch you high. Understand?"

"Got it."

He didn't question or instruct me further. "Hold up, guys," he called, moving toward the bridge. "We're going to try something."

The others drew back, watching expectantly. Ken got himself into position. He gave a small nod.

What was I doing? I should have made an excuse and slipped away when he first singled me out. But I didn't want to sneak off alone again. I was tired of being lonely, of being careful. And perhaps, just for once, I wanted to strengthen my connection with this group.

So I sucked in a deep breath and took off at a hard run. Another gust of wind hit me from behind, stronger than before. I kept going, aiming for Ken's laced fingers. Feet braced, he watched my feet intently, preparing for the moment of contact. I saw the wind rustle his hair, saw him look up in surprise. I was almost on him. He stared suddenly up at me.

It happened. Our eyes met. Straight on.

I wrenched my gaze away and stepped into his hands. *Disaster.* My father's voice roared the warning. Ken had seen. I cringed inside even as he stood and launched me hard and high. Cursing a thousand times over, I reached for that one good-sized crack. Found it with my fingers. Scrabbled for another tiny hand hold and shifted my weight for one terrifying second as I pressed tight to the wall, lifted my left leg high and made the switch with my left hand.

Toes wedged in the crack, I stood up. From here I could reach the crosswalk. Breathing hard, I scrambled up and over.

Whoops and shouts erupted from below, and from those already up and resting in the shade of the covered bridge. I ignored them all, intent on leaning over the rail.

Ken had seen. Anger and nausea roiled in my gut. Why had I been so stupid? Taken such a risk? I was sick with disappointment in myself, resentment at him, and a sudden, overwhelming grief. This was it, then. The end. I gripped the rail tight, fighting the knowledge that I would have to move on, to leave the small semblance of normalcy I'd claimed here and never see this band of guys again.

He stared up at me, visibly upset. He made a sharp motion with his hand. *"Yokai!"* he shouted.

I had no idea what he meant. But suddenly—I

didn't care.

My head came up and grief and anger faded in the face of something much, much worse.

"Storm's coming," remarked one of the guys who'd made it up earlier.

The wind was stronger and cooler here. Up high, the breeze blew steadily.

Oh, no. I let go of the rail, stumbled back a step. I knew then, what had been bothering me. It was in the wind, slightly charged with the sting of power, rich with the promise of moisture, laden with a faint, sickly sweet scent. It swirled in my hair, dragged horrid memories from my subconscious and brought tears to my eyes.

I knew the taste and the texture of that breeze. It carried something bad. Something terrifying and not of this world. The creature that rode that wind had murdered my father. And it was looking for me.

Panic jump-started my heart. Adrenaline dumped into my system.

I glared down at Ken. And then I whirled on my heel and took off at a run.

Chapter Two

I made it all the way to the College of Design before my training reasserted itself. I slowed and breathed deep, summoning discipline and calm. Somehow I pushed back that first, panicked response. Since I was already heading east, I veered slightly north and set out again at an easy, ground-covering lope.

Think. Don't just react. My father's voice again. It wasn't easy to listen. That wind—with its latent electric spark and its heady scent—it was the stuff of my worst nightmares. Only once had I seen the creature that commanded it. Once, on the worst day of my life. I'd come home to our isolated cabin to find *something*—something tall and powerful and utterly unreal—using its mastery of the air to toss my father about like a rag doll.

I put a halt to that train of thought. Reliving the horror would not help me now. Several times, through the years of isolation, I'd asked my father why we'd lived so alone and disconnected after my mother's death. He'd never answered, just pushed me to learn more, train harder. I'd come up with a hundred stories and theories to explain it, but never could I have dreamed up something so monstrous. Never could I have imagined such a creature wishing to torture and kill my father—and then turning for me. I still didn't know *why*. But my abilities had allowed me to escape, and to stay hidden for four long years.

Several times since then I'd caught a hint of the creature's presence, tasted that sickly tang in the air. I'd always run, or immediately gone to ground, and eventually it would fade. But I'd never felt it so strongly—or so close. I feared this might be the time I didn't get away.

I hunched my shoulders. Centenary was woefully bare of trees or much else in the way of cover. Reaching a group of Engineering buildings, I entered one, navigated the maze of cool, quiet hallways and went out another entrance. Sticking to the shadows of buildings when I could, I turned straight north. If I could hit Varsity at the right time, I could jump on a college transit bus. It would hide me from the air and also put an end to a scent trail.

A bus was just pulling in. I put on a burst of speed, mixing in with the crowd of kids waiting to file on. Flashing my fake student ID to the driver, I sank down into a seat. My hands started to shake, but I just clenched them hard. Now was not the time to fall apart.

I stayed aboard for just the short jaunt to Morris Drive, where I hopped off and caught another bus, this one on the main Packlink line. I took a seat near the middle door, sat back and tried to imagine what Ken Sato's role in this might be.

He'd seen my eyes. Discovered my secret. *Kawaridane*. Mutant. Freak. In recent years the Japanese word had been shortened to the derogatory *Kawad*. Call it what you will, I was marked, reviled, avoided as if my affliction was something that could be caught.

The entire planet was still recovering from the series of quakes and tsunamis that had ripped along the infamous Ring of Fire years ago. Cities in New Zealand and South America had been damaged. Japan had been utterly destroyed, and parts of California along with it. Millions killed, a civilization nearly wiped out. And everyone else was still dealing with the aftermath, much of it the result of the miasma of toxic particles, carcinogens, acids, fine insoluble matter and radiation released into the atmosphere at such a huge swath of destruction. But some of us had been more directly affected—and my mark was distinctive, so I must be extra careful.

Never let them see. It was the primary directive of my existence. And today I had failed to carry it out. Ken Sato had seen—and in almost the same moment that I sensed my enemy bearing down on me. Coincidence? How could it be?

And yet, his initial surprised reaction had come before our eyes had met. He'd sensed something on the wind, too. How, if he was not connected to it? I'd never seen another person react to that taste, that presence in the air. As much as I wished to believe in his innocence, it didn't add up. And it wouldn't matter anyway. If I escaped this time, I had to move on, find a new bolthole to settle in.

Outside, the light was fading. The bus grew crowded as students finished classes and set out for dorms and apartments. I'd been around the loop twice now. I got off with a large group on Hillsborough and headed west, toward home.

Carefully, I tested the air. Not a hint of my pursuer. I hitched up my pack and set a normal pace. Remembering what I had been taught, I let my awareness extend to the busy street, the steady flow of students, to the trees and the tops of the buildings above. All felt as it should. I tried to ignore the flash of anger and pain that came with that thought. I'd been here over a year. Long enough to grow comfortable, long enough for it to start to feel like home.

Gone now, one way or another.

Almost there. The other kids had straggled off to storefronts or apartments. Shadows reached farther, here in the lee of a small hill. I slipped into them with relief. Shadows were protectors and allies.

I stopped, suddenly afraid I might need more help than a shadow could give. Something was off. Not in the same way as before. But I felt . . . something. Eyes watching.

I veered suddenly into the parking lot of a used bookstore.

Something moved in the line of trees at the far edge, right at the spot where I would have walked past. Something large set the high branches to rustling. I moved easily, acting as if I didn't notice.

The bookstore door was locked. I cursed under my breath before nonchalantly turning to the rack of free books lining the front of the place. Picking a title, I leaned against the door and opened it. I eyed the parking lot from beneath my brim, then tossed the book back and chose another—a thick, oversized edition of Sherlock Holmes tales. Nothing moved out there. Not a branch or a leaf or a rustle of wind.

I wasn't fooled.

I hefted the book and pretended to be absorbed. Slowly I moved out, head down, nose in the book, ambling west again, but this time taking the alley behind the bookstore's neighboring houses. The lane was lined with full-grown trees, providing some cover. When I hit their sheltering darkness I tucked the book under my arm and took off at a fast, silent run.

Not for long. Something thumped to the ground, directly in my path. I skidded to a stop, backpedaling rapidly.

Panic and disbelief nearly stopped my heart. My mouth hung open.

This was not the creature of my nightmares and memories. It was something different altogether—and yet still entirely unbelievable.

On two feet, broad and heavily muscled, it stood over twice my height. Its skin was a deep, dark red, its nose large and curved over like a beak. Large, heavily muscled arms flexed as its hands opened and closed. Long, white hair flowed back to meet huge, rustling black wings.

It tilted its head in a distinctly avian gesture and peered down at me. A thin, trilling sound echoed in the alley. "So small you are, to be the cause of so much trouble."

I shut my mouth and started to back up. It shook itself and I realized it was wearing human clothing; a tunic over short breeches and a deep green vest. A tiny black cap perched upon its head and a green sash draped around the thick neck. Fluffy white pompoms adorned the sash and trembled as it stepped forward, balancing huge feet on wooden soled, geta sandals. It peered down at me, staring into my eyes.

"Come," it said. "My master awaits."

I braced my feet and sank down into a crouched, ready position, book still in hand.

It laughed with an abrasive, clacking sound. "Foolish girl. Do you not know who I am? I am Tengu." His wings spread, wide and shining ebony. "We are patrons of the martial arts. You cannot stand against me."

And it didn't know what I was, either. I waited.

It reached for me with a huge, gauntleted hand. I slammed the book down on it, pushing hard and letting the weight of the book help carry the creature's hand all the way down to the ground, then I stepped on the book, sprang lightly, pushed off his massive shoulder and launched myself past him. I hit the ground on a roll and was already running through the trees as a screech of surprised fury rang out.

There was no time for finesse, no place to hide. I pelted southwest at full speed. Too soon the trees broke and I hit a parking lot. It was full dark now, and the street lamps were lit, leaving me vulnerable. I cut the corner of the lot, aiming for Stanbrick Avenue and the thicker grove of trees at the other side. I'd just made it to the road when I heard the flapping of huge wings behind me. Something struck me hard in the back and I went sprawling.

Frantic, I reached around me, searching for anything that could be used as a weapon. My fingers brushed jagged rock—a broken chunk of asphalt. *Use what's available.* I gripped it and jumped to my feet. The creature—Tengu—was immense and strong and I didn't stand a chance. But I wasn't going down without a fight.

"Trouble indeed." He glared at me and shook himself again, like a rooster with ruffled feathers. "Someone has trained you—"

I didn't wait for him to finish. I threw the chunk of asphalt. It hit right where I aimed, between his eyes, right at the spot where his beak-like nose began. He squawked and clutched his face with a hand and I aimed a powerful kick at his knee.

Another screech, but I got no chance to run this time. He reached out with his other hand and lifted me bodily into the air. Seemingly without effort, he raised me to eye level.

"Charged as I am with returning you whole, still Tengu can be patient. You shall pay for your impertinence. I shall ask that you be given to me, once the master is done with you."

He shifted his grip and the straps to my backpack dug hard into my armpits. My mind raced. Could he truly be making it that easy? I wiggled, straightened my arms and slid free. Dropping to the ground, in a flash I ducked between the creature's legs and dashed back the way I'd come.

I made it to the parking lot. The Tengu didn't

even bother to land, it just grabbed a fistful of shirt and hair and scooped me up. It was then, legs dangling, scalp burning, and heart turning to despair, that I saw Ken Sato.

He stood in the middle of the parking lot, holding a square metal plate. The sides curved elegantly and ended in deadly sharp corners. There was a hole smack in the middle of the graceful square. Even from here I could see his light green eye blink as he stared at us through the hole.

I wondered if he had lost his mind.

And then I wondered again if he had been working with this *thing* all along.

He lowered the plate and looked me in the eye. For the first time in a long time, I didn't lower my gaze. I held my head high and glared defiantly back. God, even in the midst of this disaster, it felt incredibly good.

"You should get away if you can," he said with complete indifference. "It's thinking that it can rough you up a bit and tell its master that it happened in battle."

The creature clacked in protest as it settled to the ground. It continued to hold me high as if I were as light as a feather. I continued to stare, unsure what Ken was up to, but willing to wait to discover it. I liked my chances against him far more than against this Tengu.

The metal disk blinked in the light from the street lamps. Ken lowered it and peered at us. "No," he said firmly. "You cannot kill me and take the plate—not without losing her." He rolled his eyes. "You don't even know what it is, what it can do."

"What magic is this?" The Tengu tilted its head from side to side, trying to get a good look at the thing. "How do you know what is in my heart and mind?"

"Magic?" Ken made a sound of disgust.
"What? Are you old as well as a freak? Wake up and
smell the new millennium! I don't need magic—I
have technology. This," he lifted the metal plate
casually, "reads your brain waves. When I look at you
through this I know what you are going to do before
you do."

Tengu made a disparaging sound of his own. "I
have seen many of the wonders of this world, but
never have I heard of such a device."

Ken shook his head. "Just like I thought. Old."
He turned away.

"Wait! I should like to see this technology."

"You mean you should like to steal it." Ken
paused. "I might consider a trade."

My head jerked like a puppet's as Tengu gave a
little hop of eagerness. "Yes, a trade!"

"The plate for the girl," Ken said flatly.

"What?" My ears were starting to ring from all
the high-pitched noises this creature could make. "No!
Tengu has caught the girl. I shall claim the honor of
presenting her to the masters!"

"What else have you got?"

"I have a magic fan! Much prized!" It patted
its sash-like belt, where several implements were
tucked away.

Ken considered. "What is its magic?"

"Very good for punishing your enemies! When
you wave it before their face, it will shrink or grow
their nose."

With a little disparaging laugh, Ken turned
away again. "No, thanks. Goodbye, then."

"Wait!" Reluctantly it spoke again. "It can also
stir up a great wind. I can teach you the way of it."

"Now, that might come in handy." Ken
narrowed his eyes. "Show me how it works."

"Yes." I felt the shiver that went through the creature. "But first you must show me how to work the plate."

"Agreed." Ken approached, but stopped suddenly, several feet away. He gestured toward me. "Wait a minute. I saw most of your battle. That one is tricky. Put her down, or at least hold her away so that she doesn't try to snatch the plate."

"She is sneaky," Tengu agreed. "I will not take the risk of letting her go." Instead the creature spread his arms wide, holding me as far from his body as his long arm would stretch. "There. She cannot reach you now." From this position I could see the avarice gleaming in its eye as he beckoned. "Come now, show me."

"Sure." Ken stepped closer and held the plate up so that the sides pointed up and the hole sat at the bottom of a slight depression. "Before you use it, you must speak the code word to activate it."

"Yes? I have seen magic like this. What is the word?"

"Banished!" Ken said forcefully.

"Banished?" the creature squawked in confusion.

From my vantage point, slightly higher than Ken, I could see that the black surface of the plate had lightened, its smooth surface gone grainy.

"Yes," Ken announced in ringing tones. "Back to the realm from which you came!" He drew a deep breath and blew, sending a spray of powder into the peering creature's face. It sneezed once.

And the world exploded.

No. No. It was just the ground, rushing up to slam into me, stealing my breath and knocking me a bit loopy. That powder—or that sneeze—had sent the Tengu soaring backwards until he crashed into the black-top of the parking lot. Groaning, I gasped for breath and rolled over and away from the creature. The trees at the edge of the parking lot danced as I tried to focus.

"Gods and ancestors!" Ken Sato stood on the other side of the creature, glaring down at it with horror growing in his expression. "This is not good." He stared at me and I tried to pick one of the two wavering images of him to focus on. "He's still here! This is not good at all!"

I didn't answer, too busy trying to climb to my feet and stay there. I stared back at the guy. Gratitude swept over me, and disbelief, as well as the familiar, irresistible urge to get away.

"He should have been banished, back to the spirit realm," Ken insisted. "But he's just knocked out."

I shook my head and backed away, then followed my instincts, turning to snatch up my fallen pack and attempt a slow, unsteady run toward the trees.

"Mei! Don't run, please!"

I kept going.

"Mei, stop!" The urgency in his voice matched my own feelings. "Stop, Masuyo!"

I stumbled to a halt. My gut clenched violently. I couldn't catch my breath, suddenly. All of my limbs were shaking. It took real effort to turn and meet his urgent gaze.

"How?"

"Masuyo, please."

"How?" I screamed. Anger rocked me, and sadness, and worst of all, a fierce, forlorn hope. "How do you know that name?"

Chapter Three

"I saw," he said, low. "I saw your eyes and knew who you were."

I sucked in a breath. And another. A vortex of conflicting emotion rose up to choke me. "How?" I forced the words out. "How could you possibly know who I am?"

"I know because I've been looking for you. We've *all* been looking for you."

I cast an involuntary glance toward the creature stretched across the pavement.

"No!" he exclaimed. "I'm not with him—with *them.*"

"Then who?"

"Your people, Mei," he said simply. But he must have read the confusion I felt. "Your father's people."

I froze. Everything inside of me went icy— then blazed red-hot. The world abruptly snapped back into focus. I turned and walked away.

"Wait!" Ken scrambled after me. "Where are you going?" He fell into line beside me. "You should get inside, off of the streets."

Without warning I spun on my heel and hit him dead center in the chest with a powerful roundhouse kick.

It caught him completely by surprise. Much like the Tengu, he flew back and landed sprawling in the roadside gravel. "What the—?" He stared up at me, open-mouthed.

"My father had no people!" I spat. "He had no one—except me."

Compassion flashed in his eyes then. I glared while images and an almost tangible resentment flared before mine. I'd been interested in Ken Sato—how could I not be? I'd thought about his strong brow and square jaw, his longish hair and light eyes and his easy manner even when I wasn't on a run with the parkour guys. And he'd helped me, rescued me from that—whatever it had been. Now he looked at me with sorrow and pity—and in this moment, I hated him. "Leave me *alone*," I growled. Leaving him in the gravel, I turned and ran.

For a stretch I gave in to the turmoil inside of me and just ran, as fast and as far as I could before the stitch in my side and my common sense forced me to slow down.

It probably wouldn't help to change my appearance, but old habits died hard. I took off my cap and stuffed it away, then wrapped my ponytail up into a sloppy pile on top of my head. Wasted effort, most likely. It was dark. There was no reason to hide, anyway. Both Ken and whatever lurked out there knew about my . . . affliction.

I kept to a purposeful walk, backtracking and then turning west when I hit the alley where the Tengu had first landed. My steps slowed when I drew closer to my—what? Home? Not really. My refuge, I guess. My safe spot.

I turned out of the alley, into a narrow strip of weedy green between a rental house and the parking lot of a sub shop. The house, for some reason painted a deep purple, was brightly lit at the front but dark and silent in the back. Music and masculine voices echoed back from the porch. Next door, the shop had a few customers, but no one lingered outside. Listening intently for signs of someone behind me, I hesitated, then ducked quickly behind a large stand of overgrown shrubbery at the back corner of the house.

It was dark back here, the lights from the sub shop only penetrating the thick brush in pinpoints. I didn't need to see, anyway. Two steps and my hand encountered a rail. Moving quietly I climbed the few steps to a small landing.

The door was unlocked, as always. *Easy in, easy out.* I touched the knob and it swung silently into darkness. I put a hand across the threshold and paused, as I did every time. Letting my senses move into the room before me, I tested the silence, the stillness, the very air.

The boarded up set of rooms, completely hidden from the other, legitimate occupants of the house, felt as empty as ever. This was my quiet, cave-like haven, where I felt safe, hidden away from the rest of the world. I closed the door and flipped the switch to light several small, scarf-draped lamps throughout the room. They gave off a soft, warm, welcoming light—and nearly cracked my heart in two.

It only proved my mistake. Too long. I'd stayed too long, grown too comfortable. I'd become too used to the rhythm of life here. I'd grown fond of even the idiot college guys who unwittingly shared their house with me, let myself become used to their schedules and idiosyncrasies, though in a far lesser fashion than I'd allowed myself to know the freerunners. *Stupid. Stupid.* I'd let myself dream of connections—and now I had to pay the price.

Sitting on an overturned five gallon bucket next to the door, I took off my shoes, then I rose and pulled my hiking pack from the closet. Rifling through my possessions, I began to make harsh choices, picking and choosing with an eye only to weight and survival. A couple of pairs of close-fitting, dark pants, several tanks and my military-style jacket made the cut. I shoved the clothes into the pack, on top of the dried rations I always kept in there and ready to go. After a moment's hesitation, I placed my Feiyus in there too.

Ruthless and methodical, I stripped my gear to the bare
minimum, lightweight and easy to carry. It wasn't
until I got to my workspace that I faltered.

Not tonight. I couldn't face that particular
goodbye tonight.

Instead I retreated to the tiny bathroom. All the
activity in the house was still focused on the front
porch—and likely another keg set up there. I took the
chance and took a hot shower—it might be the last I
got for a while. Then I crossed to the pallet on the
floor in the corner, pulled the covers over my head—as
if that could block the pain, regret and multitude of
questions whirling in my head—and reached for sleep.

Eventually I found it. And of course, I dreamed
during the night. Always the same, it was the dream
that comes to me whenever I'm particularly troubled
or scared.

I walked through the familiar contours of a
lovely, Japanese style garden, following a stone path
that echoed the course of a sparkling, clear stream.
Lush greens and delicate blooms surrounded me. Soft
blossoms floated in the air, carrying a soothing scent.
I am at peace, reveling in the heady feel of so many
green and healthy growing things. As usual, I wallow
in the serenity of the place—until I see the lady,
walking away from me in the distance.

I call, but she never hears me. I follow her as
she moves smoothly across the landscape. Tonight she
wears a fabulously embroidered robe of soft pink. Her
hair is ebony, elaborately coiffed and adorned with
dangling jewelry. I'm almost ashamed to catch up to
her, looking as I do in my grubby clothes, but I am
irresistibly drawn to her. Her head bows low tonight,
her shoulders droop. I have to catch her, to hear her
story and try to ease her pain, but she never knows that

I am there, trailing behind her.

She reaches the pretty, arched bridge too soon and crosses over to an island in the center of a pond. As always, some force blocks me from following her. I stand at the edge of the bridge and watch her lay a flower before a small, stone temple. The scent of the incense she lights wafts over to me.

Frustration fills me, and overflows in the form of helpless tears. I strain against the invisible shield holding me back, pound my fist upon it in frustration. The blow sounds unnaturally loud and harsh in the peaceful scene—and for the first time, in all the times that I have dreamt this, the lady looks up. My breath stops as she turns a head over her shoulder.

Startled, she meets my gaze—

And I awake, not befuddled with remnants of the dream, but clear-headed and in a far better frame of mind. The air felt warm, closer than usual, but it didn't matter. I rolled out of bed, filled with purpose. I knew where I'd gone wrong, why I'd felt so conflicted last night. I'd done it to myself—first by betraying the most basic rule of my existence, by even subconsciously letting myself dream of settling in one place, of creating any sort of permanence.

I knew better. A home, a semblance of a normal life—none of that was possible for me—not while that wind creature was out there, hunting me. Yanking on my most comfortable boots, I laced them tight. I'd been running for so long, not even sure what I was running from, let alone how to fight it. I'd had no answers, no information, and no place to turn to find them.

Until now.

I hadn't been quick enough to grasp what had happened. Now I have access to someone who knows *something*. More than I do, at least. That had been my second mistake. I shouldn't have abandoned him last night. I gave myself a bit of a pass—the instinct had been ingrained so thoroughly . . . but now for the first time, I had something to run *toward*.

I had to find Ken Sato. And I had to get the hell out of Dodge. In that order.

But first . . . I approached my workspace with a heavy heart. Dropping to my knees, I surveyed my collection of supplies. Making paper, or *washi*, was my joy, my creative outlet, and the one connection I had with my mother. It had also become a means of income after I exhausted the local stores of cash and supplies my father and I had set up. Moments of happiness and satisfaction had been few and far between since his death, but many of them had occurred right here. Having the luxury of space and time to create *washi* was the other reason for my attachment to this place.

My ill-advised and mistaken attachment. I sighed and traced a prickly bundle of dried fibers. Maybe Ken Sato knew something of this wind creature—maybe he knew how I could defeat it. Once I had killed this demon, I could set myself up a real studio, with bigger tubs and larger screens. I could obtain traditional components and practice the old techniques. I could make the kind of fine, quality paper I'd only dreamed of.

But for now I had to leave most of it—fibers, soda ash, tools, all the dried flowers, needles and leaves I'd harvested—behind. Resolutely I picked up my *sugeta*—the hinged frame with a removable bamboo screen used for forming paper sheets. It was old and shiny with use—and it had belonged to my mother. Despite its awkwardness, I would take it along. Rearranging my pack, I padded the hard frame with items of clothing and made it fit. I sat a moment longer before I picked up a small stack of finished paper.

The high-end shopping complex located just a few blocks from campus held several stores that were willing to sell my handmade, decorated papers—but this stack I had never been able to part with. Each unique, colorful sheet represented something, some fragile bloom or gorgeously painted arch from my recurring dream. I'd thought of that lovely, lonely lady in the garden as I crafted them.

Though it made me wince, I folded the papers over on themselves. I couldn't leave them behind. Carefully I placed them in the front pocket of my pack. That was it, then.

It was time to go.

Chapter Four

Ken Sato awoke to the tantalizing smell of fresh baking bread and the small, cheerful sound of a young robin chirping in his ear. *Dawn draws near*, it told him, hopping from his shoulder to the top of his head. *Nearly time to greet the sun.*

Ken thanked the fledgling, sitting up carefully so as not to dislodge it. He needn't have bothered; the young one was too flighty to sit still for long. It fluttered to a nearby metal hood, then onto the low wall that edged the rooftop of the deli sandwich shop.

Ken followed, stretching. Not the most comfortable night's sleep he'd ever had, but not the worst either. He'd endured many sorts of danger and discomfort in his quest to find Masuyo Barrett—and he'd gladly do it again.

His heart rate ratcheted as he glanced over at the purple house. It lay dark and quiet, but he knew she was there. He'd followed her last night, moving as silently as a breeze. She'd be inside now, preparing to leave in the still, dark time before the dawn. How did he know? He yawned and rotated a shoulder, gone stiff from sleeping on the rough surface. He knew because that's exactly what he would do, in her place.

He'd found her. He took a moment to marvel, to soak in the triumph. So many people searching for so long—and he'd been the one to find her, just as he'd always dreamed.

It had been a near thing. He'd joined the parkour group as a good excuse to spend time on campus, to meet young people and range over the length and breadth of the university. He'd actually attended two sessions with Mei and just thought her cautious, an athletic girl who used the trappings of a tomboy to keep strangers at bay. But he'd noted that she always wore a cap, and kept her head down. Niggling suspicions began to creep in, but he could hardly conceive of the infamous Masuyo Barrett hanging so casually with a bunch of ragged freerunners.

He'd started to watch her, then, and he'd seen how good she was. How she didn't show off or brag, but she surpassed them all. He could scarcely believe how incredibly in control of her body she was. He'd planned that bit at the bridge, hoping to draw her out— but there'd been no need. He'd seen her eyes, and he'd known.

The girl with the stars in her eyes. She was a figure from his childhood bedtime tales, a character he'd heard of his whole life, but still her eyes were not what he'd been expecting. Almost, she could pass for normal. Her eyes were shaped like any other mixed blood girl's, but the iris was big and an impossible dark blue. The pupil though, that's what shocked you. Not round at all, but shaped like a starburst. Not black, but silver—and when the light changed they grew or shrank accordingly, like the continual birth and death of a far-off star.

No, not what he'd been expecting. They were nothing like—

The fledging chirped—just one short note of warning—and Ken froze. After several long seconds, he sent the young bird a silent but fierce message of thanks.

The Tengu moved below. Another mystery. This avian spirit creature did not behave as he'd been taught to expect—and neither was it alone. The Tengu was not what he had scented on the wind yesterday. He had no idea what tainted the air like that—but Mei did. She'd run instantly, without hesitating a second. He'd been lucky to spot her later, trudging up

Hillsborough. Lucky to have been able to help her escape the man/bird mash-up that crept below him now.

Slow and quiet, it advanced from the alley. Its wings were outstretched, its head tilted. As Ken watched, it sucked in a deep breath, moved its head in the other direction and breathed in again. A flap of its great wings and a little hop and it was in the sparsely grassed area between the house and the shop. It circled below him, sniffing deeply, moving between the shop beneath him and the house beyond. It stopped in the middle, wingtips flicking indecisively, then abruptly it rose into the air. He ducked as it searched out a perch in a low spreading tree behind the house, where the neglected shrubs grew as thick and close as a jungle.

Ken held his position. Cursing silently, he moved the fingers of one hand slowly, until they pressed on the mark scored into the tender flesh of his forearm. Concentrating, he called up a slight wind, ensuring that his scent drifted away from the creature across the clearing and hoping it couldn't detect that slight bit of *minding*.

From below came the softest snick of a sound. A turned lock? The Tengu heard it too. It snapped to attention, crouched low and ready on its branch.

Mother of all monsters, but something wasn't right here. He'd tricked this thing last night and blasted it with the *kayaku* powder too—it should have been sent hurtling back to its spirit realm. Yet here it sat, still hunting on the earthly plane. The Elders would need to know. They wouldn't be happy—not with him, either, for now he was going to have to expose himself, and likely use his precious *seihoukei* too.

Long minutes passed and nothing further

happened. *Good girl*. Someone had trained her—it
helped explain how she'd stayed hidden for so long.
He used the time to call upon Kuji-in, one of the
sources of mental and physical strength. Closing his
eyes, he folded his hands in the first seal and focused
on Rin, the seal for power and strength in mind and
body.

Across the way, the Tengu lost focus. It hopped
about on its branch, its feathered wings ruffling.

Only Ken saw the faint movement behind the
bushes below. Mei was moving stealthily away from
the door. Not until she reached the end of the
protected sidewalk did the creature realize its mistake.

With an ear splitting screech it leaped—and
landed at the end of the paved walkway where Mei
should have been—but wasn't. As soon as the first
hint of sound broke the stillness of the morning, she'd
reacted. Over the low railing and through the brush,
she was running full tilt before the bird-like creature
got over its surprise.

The Tengu squawked in anger and took off after
her.

Ken stood. With a soundless leap he took to the
top of the low south-facing wall. Pressing a finger
against his scar again, he called up a blast of cool air.
With fierce concentration he hurled it, willing it into a
sweeping arc that circled the flying creature, then
swept up from beneath it, wrenching one wing high
and causing it to land with an awkward thump, several
feet short of its target.

It whirled, beady eyes searching, and Ken
dropped to the roof. In his mind's eye he pictured the
scene below. Something odd was going on down
there. It had seemed almost as if the trees had leaned
in, closing after the fleeing girl.

He shook his head—he needed to distract the

creature again. He searched his memory—and recalled the restaurant's dumpster below.

One hand circling his marked arm, he summoned a quick, sharp burst of air to flip the dumpster lid closed.

The avian monster didn't fall for it. It turned south and headed after Mei again.

It didn't have to go far.

She'd gone to ground. One of the university's endless construction sites lay directly ahead in her last trajectory. There was no sign of her on either side of the sagging, chain-link fence, and no betraying sound to alert the Tengu to her location. Ken nodded his approval. Better to hide. Or to confront. She'd never outrun the big bird/man.

"Come out, child," the creature called from atop a leaning fence post. "It's no use fighting. You cannot win against Tengu."

An easy assumption, had Mei been a girl alone. Ken darted from one shadowed section of alley to the next, moving silently but swiftly after the thing, using his air *minding* to keep his touch upon the ground light and soundless.

She was not alone.

He only hoped she had a weapon to keep the thing at bay until he got into position.

The Tengu drifted down. Its massive fists clenched and it sent out an agitated clicking as it began to move through the tangle of construction equipment and vehicles. The sound bounced, echoing strangely in the cluttered space and rattling the bones in Ken's ears. He shuddered as he approached the fence, watching carefully.

In abrupt contrast, Mei made her move in silent, spectacular fashion. The creature's shock of white hair scraped a front loader's raised bucket as it passed beneath it. As it moved on, Mei rose out of the bucket and launched herself, taking a great leap and landing on the creature's back. She gripped its thickly muscled neck with one hand and began tearing out feathers from its wings with the other.

Tengu's cry of rage was terrible. It reached for her, trying to pluck her off, but the angle was awkward and she clung fiercely. Shivering, flapping its wings, trying to beat her with them, it leaped about, until it finally reached a tall pole sunk in concrete and used it to scrape her off like a barnacle.

She landed on her feet and crouched into a ready stance.

The creature gave a menacing laugh. "I was hoping you would be foolish, young one, but you have surpassed my expectations."

"I was hoping you would be smart and move on."

"A futile wish."

Ken smirked even as he moved into the yard, looking for a high spot. Tengu may be big, but its wit obviously was not.

"My masters want you," Tengu continued. "They will have you." He shook himself and a few stray feathers drifted away. "But first you shall pay."

She shrugged. "We shall see."

"Were you not listening last time? We Tengu are masters of all of the martial arts. We taught you humans everything, all that you know."

She raised a brow, mocking the creature. "Then perhaps it is time you learned something."

Again her move was swift and silent. She leapt forward. The Tengu reacted, raising fists and wings. Mei slid, gliding under and past, grabbing another handful of black feathers as she went. This time she didn't run, but turned to face him, still clutching a fistful.

The monster whirled, lashing out with a sandaled foot, but Mei avoided it easily, backing toward a cleared space before the building under construction.

"I shall carve an equal bit of flesh from you, insolent girl."

"You can try," Mei answered. "I'd go for a crippling spot, if I were you. An eye for an eye, isn't that what they say?" She shook her hand and feathers flew. "These are primary flight feathers. Let's see how you fight when you don't have the advantage of attacking from the air."

Ken's heart sank even as the Tengu threw back his head to laugh. "You betray your ignorance. I am *Tengu*, I do not bow to the physical limits of your world."

Clearly Mei had not encountered a spirit creature before. The avian horror was right, the laws of physics were easy to bend—for a *yokai* from the spirit realm. He scanned frantically, looking for a spot that would give him the best advantage.

The Tengu, meanwhile, pumped its wings. Unable to let her challenge pass, it clearly meant to prove her wrong.

Except—it was having trouble getting aloft.

It pumped harder and lifted a few feet—but clearly had to work to hold steady.

Ken's mind was racing. What was this? How had she done that? It was a huge advantage—if only for the shock it had clearly dealt the creature. The gears in his mind whirled and he leaped for the front loader Mei had been hiding in. Climbing up the extended arm, he perched at the apex, straddling the joint that attached the bucket. Clamping a hand over his scar, he called up, not a big blast of air, but several small ones. The Tengu was concentrating fiercely on its injured wing—he sent his projectiles of air racing toward the healthy wing, where they played havoc, lifting, shifting and misdirecting the long feathers that achieved and directed flight.

The creature faltered in mid air. It squawked in outrage and confusion—then it turned its anger on Mei. Abruptly, it folded its wings and dropped.

The force of the blow sent Mei sprawling. In a heartbeat, she was up. She knocked aside the next punch and darted in close, delivered a hard elbow to the bridge of the creature's nose, then flitted away.

The battle was on. Ken pulled out his precious *seihoukei*, knowing he must use it. He gripped it, half of his brain noting for the last time how precisely it fitted his hand, how elegantly it presented as much a work of art as a weapon. He pressed the button on the side, releasing the sharp spikes from the corner that made the thing deadly—and waited.

Mei was formidable. He would find time to reflect on her incredible show of skill later. He'd never seen someone so fast. The Tengu struck again and again, but time and again she was already gone by the time the blow landed, in a new spot and searching out another way to move in and strike back. She got several good blows in, but the Tengu barely noticed. His strikes, on the other hand, inflicted damage when they landed. She was hurting after a few minutes of intense exchange, and beginning to tire.

The Tengu knew it. He held back, eyeing her carefully, and at the next strike he allowed her to land it—then reached out and grabbed her as she retreated.

The creature's screech of triumph turned to a shout of anger and pain and abruptly she dropped to the ground.

Tengu shook out a bleeding hand and she

grinned at it, reaching beneath her tank to pull off a rough, homemade belt made of burlap spiked with nails and other sharp objects. She swung it over her head and danced backwards—and tripped over a stray metal pipe, sprawling on her back.

Tengu leaped. Ken was already moving too. He knew the Tengu would spread his wings and launch at her a split second before it happened. He jumped up to brace himself between the loader's bucket and arm. Loosing a thick blast of air, he willed it to travel fast and wrench the creature's wings back, knocking it aside.

It whirled in his direction. "You!" The creature snarled up at him. "I knew I smelled *minding* on you!"

In a hurry now, it turned from him, reaching for Mei once more, and Ken didn't hesitate. He leaped from the bucket and launched his weapon. It spun, shining silver in the morning light and hit the Tengu dead center in the back, right between its wings.

And something else strange and unexpected happened. The creature should have slid instantly away, propelled back to its spirit realm. Instead it gave an odd chirp. It stared at him while the edges of its form glowed, then darkened. A deep, utter blackness etched its outline, covering the creature's form entirely and began to creep inward, somehow pulling the Tengu's mass with it, contracting and constricting until there was nothing left except a whirling sphere of darkness—and then with audible *pop*—it was gone.

Something small dropped to the ground.

Carefully, Ken approached it. He crouched down. A small resin figure lay in the dust—a bald eagle with talons extended and wings spread. He picked it up. It was slightly warm, but otherwise looked just like any child's toy. He considered pocketing it, but instead stood and tossed it further into the construction site. Then he turned to Mei where she still lay, half reclining on the ground.

He reached out a hand to help her up.

"Come on," he said. "We'd better get out of here before the other one shows up."

Chapter Five

I leaned on my elbows and stared. "What *are* you?"

"A friend," he answered simply.

I shook my head, suddenly afraid that Ken Sato was a worse monster than that *thing* he'd just dispatched. "I don't have friends."

"I think it's time you did."

If he'd tried it earlier, if he'd uttered those same words four years ago, I would have fallen for it. I'd have drunk them in and followed him anywhere. But I'd found the hard way what happens when someone offers you everything you wanted. I clenched my fists. And a few dirt bags had learned that not every lonely little girl was easy meat.

"Mei, please."

I ignored his outstretched hand and climbed to my feet without assistance. Maybe Ken Sato needed to be taught that lesson.

A slight wisp of a breeze brushed across my cheek—and I started, raising my face to test the wind.

"What is that thing?" Ken's nostrils were flaring too.

I glared at him.

He glared back. "It's only fair that I know what I'm facing."

As if he didn't.

My scorn must have shown in my expression, because he moved quickly to my side. "No matter what you think, I'm not associated with Tengu, or with that—that thing you smell on the wind. Or with any of the rest of them, either."

The rest of them? Chilled, I hesitated. "It's a killer," I said eventually. I let my bitterness bleed through into my tone.

He didn't hesitate. "Let's go."

I jumped up to retrieve my pack from the bucket of the loader I'd hidden in. "Go, then."

"Seriously?" For the first time his temper flared. "I saved your Shitake Mushrooms twice in the past twelve hours. And still you won't trust me?"

Despite myself, I laughed. "Shitake Mushrooms?"

"You know what I mean, Mei."

I raised my chin and met his gaze. He stared intently at my eyes. And I let him. I knew what he saw, what had made my life into this mess. *Starburst*, my father had called it affectionately. The iris of my eye was larger than normal and unusually colored— unusually *multi*-colored.

"Beautiful," Ken whispered.

I wished I could believe him. But they'd cost me too much for me to think of them as anything but a burden.

"Listen," he said slowly. "Those things will kill me as quickly as they will take you. "And I'm tired. The *minding* saps your strength."

"*Minding*? Is that what you did with the air?"

He blinked, then frowned. "Later, okay? That thing is looking for us and I'll be moving slow for a while, so why don't we head out?"

"We?"

He sighed. "At least we can work together to get away from here?"

I wasted another long few seconds looking him in the eye—and then I made the only decision I could. "Fine, but I have questions. And I'll want answers as soon as it's safe to get them."

He nodded. "I have a few questions for you, too."

I shrugged. "Come on."

We struck out, heading west toward the interstate, keeping to the back alleys when we could.

My nerves were frayed. It startled me that he moved as quickly and quietly as I did. I kept stopping myself from glaring over at him. Everything that had happened in the last day—the return of the wind demon, the loss of my home and the parkour guys, the attacks of the Tengu—and still the strangest feeling came from traveling side by side with a stranger.

Not *really* a stranger, I guess—but clearly Ken Sato was no mere college student. My brain churned with a thousand questions. I wanted to hurl them at him, drag the answers out of him, but I concentrated on getting distance between my nemesis and us.

We were forced to take to the main roadway when we reached the fenced in land of the arboretum. We'd just made it past and were heading into the maze of back roads again when I felt the questing taste of the demon in the air.

"It's getting stronger." Ken warned. "It must be close."

"I know." I cast about, suppressing the panic that tried to rise out of my gut. We were near the State Fairgrounds. Beyond the gates people stirred in the early morning light. Vendors for the weekly flea market were setting up and early shoppers were trying to beat the heat and the crowds.

"Let's go inside." I nodded at the gates. "We might avoid its notice if we can get in the midst of a big enough crowd."

We entered, the only ones on foot instead of in a car. There were only a few bargain hunters roaming the outside stalls, so we followed our noses to one of the buildings and the largest crowd we could find. A baker's stall was drawing people in with the smell of fresh coffee and hot pastry. I glanced at Ken and noted how he breathed in the scents.

"You'd better eat something," I told him. "You've gone pale and there are circles under your eyes."

He nodded. "It's the—" He paused. "I used a lot of energy."

I reached for my pack, but he shook his head and took a wallet from his pocket. He ordered an egg sandwich and tea and, keeping my head down, I leaned in close. "We'll stay in here a while. Strong scents can confuse it. It might move on."

He nodded his head toward the cashier as she gathered up his order. "What about you? You should eat, too." He lifted his wallet. "I can float you."

I paused, unwisely savoring the feeling the offer brought on. Such a simple thing, a basic kindness that I hadn't felt in so long. "Thanks, but I ate this morning before I left." I urged him to take one of the seats close to the bakery case. He fell on the food, eating quickly while I kept testing the air and avoiding anyone's direct gaze.

Relieved, I saw some of his normal color return. I waited until he finished before I let loose the tight rein I was holding. "Ken." I took a deep breath. "Before we go any further, before any other strange and insane thing happens to us—I have to ask. What do you know about my father?"

He pushed his coffee aside and met my gaze directly. "I met him, when I was small."

I clenched my fingers to keep them from trembling—or from reaching out to grab him. "When? Where?"

"Listen, I know Brian Barrett had no blood relations left alive, and I'm beginning to understand that you don't know anything of it, but Mei, your father had a family, of sorts. A whole village full of those he cared for and who loved him in return."

Pain twisted in my gut. "How? How can this be true and I don't know it?"

"I've been wondering the same thing myself. The only thing I can think of is that he was trying to protect you. Perhaps he didn't trust someone at Ryu?"

"Ryu?" I frowned.

We both forgot the question as an enormous roaring, *whoosh* sounded.

I froze. Everyone stopped, in fact, as the walls of the building rattled and a wave of sickly sweet tainted air blew through.

"Outside," I whispered. "And not far off."

"I wonder—that bit of Tengu that was left—you think it found it?"

"Let's go."

We pushed through the crowd to the door. Outside, shoppers were talking excitedly, helping to lift fallen racks and return goods to tables and shelves.

"Do you think it was an earthquake?" a woman asked.

"An explosion, I think," her friend answered.

I broke free of the group at the door—only to pull up short. My gaze locked in horror on the fencing between the fairgrounds and Hillsborough Street.

"Look," I whispered to Ken. I pointed with my chin.

"At what?" He glanced wildly about.

"Look—*really* look! Coming over the fence."

He stiffened. They were difficult to see if you didn't know what to look for. Distortions. Long tentacles formed of spirals of swirling air. They were extensions of the creature that had killed my father, under its control like extra appendages. Several were cascading over the top of the fence. I could see a couple more questing over rooftops and a few others crawling along the ground.

"What is it?" Ken breathed.

No one else had noted them yet, but a dog near the fence barked frantically at the nearly transparent moving spirals. His mistress, a girl about my age, tried to calm him.

"Don't let them touch you," I warned.

Ken shuddered. "I won't. Let's go."

But I stood, transfixed. I hadn't been this close to the thing since that awful day. I couldn't tear my gaze away as the biggest tendril dove under the dog's legs and reached for the girl.

"Hey! Watch out!" I shouted too late. The spiral split into long fingers. They snatched her up and gripped her tight. Her cry of fear and surprise was cut short as two invaded her nose and mouth. The dog went berserk.

"No," I whispered. The girl was lifted, shaken like a ragdoll and tossed aside.

"Come on," Ken urged. "We have to get out of here." He paused. "Listen!"

But I only heard the calls of the crowd as others noticed the girl collapsed on the ground.

"Let's go," Ken repeated. He pulled at my arm and I stumbled after him, following blindly. It wasn't until we reached the gate we'd entered by that I came to my senses.

"Wait," I called. "You're going the wrong way." I gasped as I looked past him. A thick, dark column rose over the construction site we'd fought in this morning. It looked like a swirling tornado, but it held still, fixed over that spot while dozens of tentacles stretched from it in all directions. "Ken! You are running towards it!"

I skidded to a stop. I'd thought the thing was big the first and last time I saw it, when it filled our small cabin with swirling robes and red eyes and debris-filled whorls of air. Now it towered above the two stories that had been completed at the construction site.

"Yes," he said, low and urgent. "It's already searched here! And that's where we're going," he pointed.

I followed the line of his finger across the intersection at the corner of the fairgrounds, where cars were stopped and people were climbing out, staring and taking pictures and videos of the massive tower of air with their phones.

"Aim for that platform," he called, winding his way through the stopped cars and leaping over a questing tentacle.

Cursing, I followed. "The train platform?" I could hear what must have caught his attention before—the warning whistle of an approaching train. "I don't think it stops here!"

"It doesn't," he answered over his shoulder. He'd pulled ahead of me and was continuing to make better time. "It only stops here during the State Fair."

"Then what—"

"Just run!"

I put on a burst of speed.

"Look at the cars," he called over his shoulder. "They have ladders built into the sides. Easy to jump and catch onto."

"Easy?" I gasped.

"Easier than making it up that bridge yesterday," he said with a breathless laugh. "Let's go." He was off again, sprinting fast and pulling ahead. He reached the wooden platform before the train did, turned and beckoned me on. "Faster!"

I ran at top speed. Gauging the approaching train, I thought I'd reach the platform just after it did, which should give me plenty of time to pick a car and make a jump. Ken's eyes were alight with excitement as the horn blared and the engine swept past—but then they rounded in horror as a thick tentacle of air reached up and over the moving train. The biggest one yet, it came down at the base of the stairs and surged forward, seeking.

Right across my path.

I put on the brakes, tried to back pedal, but I knew it was useless. I was going to plow right into that thing and the instant it touched me, I knew, the wind demon would have me.

"No!" Ken shouted. I saw his hand rise in the air.

Cursing, I fell back, trying to stop my forward momentum, but then my head jerked and all my limbs flopped as I was lifted straight up at top speed. Kicking and screaming in panic and rage, I fought against the column of air that had formed around me and snatched me twenty feet off the ground.

"Mei!" I heard Ken shout. "Stop! It's me! Stop fighting or I'll drop you!"

I stopped and hung there, motionless, supported only by the surging, swirling air beneath me. Below, I could see the demon's tentacle surging on, uninterrupted. Ken stood, one arm raised, the other hand wrapped around it. His eyes had gone wide and the strain of supporting me showed in his face. Gradually I began to drift down and toward the platform.

Gratitude and resentment warred inside me. My heart pounded—and not just from exertion and fright. Three times. Three times in the last day he'd come to my aid—and with powers that appeared to be sinisterly similar to my enemy's. I knew I should be grateful, but I'd learned not to depend on anyone.

I dropped the last few feet to land beside him, my hair still blowing wildly in the wind of the passing train. I grabbed onto him to keep from falling, but we were both unsteady. He'd gone pale again and I felt the sheen of sweat on him.

"Go on," he said in a dry, cracked voice. "Train's almost through. Jump."

"No," I said firmly. "After you."

He nodded and shambled to the edge.

"Now!" I shouted and he jumped, nearly without looking. He just made it and hung on, speeding away.

Adrenaline still surging in my system, I leapt for the next car, then climbed up to the top, hopped across to his, then reached down to pull him up.

He sprawled across the top of the flat container car, his bangs lifting in the fast passing air.

"By Jugoya's moon, but I need a nap," he groaned.

"The next time, I'm saving your Shitake Mushrooms," I grumbled.

"I look forward to it," he said into the warm metal beneath him.

Looking back, I saw the thick, questing coil fall flat as the last of the train's cars traveled past the tiny platform. "I think we made it," I breathed. The great twisting cloud looming in the sky grew smaller as we moved away.

"Good. Because I'm not moving anytime soon."

I stood over him, holding my blowing hair out of my face and watching not only my enemy, but also Hillsborough Street and the university campus fade into the distance.

"How long?" He peered up at me with one eye. "How long have you been here?"

"Too long it would seem," I answered with bitterness. "Almost a year and a half."

"I'm sorry," he whispered.

I sighed. "So am I." But I'd grown used to the pain of moving on, become accustomed to the hardship of starting over. I glanced down at him. Except this time I wasn't doing it alone.

But was that a good thing?

I buried the suddenly optimistic part of me that hoped it was.

Chapter Six

"Just stay down and rest a minute," I told Ken. "I'll see if I can find us a spot to hide away."

"I'll try not to fall off," he groaned.

I snorted and walked over to the edge of the car. This one and the next one were the shipping container sort, the same kind of plain rectangle you saw stacked on ships and docks. The one after that, however, was the old-fashioned boxcar you imagined when you thought of trains—I might have luck there.

I made it over and struggled to push the sliding door open from above. After several failures I got a rocking rhythm going that loosened the latch. I slid the door open enough for me to lean over and peer in.

Score. After my eyes adjusted, I realized what had been stacked high in there and wrapped in thick plastic—automobile seats. I lifted my head and called over to Ken. "Get over here, princess! Your bed awaits!"

"Bed?" He lifted his head.

"I'll just go and turn it down, put a chocolate on the pillow for you, shall I?" I called snarkily. With a grin, I gripped the edges of the car and flipped inside.

I dropped down, landing on a shaky stack of captain's chairs. At the bottom were the bench seats. I shifted piles, clearing a bench for Ken and cutting through the thick plastic with my knife. By the time his head poked in above, I was working on opening my own plush leather driver's seat.

"Yes!" he moaned. He pointed a finger at me. "Just don't watch me get down."

"Not feeling like your usual graceful self?" I threw myself into the seat. "I couldn't care less right now."

"Feeling like death warmed over," he corrected.

"If I had an ounce of energy to spare I'd float down, just to try to impress you."

I sat up. "Yes, we must discuss this ability of yours."

He climbed down the last few feet and flopped back onto the bench with a moan of pleasure. Arranging his pack for a pillow, he turned his back to me and curled into a ball. "Later," he yawned.

I didn't argue and within minutes he was breathing deeply, sound asleep. My own mind was awhirl. I felt adrift and uncomfortable. I liked to have a plan in place, a goal in mind. Right now my only goal was to question Ken. Anything else would depend on his answers. I hated delaying the conversation, but there was no denying his fatigue—or the fact that he'd come by it on my behalf.

So I methodically went through my pack, fixing my supplies firmly in mind, and then I settled back into the padded chair with both arms threaded through the straps so that I was wearing it backwards, essentially. With my worldly goods and my mind as ordered as I could make them, I drifted off.

I don't know how long I slept, but I bolted awake quickly enough when the big door slid abruptly open. Blinking at the suddenly blinding light, I leapt up, but could only make out a stubby silhouette peering in.

"Oh, fer the love of—" The creaking complaint died under the weight of a raspy cough. "Bill! Bring the stick! We gotta couple o' stowaways!"

I poked Ken and adjusted my backpack into the correct position as he rolled off the bench into a crouch. "Time to go," I told him.

The railway official had fixed on me. "Dammit! It's a stinkin' *kawad*," he yelled. "Hurry it up, Bill!"

I didn't wait for Bill and his stick. I leapt over the first man's head and rolled when I hit the ground. I was up and facing him in seconds. He turned, sneering, as Ken leaped out after me.

"Listen—we're s'posed to take you up." The short man eyed me with loathing. "You done defrauded the railway. We can use the stick on you, did we want to." He gestured toward another employee, brandishing what looked like a cattle prod as he approached. The end sparked a bit as the man raised it. "They'll want to charge you for the ride and fine you extra besides." He held up his hands. "But I don't know what's wrong with you and I don't want to know—and I durned sure don't want to catch it."

"Try not to be such a stereotype," Ken snorted. "There's nothing wrong with either of us."

"I got no mind to mess with no dirty *kawad*." He tossed his head. "Just get away from here, the both of you."

"What are you going on about?" Ken's exasperation was growing, a funny twist on the situation, since technically we were the ones in the wrong. "So her eyes are different. It's a side effect of the radiation in the atmosphere, it's not like it's contagious."

"Get on with you, I seen the vids." The man shuddered. "Seen the freaks what could dissolve your flesh just by lickin' you with their acid tongues."

"I promise not to lick you," I said wryly.

"It's not funny," Ken complained. "They can't control how they are affected by something that happened before they were born."

"The shenanigans those gangs of freaks get up to ain't funny, neither. Seen what happens in the bigger cities. Not going to happen 'round here 'cause we're not going to tolerate them hanging around."

"Maybe they wouldn't act that way if they were treated better," Ken spat out.

"Never mind," I told him. "Let's go." I headed toward a sliding gate in the fence surrounding the train yard.

"Not that way," the man said with exasperation. "You'll get me in bigger trouble." He hitched a thumb over his shoulder. "Amtrak just came in. Just head for the platform and mingle with the other passengers. Go out through the station."

I started moving, pulling my cap from my pack as I went. I donned it again and kept my head down, only looking up long enough to read the signs posted up high at passenger eye level.

"Greensboro," I said to Ken.

"Good." I could see him trying to let the news wash away some of his annoyance. "I was hoping we'd head west."

My spirits were lifting a bit, too. Greensboro. It had been a long time, but some things would not have changed. "We'll head north. We have to find Battleground Avenue."

"Why?"

"Because we're going to need a place to hide away, get some rest and sleep for the night."

Ken shrugged. "As good a plan as any, for right now." He sighed. "I could use a good night's sleep, that's for sure."

We left the station and set out. I sighed as we ran into another group of hate mongers.

"Round them up!" They wave their signs at the passing traffic as they shout. "People have rights, freaks do not!" Some of the signs feature images of horrific mutations, extra bug-like appendages, twisted spines, barbed spikes. I swallow my sorrow and bite back anger.

"Look!" Ken points across the street and I see a group of counter protesters. Some of them carry the more benign, even pretty variations of change. A girl with skin tinted pale blue shouts at the group on our side. Another with long, brilliant white hair watches sadly. The haters ignore the harmless, pretty effects and focus only on the ugly and grotesque. They revile those that are born with them instead of helping them, sympathizing with them. Others imitate the lesser changes, even going so far as to permanently dye their skin or surgically enlarge their eyes.

It's all a complicated, jumbled mess and I wish for the thousandth time that I was just *normal*.

I keep my head down and remain quiet and alert while we are in the city proper. But as Battlefield Avenue soon turned into a multilane street, I drew up alongside Ken.

"I've been thinking," he said. "I'm sorry you had to leave Raleigh. I get the feeling you'll miss it."

"Parts of it." The twang of grief in my chest when I thought of my Parkour guys would take a while to fade, I guessed.

"That thing back there, though, it's looking for you and I don't think it's going to give up."

I bit off a harsh laugh. "It hasn't in four years. I can't think why it would now."

He stopped walking and stared at me in horror. His eyes widened and I was struck suddenly. "Your eyes—you are not full-blooded Japanese, are you?" The question came out more harshly than I'd intended.

"My grandmother was Scottish," he replied, but quickly moved back to the subject at hand. "You've been running from that thing for four years?" I could see him cast back in his mind. "Ever since—"

"Since it killed my father."

I'd shocked him again. He took a step and then

stopped, turned around and began to walk in a circle. "That thing—it killed your father? Oh, this is bad." He stopped again and stared at me, then started walking, faster than before. "There are so many things I must tell the Council." His gaze softened as I moved to catch up. "I know you've been alone for a long time, Mei, but you don't have to be alone anymore. I have to go home—and I hope you'll come with me."

I snorted and moved away, edging closer to the side of the road. "Heard that a time or two before."

"Mei." He followed, stopping close behind me. Dropped a hand on my shoulder. "It's your home too, or it should be. Come home with me. To Ryu."

I ducked away from Ken's hand. "Whoa! Let's slow this down a bit, please?" My shoulders were hunched nearly to my ears. "I don't even know how to walk along beside you without being weirded out."

His expression dimmed.

I couldn't worry about his state of mind. I was having enough trouble holding on to my own. "I don't know you." I bit my lip hard to keep a swell of dangerous emotion at bay. "I don't know anything."

He raised his hands. "You're right." He stepped back. "You're right. I'm sorry. I'm handling this badly. It's just . . . none of this is happening the way I imagined it would."

"Yes, let's start there." I despised the shakiness of my voice. "How did you know to expect anything? How could you possibly know who I am? Where to find me?" I glared at him. "How is it that you've met my father?"

He gave me a little smile and gestured, inviting me to keep walking with him. "I grew up hearing stories of him. We all did, where I'm from."

Ryu, he'd said. I knew it meant school, in Japanese. But I wasn't ready for that yet. I wanted to hear about my dad.

"Brian Barrett was a legend. Beyond his master smithing skills, I mean. His work is still prized highly in the village. Such lethal beauty, he produced." He cut a glance my way. "A few lucky men possess one of his katanas. Others have throwing knives, that sort of thing."

I caught my breath, suddenly and forcibly reminded of the heat of my dad's forge, the sudden brightness of his smile in a soot-lined face, the ring of metal meeting stone.

"But it was the stories of his fighting that my friends and I loved, all the adventures he had, fighting the *yokai*, and the hair-raising tales of his missions.

I frowned. "*Yokai*? Missions?"

He watched me carefully as we walked. "Your father lived and worked in Ryu, at one time. He was one of the most successful scouts we had. Much of the knowledge we have of the enemy, we owe to him."

"The enemy," I said flatly, filing away the rest of the new information. "That . . . thing out there? The one hunting us? He *spied* on it?"

"And others like it. And on their master, as well."

The rest of them. The words echoed again. *Their master?* My head was about to explode with the sheer number of things I needed to ask, but stubbornly I clung to the thread that included my father—and the things I hadn't known about him.

"We heard stories, too, of his love for your mother, how he fought his way into Japan after the quakes—and risked everything to get her out. How they married there."

How I was conceived there, amidst the wreckage and devastation. He didn't say it out loud, but I knew he was thinking it. This part of the story I knew, but my heart cracked a little, hearing him speak of my family history like it was a fairy tale.

"Did they speak of her death as well?" I asked harshly.

Hesitant, he nodded. "Yes, although no details are known, only that she died when you were very young—and then you and your father disappeared."

I didn't know much, either, about that terrible night. I only remembered waking to screams and shouts, to a loud roaring sound and flashing lights, and then utter darkness. Almost, I could feel again the heaving of my father's chest, hear the harsh rasp of his breath in the dark as he snatched me away, never to return.

"Maybe you'll cut me a break, then?" Ken asked. "For handling this so awkwardly. I wanted to be the one to find you, have imagined it for a long time. But now—walking along, talking so casually to someone out of legend . . ." He bent suddenly and scraped his long hair back into a pony tail. Took a black band from his wrist and secured it. "It's a bit . . . strange . . . talking to someone from my bedtime stories—I'm a little freaked out."

He was freaked out? I was struck dumb. For so long we were alone, just my Dad and me, seemingly against the world. And then it was just me. Isolated and hidden. Always hiding, even when in plain sight. Four long years, every moment spent lonely, most of them battling fear. And all that time, somewhere, people knew of me. Spoke of me. Told their kids bedtime stories—about me.

It was surreal. Almost unbelievable. I blinked at him, trying to absorb it, until something he'd just said connected with something I'd heard earlier. "Wait," I protested. "You said you'd been looking for me, that you wanted to be the one to find me. Does

that mean there are others, searching for me? Besides
that thing, I mean?" I flicked my fingers skyward.
"People?"

"Quite a few." We'd paused, waiting for a
chance to get across a cross street. "The stories about
you and your family are still spoken, but there'd been
no new information since I was small. All we knew
for certain was that you and your Dad were missing.
But four years ago, the Elders made finding you a
priority. They didn't explain, just said it was
imperative that we keep you from falling into enemy
hands. They sent out scouts."

Four years ago? When my father was killed.
Anger flared high, choking me. Maybe we had not
been as isolated as I had thought.

"When I came of age, I volunteered," he
continued. "The scouts had already searched far and
wide, even all the way to JanFran."

JanFran. Like *kawad*, it was another relatively
new term—describing what was left of San Francisco,
a wreck of a city, abandoned by millions when
earthquakes and flooding ravaged the area and
separated the peninsula from the mainland. But many
refugees from the devastated islands of Japan had
gathered to settle there, stubborn and determined to
forge a new home, and salvage something of their lost
land and culture.

Just hearing the word made me wince. JanFran
was the place where I'd been born, where we had spent
my early years. Where my mother had died.

"I took a chance, though, that you'd be closer."

I wrenched my thoughts back to Ken. "Why?"

He frowned. "It made sense. They were only
looking for you, which meant that something had
likely happened to your dad and the Elders knew it.
Perhaps the two of you had been close all along. I

thought perhaps you might still be."

"Why?" I rasped. "What do they want of me, these people? Your people? Why should they care what happens to me?"

For the first time I saw something close in his expression. "They want you safe. They wish to welcome you, and to exchange information." He looked away. "Beyond that, I cannot say."

One simple glance of avoidance—it spoke volumes and bludgeoned the desperate hope of trust I might be clinging to. Doubt was a fist, squeezing my heart.

I didn't let it show. Instead I pointed to a brown sign with white lettering. Kur-Mall Park. "Look. That's where we're headed."

Chapter Seven

I'd been feeling a little better with every step that took us out of Greensboro's city limits and into a more suburban region—but I felt a huge sense of relief as we crossed into the open acres of the park. I sucked in a deep breath. The soothing scent of green, growing things washed over me, easing the sharp edge of my disappointment.

I stepped up my pace. Shards, but it felt good to drink in the feelings of safety and familiarity that came with the sight of the manicured lawns and the surrounding woods.

"It's pretty," Ken remarked. He'd begun to slow. "But where are we heading?"

"Not far." I struck east, heading for the road that would take us past the driving range, the clubhouse and the more populated areas of the park. "There's shelter here."

He shrugged and I didn't explain further. I'd stayed here twice before and this place had become a safe haven in my mind. I left the main road, heading north, and bypassed the picnic shelters. I was aiming for the area near the smaller of the park's two fishing ponds.

I stopped at the first sight of the water and sighed. Just as beautiful as I remembered it. The calm surface reflected the dazzling blue of the afternoon sky.

Ken caught up to me. "A nice spot. Do you mind if we take a second to rest? I'm starting to wear down."

"It's not far—"

He'd already plopped himself down in the grass. "We're not in a hurry for once, are we?"

I glanced around, sinking down beside him. "I

guess not."

The meadow grass was a bit on the long side.
A couple of kids played on the far side of the pond,
where a stream headed for the lake and the ground
stayed marshy year-round. The springtime sky was
clear and gorgeous, free of the coming summer haze. I
breathed it all in and stored it up, drawing strength
from the feeling of freedom and the beauty of the
scene.

Ken had stretched out in the grass, and after a
moment, I did too.

"I wonder what time it is?" I asked idly.

He turned his head to look at me. "Well, I
guess that answers one question. You're not jacked."

I bit back a scoffing snort. No, I did not have
the implants that were all the rage amongst the young
these days. Placed into their temples or wrists, the tiny
devices kept them 'plugged in' in a way that I could
not risk. "No, a direct satellite connection is not
conducive to staying hidden."

He nodded. "We don't have them in Ryu,
either."

Because they were staying off the grid as well?

"Well, we've got a few hours until the light
fades, at least, I'd say."

He nodded, but his attention had shifted.
Slowly, he sat up, staring across the expanse of green
to the pond. "Odd, isn't it?" He nodded toward the
pond. "Don't you think that's strange?"

"No," I said automatically, then laughed.
"After the last two days? What about this peaceful
scene could seem strange?"

Ken didn't crack a smile. "I don't know. Those
kids. Playing out here alone near the water, with no
adult supervision."

I stared over at the pair—a little boy and girl

scampering along the water's edge. "There are tennis courts that way," I gestured. "Maybe their parents are there."

"Maybe," Ken conceded. "They just look small, to be left alone."

I thought back. "It seems like there were always kids hanging out around here." I shrugged. "I never thought anything of it." And I'd done my best to stay away from anyone.

"I guess you wouldn't," he said thoughtfully. He wasn't looking at the kids any longer, anyway. Instead he was frowning and looking about at the ground around us.

I dismissed the matter and sat back, soaking in the warmth of the sun, but my calm state had been ruined and after a few minutes I rose and headed around the other end of the pond.

Ken caught me as I was searching along the tree line. *Ah.* There was the break I'd been looking for, a small gap in the marching line of trees, beyond which lay a small track, hardly more than a slight groove in the forest floor—nothing like the wide, paved greenways that served as trails in other areas of the park.

"This is it," I said after we'd walked a short stretch. I stared down at the small, sunken hollow and the mostly forgotten shed in the midst of it.

Ken was staring about. "Interesting," he said. "What?"

"You said you could evade that thing by blending in with a crowd, or by disguising yourself amid strong smells."

"Yes, that's part of it." Early on I had tried to live alone in the forest, at some of the hidden campsites that my dad and I had kept stocked. But I'd had several narrow escapes and desperation had driven me into more populated areas. It had been the right move, for I'd found that the higher the population, the longer the intervals stretched before I sensed my pursuer.

"It seems a miracle that you've lasted so long, with that thing after you."

I stiffened. "Yeah, it feels that way to me, too."

"If it's tracing you by scent, then this place, settled down lower than the lay of the land, must make it more difficult."

"That's the general idea," I said. "Wait here while I check it out."

I moved forward, treading silently through the forest's detritus, but already my fears were easing. Last year's fall leaves covered the trail and piled before the door. A coat of grime had settled undisturbed over the windows. I peered inside as best as I could and waited, but there was no sign of movement or hint of noise.

Carefully, I eased the door open. When it stuck on a built up layer of soil runoff, I relaxed and yanked it fully open.

It looked the same. Small and dim, with spare rods, oars and poles from the nearby fishing pier stood in one corner. In front of them lay stacks of wadded nets. In the other corner the pull out bunk was down and still made up with the blankets I'd left.

Turning, I gestured for Ken to follow. He came up to peer over my shoulder. I sucked in several deep breaths, then moved aside and, for the first time in my life, invited the outside in.

"It'll do," he said, moving in to inspect the tiny room.

I did my best to ignore the strange, uncomfortable sensation of seeing a stranger in what I considered my space.

With a massive sigh, he collapsed on the bed, his pack at his feet. "We'll be warm and dry tonight, at least."

My gaze stuck on his pack. Suddenly I realized it was the same one I'd seen him carrying at gatherings of the parkour group. "I guess you never were just a college student, were you?"

He shook his head. "No. I was looking for you. I've been concentrating on college campuses. I have to say, there were some places that I felt like I would never fit in, but your free runners made me feel very welcome."

I sighed. "They did the same for me." The log I'd dragged in and positioned upright at the window was still there. I perched on it and looked out at the gathering evening, more advanced here under cover of the trees. My mind drifted back to the very surreal danger we were in and all that happened today. "Tell me about that thing you do with the air."

He slumped back against the wall. "It's called *minding*."

"*Minding*." I tried it out. "May I . . ." I paused, feeling awkward. "I noticed . . . your arm . . . May I see it?"

He shifted, as if embarrassed, but he held out his arm and pulled up his sleeve. "It's a scar."

I moved closer, the better to see it in the dim light. Very fine, thin raised lines marked the tender skin of his forearm. They were white now, long healed, but it must have hurt dreadfully, for the design was not small, even if it was elegant—a collection of swirled lines that were meant to represent wind.

"I've seen you grasp it when you are working the air . . . *minding*."

"Yes. It's like a . . . trigger. It's part of our training. A touch to your mark helps you collect your energy, focus your will, direct your power."

"Do all of you—your people and these . . . creatures . . . do you all have powers of flight or related to the wind?"

He jerked away. "What?" He frowned. "I guess I can see why you might think so, but please don't lump my people in with the *yokai*."

"*Yokai*. You said that at the bridge. What is it?" I moved back to my seat at the window. He looked like he could use the space—and I was more than sympathetic with the notion.

"It's a general term for a supernatural creature. There are many different sorts of *yokai* in Japanese mythology."

I stared at him and asked the question that scared me the most. "And you are not one of them?"

His face changed, softened a little. "No, I'm human, just like you—as are the people of my village. We are . . . special . . . though. Our ancestors were given a serious task. Throughout the centuries we have honored their promise and continued to carry their burden."

"What burden?"

"That will be explained to you later. Let me tell you now though, that in exchange, some of our people were given certain gifts. We never know who will show the signs or how it will manifest, but it is most often expressed as an affinity for some aspect of nature."

I thought about that. "You mean, like the elements? Air, Earth, Fire, that sort of thing?"

"Sometimes. Elemental affinities are the strongest and the most prized—"

"Like you, with air," I interrupted.

He flushed a little and looked away. "Yes. But the gift can show itself in many ways. As sharpened senses, perhaps—"

"That could be uncomfortable."

"Yes. The gifts are varied." He turned redder still. "My father, for example, has an affinity for mushrooms."

I bit back a grin. "Mushrooms?"

"Yes. He's a farmer. His specialty is fungus and mushrooms. He can whisper and make any of them flourish and grow—to shocking sizes sometimes."

I nodded. "It seems the perfect, useful gift for a farmer. And you'll never go hungry."

"It is—and no, we never did. He's also found that he can enhance the . . . intensities of some mushroom characteristics. It's made him more valuable to the village. He leads a quiet, simple life and finds himself very happy."

I cocked my head at the slight change in his tone. "But you wanted more?"

The fading light couldn't hide the slightly shamefaced cast to his expression. He nodded.

I shrugged and propped my elbow on the slight edge of the window. "Well, then. It's a good thing you got your particular gift."

He nodded.

"Are there others like you? In your village? Those who can manipulate the air?"

"No. There are other elemental gifts, though."

I made a face. "I can only imagine what that must look like. Can they control tongues of fire like you do with columns of air?"

"At least one does. It takes years of discipline and practice before you can practice such skills."

I looked at him with new respect. "If there's one thing I know about it, it's long hours of training."

He leaned forward. "What about you, Mei? Do

you have an affinity, a special ability or relationship
with a certain aspect of nature?"

"No. I know how to fight, to hide and a few
other things, but whatever skills I have come from
long hours and lots of sweat."

He looked almost as if he didn't believe me, but
he let it drop.

"I didn't mean to insult you earlier." I hoped I
could manage a credible apology. "It's just that your
abilities are a bit similar to that . . . wind demon's.
And the Tengu had flight . . ." I trailed off.

"I know." He frowned. "Wind demon? Is that
what that thing is?"

"I don't know what it is." I took a deep breath.
"That's just what I've called it in my head."

"It's as apt as anything else."

"Do other *yokai* have elemental powers too?"

"Some do. There are many different sorts of
yokai in Japanese folklore. Many are associated with
nature. Some are the spirits of men. They are as
varied as the rest of life, and can be gentle, or
tricksters, or kind." His eyes narrowed. "That wind
demon—it is not kind. I could feel the anger and
malevolence coming off of it."

"I know," I whispered.

He was thinking. "Masters, the Tengu said. He
wanted to be the one to hand you over to the masters.
I don't know for sure, but I suspect that your enemy
must be in league with ours." He sat up. "That's why
I want you to come to Ryu with me, Mei. Beyond the
Elders' wish to see you, I think they might be the only
ones to have the answers that will help you."

He stood and took the couple of steps that
brought us together. My heart began to pound. He
knelt in front of me and put a hand over mine. "I want
to help you, Mei. I swear, I will do all I can to help

you defeat that thing. But first we must get safely back to Ryu."

I nodded, but uncomfortable with the contact, I pulled away and stood. "Yes. I'll go with you. I want to know everything your people do about that creature."

"Good." He sighed, looking both relieved and a little abashed. Turning back, he reached for his pack. "Another thing about *minding*—it's all about balance. It takes its toll. Translation: I'm starving!" He pulled his pack open. "I've got a tiny camp stove in here. Big enough to cook some noodles, though. Can we crack that window and get it going?"

Still uneasy, I nodded. "Do you have enough energy to go back the way we came? The picnic shelters have collapsible fire buckets in their emergency kits. You can tote some water from the fountains or restrooms there." I snatched up a net sack I'd fashioned when I was last here and seized upon the excuse to get out on my own for a few minutes. "I'll head out and gather some greens to go with it."

Before he could answer, I was gone and breathing a sigh of relief as I hit the solitude of the woods. I melted away from the shed, moving swiftly and following old habits. The trees and the underbrush, they were old friends. I'd done this a hundred times. There. The freshest shoots of kudzu were tasty. The new, small leaves of Spring Beauty. And, ah, a messy, sweet pile of mulberries, blooming early. I let the familiarity of the search soothe my jangled nerves.

I was battling my own innately distrustful nature, my woeful inability to sustain a long conversation—and a total lack of knowledge about how to act with an attractive male close to my age. Everything was about to change. My solitary existence had come to an end—at least temporarily.

I could handle it. I was trained to deal with the unexpected, to adapt and persevere. To survive. I would.

Right after I lost it. Just a little.

A break in the woods showed me a glimpse of the nearby pond. I remembered the cattails that grew at the marshy edge. Chopped up, their stalks would add a nice crunch to my salad.

I took my time finding just the right stalks. My knife—looking at it now made me think of my father and what Ken had said about his workmanship being prized—made short work of the thick outer layers. I scanned the marshy soil around me and frowned, surprised to see some unexpected plants, if my eye was right. Shrugging, I decided I'd gathered just enough—when I felt a shiver go down my spine.

Still crouching, I whirled around.

The kids. It was just the two kids. They'd come up behind me, making no noise on the soft ground. I lowered my knife.

They smiled. "Hello," they chorused in unison.

I blinked—and clutched my knife close again.

Chapter Eight

Ken fell back against the bunk again as Mei took off. His face flamed, even though he was alone.

He was handling this badly. For years he'd hoped to be in this exact position and now he was screwing it up. Royally.

He'd imagined it a thousand times. He'd envisioned discovering Mei and finding her shy, exhausted perhaps, from her long ordeal. Grateful. He'd never imagined that she'd be so . . . different. He'd never thought she'd be so distant . . . cagey, almost. He could never have predicted the depth of her skills or the quick bite of her tongue—or how pretty she was.

He would never have believed just how much he liked all of those differences.

He sat up. There was another thing different about her too. Something he didn't understand and that she appeared to be unaware of. But he couldn't shake the memory of those trees this morning—they'd bent over behind her as if to block the Tengu's pursuit. And earlier, when they were lolling in the grass—much of it had still held the winter's edge of lifeless brown color. And yet—he could have sworn that the patch of grass around Mei was greener than any other bit—and greener when she stood up than it had been when she sat down.

It was a puzzle that he needed to discuss with the Elders and for that he needed to get them both safely to Ryu. And for that he needed to get his strength back.

Leaving his pack, he set out for the closest shelter. A little brown wren followed him, swooping from tree to tree in his wake, but before he'd left the shelter of the woods it had perched comfortably on his shoulder, twittering happily and sharing all the forest gossip regarding the best nesting sights and who was tending eggs with whom.

He listened with half an ear, used to the small confidences of birds. Their friendship and fascination had begun when Ken was small, right after he began to show signs of his *minding* ability. Regarding it as an offshoot of his gift, he'd always found it useful and comforting. He'd been on his own, searching for Mei for over a year now, but he'd never really been alone.

The wren left him while he collected the bucket and water. Ken was heading back, feet dragging from the weight of his exhaustion, when the little bird came darting back. It fluttered about his head, its tweets gone raucous with some strong emotion. It landed on the bucket handle, then lifted off again, zipping about before settling to his shoulder again. *Trouble*, it said, feather's ruffling. *Girl. Water. Big Trouble.*

I nodded back to the pair. "Hello to you, too," I answered. A boy and a girl, they both looked to be about eight years old. He wore a shorts and a tunic-style shirt. She twirled the skirts of her brightly patterned dress and had a finger in her mouth.

My initial grin at their greeting was still fading. Something was off. They were both spotlessly clean—fingers, faces, clothes and shoes—despite the fact that they'd been playing along the water for hours.

I stood, tucking the cattails into the net, but keeping a hold on the knife. "Well, goodbye, kids. It's getting late. You might want to find your parents."

The girl popped her finger out of her mouth. "You wouldn't happen to have any cucumbers, would you?"

I shook my head and began to back away.

Cucumbers. It triggered alarm bells in my head. Cucumbers were important. I searched desperately for the reason why. "Sorry. Only cattails."

"That's too bad," she said forlornly.

I started to turn. "Have a good night."

The boy reached for me. "Will you help us pull out our boat? It's stuck in the mud, down by the water."

I pulled my hand away so that he couldn't reach it. It was coming back to me. I'd spent a lot of time in libraries over the last four years. My search for information had centered on creatures associated with winds, but I'd ended up reading a lot of folklore from all over the world. Cucumbers. Water. I struggled for more.

"We haven't been properly introduced," I said, looking from one to the other. "My name is Mei." I gave a low and deferential bow.

They looked surprised. The girl immediately returned the gesture, quick and graceful. "I like her," she said.

The boy initially looked pleased, but his smile faded. He stared at me a moment, then gave a less perfunctory bow in return.

I held very still. Yes, there it was. I couldn't see it, but I heard the sound of a thin stream of water hitting the ground, and saw the spot before him grow wetter than before. He rose up quickly. "That's all you'll get," he snapped. "It's been a very long time since I fell for that particular trick."

"I have given you my name," I said evenly. "The polite response is to give me yours."

"She's right," the little girl said. "My name is Kaoru."

He scowled. "And I am called Hayate."

"I know what you are," I said. "Why not show

me your true forms?"

They looked at each other—and I stifled my reaction as the illusion of the two, pretty human children abruptly winked out.

In their place stood two small, green figures—still obviously a male and a female. Both had thick, stocky torsos and spindly limbs. Hands and feet were webbed. The changes in their faces were most startling, as out popped large, owlish eyes and a carapace—like a turtle's—for a mouth. But it was their heads that marked them for what they were—Kappa. Fringed, dark hair ringed a bowl-like indention at the top of both of their skulls. Water pooled in the bowls—the same water that had spilled out when Hayate bowed. I recalled from the old, illustrated legends the fact that Kappa must keep at least a bit of their home waters in those bowls or lose all of their strength.

I bowed again. "I am honored."

"Are you sure you don't have any cucumbers?" Kaoru asked wistfully. "I do like her," she told her compatriot.

"Well, stop it right away—look at her eyes—and then just give her a sniff."

The little female looked puzzled, but leaned in and smelled me—and abruptly shrank back. "Oh, no."

"Yes, we knew something was stirring," Hayate said to me. "We could taste the faintest whiff of it on the wind—and now here you are."

"Here I am—what?" I asked.

"Here you are with starburst eyes and smelling of several different *yokai*."

Kaoru took another deep breath. "Is that Mountain Troll or Tengu?"

"What's the difference?" Hayate sulked. "That's not the bothersome one anyway—or the right question. The right question is—Do we eat her or just run her off?"

"Eat me?" I took another step back.

"Either one will bring us trouble." Kaoru said mournfully.

Hayate leaped forward suddenly and locked his hand around my wrist. "We already got trouble, didn't we—and that was when we weren't involved at all. Now we've seen her—and what do you think will happen? Nothing good." He scowled. "We might as well get our revenge in now."

I pulled, but couldn't break his grip. "You don't want to eat me!"

"Oh, but I'm afraid we do," Kaoru said sadly. "We do get a few cucumbers in the summer time, when people are out for picnics, but that's been months. We've had nothing but frog and snake for ever so long."

"It's not like the old country here," Hayate complained. "They had sense in Old Japan. Right up until The Rift, they'd put a notice up by the water and if you were foolish enough to get caught, no one blamed us. You had to be careful not to take too many or people would get riled up—but that was in the old days. We were lucky. For the last hundred years, we had a talisman that gave us the means to survive without killing. We lived peacefully with our neighbors. It was ideal."

"Your nasty, windy friend ruined that, though." Kaoru frowned.

"Now we are forced to go back to the old ways—and yet in this place you cannot take someone without a great clamor and men and dogs everywhere—even in the water searching beneath every sunken log." Hayate began to yank me toward the water.

I struggled to break free, but his grip was tight and his pull inexorable. 'I don't know what you're talking about. I don't have any friends, let alone one who is a *yokai*." I had a fleeting moment of guilt when Ken Sato's face flashed up in my mind. But I was glad he was not here facing such an awful fate.

"His scent is on you. And we have a grudge against that bag of wind."

"He really did hurt us—and all because we knew nothing of *you,* a girl with starburst eyes." Kaoru sighed. "We were lucky to have help in leaving Old Japan. The water there—tainted after the Rift— was poisoning us. But here—it was lovely. Peaceful. We could live without really harming anyone, until your breezy friend came along."

I dug my heels in. "The wind demon?" I yanked hard to make him stop. "He's my enemy, not my friend!"

Kaoru, trailing along, asked, "Perhaps we can work with her, then, Hayate?"

The male Kappa shook his head. "Against him? No. Better to get our kicks in now. He's going to punish us no matter what we do, so we might as well deserve it. We'll deprive him of his prey." He started to pull again. I didn't know if it was because of his low center of gravity, or because he had supernatural augmentation, but I found I couldn't resist his insistent draw.

"We can work together!" I struggled, knowing I couldn't let him get me in the water. I remembered clearly that a Kappa would drown their victim before feasting on them. "A challenge!" I shouted suddenly. I'd also just remembered something about Kappa being unable to resist a challenge. "Let's have a challenge!"

Kaoru clapped her hands. "Oooh, we do love a

challenge? What do you propose?"

I cast about desperately. My eye fell on the cattails and I remembered suddenly what I'd seen earlier. "Cucumbers! I'll show you how you could get a hundred cucumbers this summer."

"Oh, that is tempting, isn't it Hayate?"

"No," he answered flatly. "It's time we were smart about this, Kaoru." He eyed me, considering. "This time we'll issue the challenge."

I seized upon the opportunity. "And if I win—I go free."

He hesitated, but then nodded.

"And you'll tell me everything you know about the wind demon?"

"Fine. But if you lose, we eat you."

I swallowed hard. "What is the challenge?"

Abruptly, Hayate let me loose. "Come. I'll show you."

He and Kaoru set off. After a moment, I realized they were heading in the direction of the tennis courts. I briefly considered running away. But something held me back. They were enemies of my enemy—and oddly enough, I sort of liked them. When they weren't trying to eat me. And there were heading *away* from the water. I wanted to see if I could possibly help them out—and there was plenty of time to fight later if I could not.

We'd just come in sight of the tennis courts when Ken came rushing up behind us. We turned and I noticed a little brown wren dancing in the air about his head.

Kaoru eyed it hungrily. "It's been a long time since I had a bird," she said. "Its chi tastes like dark meat—a nice change from frog."

"Wait. You devour chi?"

She eyed me curiously and I realized that they

had both switched back to their human disguises. "Of course. Did you think that we would eat your flesh?" She grimaced.

My sense of relief was ridiculous. I would be no less dead if they drained my life energy away, but still, it sounded better than the thought of them gnawing on my bones.

"Mei, wait!" Ken called. "Wait up!"

I glanced at my escorts, but they had both paused to allow him to catch us. Ken huffed up, his eyes on me and his eyebrows dancing, trying to convey an unspoken message. "Mei, I'm afraid all is not as it seems. We must go. It isn't safe here anymore."

I raised my own brows. "It's all right. I know who they are. Kappa." I gestured. "Why don't you two show him?"

He blinked as their true forms appeared. The little bird perched on his head let out a cheep and took flight, heading for the forest.

"There," Hayate said, turning to point toward the tennis courts. "There lies the challenge." He and Kaoru began to trudge in that direction again and I set off after them.

"Mei, what are you doing? Those two are dangerous."

"I know, they've threatened to eat me."

"Then let's go. Perhaps together they might have stood a chance against one human, but they can't hope to overpower us both."

I raised a brow. "Have you eaten?"

He shook his head.

I noticed his shirt was wet, as if he'd spilled the water he'd gone to collect. "Then you won't offer much resistance, will you?"

"I can run, at least! Come on, let's get out of

here."

I didn't know if I could explain what I was feeling. "I want to hear their challenge."

"Why?"

I ignored his exasperation. "Listen, they didn't come after me because of who I am, but because they are trying to survive, just as I have been for so long." I wasn't sure if he could understand how significant that felt to me. "And they've suffered at the hands of that wind demon, as I have." I shrugged. I had no experience explaining myself, but I felt an affinity for these two. They were different too. Out of sync with the normal world. But they weren't evil. "I may not be able to, but I want to see if I can help them."

He huffed out a sigh. "Fine. Just don't do anything stupid, okay?"

I shrugged. "We'll see."

But I didn't see. Hayate had stopped and was gazing upward at the court lights. "There," he said.

"Where?" I asked.

"At the top, between the two light fixtures. See the main bolt holding the cross arm? There's a ring hanging from it." Hayate looked me over. "Climb up and bring down the ring."

"What?" Ken sputtered. "Don't be ridiculous."

I looked at the incredibly tall metal pole. It was not wide at the base and only got narrower on the way up. How had the ring got there? I thought I knew.

I looked from Kaoru to Hayate. "Why?" I asked.

"Do you think she can do it?" Kaoru asked.

"She's got a better chance than we do," her partner answered.

"We need that ring," Kaoru said. "It was a gift, from the last daimyo that ruled over our old home. It lets us siphon off just a little bit of chi from a person, so we don't have to destroy them to eat."

"How does it work?"

"They wear it, like a piece of jewelry, mostly." Hayate looked upward toward his prize. "It can change circumference from ring to bracelet to a circlet crown."

"It's usually easy for a child to talk someone into trying on their crown," Kaoru said with a grin that looked odd on his turtle-like carapace. "The ring collects the chi and when we take it back and wear it, it is transferred to us."

"So you don't kill them—but what does happen to them when they lose their chi?" I asked.

"We can survive well enough only taking a bit from each person. It's easy enough for them to regenerate it."

Totally worth the risk, then. Glad I had trusted my instincts, I examined the slick pole once more.

"That wicked *yokai* put it there. He might have taken it, or destroyed it, but he wanted to taunt us, knowing it was so close, but we could never reach it." Hayate gestured to his short trunk and spindly legs.

Ken was staring at the narrow metal pole. "You can't think to try to climb that?" he barked, incredulous.

I eyed him. "Could you lift me again, with a funnel of wind, like you did earlier?"

His shoulders slumped. "Not right now. I'm depleted. I can't even summon up a breeze." He looked at the Kappa. "If we hold the challenge until morning, though, I can easily get it for you."

"The challenge is hers," Hayate said sternly.

"I don't think you should stay here, in any case," Kaoru warned. "The wind demon knows you were here before," she said to me. "It took our ring because it didn't believe you'd been here and we knew nothing of you." She shook her head. "It will not give up. And it is not likely to be working alone. Sooner rather than later, something will turn up here, looking for you again."

Ken moaned. "But I need food and sleep—or I'll never get my *minding* back."

"Ah, that's what it is about you," Hayate said. "I knew there was something."

"We'll go," I said, "but I'm going to try first."

Ken started to protest, but I cut him off. "I climbed loblolly pines at home and some of them were about the same diameter. They even narrowed at the top like these—but they did also have bark and texture."

"I have rope in my pack, but not near enough to reach the top of that," Ken said, resigned. "What else can we do?"

Thinking, I stared off into the woods, then turned to the Kappa. "Listen. I'm going to try my best, but I'll have a better chance at making it up there if I can collect enough sap to coat my hands and the bottom of my shoes. There's a stand of small pines not far from here. Let me go and cut some, and I'll come right back, all right?"

The strange little creatures glanced at each other, then both nodded.

In the end, I hacked more branches and gathered more sap than I had initially planned, and I thickly coated my hands and feet, the insides of my knees and the net sack too. Everything else I left on the ground. I didn't want to carry any extra weight up there.

Walking up to the pole, I flexed my sticky hands. The sap might not help, but I didn't think it would hurt. Experimentally, I placed my hands on the smooth metal. It did make gripping the smooth metal a bit easier.

"Be careful," Ken ordered.

I had to admit, the concern in his voice warmed me. I didn't let it show, though. I just shifted my grip higher and took a deep breath.

"Wait!"

I glanced over, caught by the excitement in Ken's tone. "The *futari jinba*! We could get you a good ways up there with it!"

I blinked. "Why didn't I think of that?" I grinned at him. "You're brilliant!"

He flushed pink, then so did I.

"How sweet," Kaoru said.

I shook it off. "Let's get this done." I gestured for him to take his spot and backed up, giving myself a good sprinting distance.

"Ready," Ken called.

I nodded—and took off. It worked as beautifully as it had the first time. Our timing was perfect. I stepped in Ken's palm and he launched me high. I was nearly half way up when I grabbed on.

I immediately began to slip, but I tightened my knees and locked my feet and I stopped. Carefully, I began to climb.

I did well at first. I had to fiercely concentrate on several things at once—gripping with one part of my body and reaching or climbing with another—but it was not too much of a struggle to climb another quarter of the way up. At that point, though, the pole narrowed so much that my perch began to feel precarious.

Grimly, I continued to inch higher. I was still a couple of feet below the cross bar when I began to feel truly unstable. I stretched, reaching for the ring, but I was still too far away.

Frustrated, I let my forehead rest against the

pole. I refused to give up. The Kappa deserved to be happy—to have the chance to live without harming others.

I tried again to climb further, I kept slipping down.

"Come down," Ken called. "Before you fall! We'll wait until tomorrow!"

I shook my head. Kaoru was right, we shouldn't stay if my association with the place was known. But there was something else, too. I wanted to be the one to help the Kappa. I felt that I understood them, shared some of that hard edge that came from having to fight to survive.

But I was stumped. Any higher and I'd never be able to stay on.

Stay on . . .

Inspiration struck. I carefully reached down to unhook the net from my waist. It was a struggle to hold on with one hand, but I gripped hard while I eased the thing through my fingers until I had a hold of one end—then I swung it up towards the ring.

The first and second time, I missed completely. I had to make this happen quickly though, because my arms and legs were trembling with the effort of holding on.

The third time I hit the bolt that held the ring— to no effect.

Cutting off a curse, I grabbed the pole with both hands and rested as well as I could. Then, gathering strength, I tossed the sticky net again.

This time it hit the ring solidly, and hung there. I yanked—but nothing happened. The ring and the net stayed put.

I bit back a frustrated sob and thought furiously. The angle was wrong. I hung on tight to the end of the net and began to flap my wrist, sending a wave through the thing, all the way to the top.

It worked! The ring slid off of the bolt. Still entangled in the net, it swung down until it hung below me.

"Heads up, down there!" I called. And I let the net and its precious cargo drop.

I only dimly heard the resulting hubbub. I was concentrating on getting down. It was definitely easier going down, but I was still spent when I jumped the last few feet.

I nearly fell over when Kaoru launched herself and gripped me tight about the legs. "I knew I liked you." Her big yellow eyes blinked up at me. "Thank you."

'You almost gave me heart failure," Ken stated. "When you got to the top . . ." He shook his head. "It nearly killed me, watching you, knowing I should have been able to fetch it easily."

Hayate shook his head. "No, as I said, it was her challenge." He bowed to me, deeply and without care for the water that spilled from his bowl. "You have done us a great service. I would give you gifts in return."

He stepped toward Ken and reached out a hand. I saw he wore the band of metal as a bracelet—and that it was carved in unrecognizable symbols. "Come," he told Ken. "Give me your hand."

With a quick glance darted in my direction, Ken reached out toward him. Hayate grasped his hand, and I saw surprise light Ken's face. I thought I knew what was happening, could almost see the transfer of life energy flowing between them.

Ken stared at his palm when Hayate released him. "It's back! Just like that. My balance—my energy!" He clapped the hand over his other arm and shot a blast of air into the sky.

"I have given you my chi—don't waste it," Hayate admonished. "I'm afraid you will need it."

"Gifts!" I exclaimed, remembering both Hayate's pledge to tell me what he knew about the wind demon, and the challenge I had meant to issue the Kappa. "Kaoru, you can still have a hundred cucumbers this summer. You have some seedlings growing in the marsh, near where you found me."

The female nodded. "We planted them. But they never seem to thrive. They always shrivel and die away."

"It's too wet there," I told her. "I tended our garden growing up." I grinned. "Plants are like people. You just have to spend a little time listening to them and you'll discover what they want and need. Cucumbers will do better if you plant them further away from the water. They like warm soil, but kept evenly moist. And scatter some pine straw under the vines when they grow, to keep them free of rot."

She patted my arm. "We will. Thank you."

Hayate stepped up to me. "Yes, we thank you. And I offer you a gift as well."

I crouched down and looked him in the face. "I only want what you promised. I want to know everything you know about this wind demon."

He shook his head. "He is a dangerous enemy. You should not provoke him further."

"I have not provoked him, only eluded him," I said sharply. "He killed my father and has been chasing me ever since."

Kaoru let out a sorrowful sigh.

"That is provocation enough," Hayate said sadly. "He was a vain, prideful man in life and has only grown worse in his many long years as a *yurei*."

"*Yurei*? That is different from *yokai*?"

"Yes. A *yurei* used to be human," Ken offered.

"But after death has become a vengeful spirit."

"Yes, vengeful. Fuma Jinnae was that, and greedy as well."

"Fuma Jinnae," I breathed. My enemy had a name.

"He was a skilled ninja and a prized warrior in an ancient clan known for their incredible skills at stealth."

"It was said a man of his clan could disappear right before your eyes," Kaoru remarked.

"How did he come to be the . . . *monster* that he is now?" I asked.

"He led a mission for his clan leader. They were often hired by a daimyo to discover the secrets of a rival. This time they were hired to find the secret way into a daimyo lord's palace. It was an easy job for Jinnae and his men. But he could not resist teasing his victims. He sat in a teahouse and praised the villagers for their watchful guards and sharp security measures. The men of the village were proud and boasted of their efforts, and jeered at the notion that their defenses could be breached. They scoffed at the reputation of Jinnae's clan and even mentioned him by name. He was furious at the insult. When he returned home, he gave the sought after information to his clan leader, but he also sold it to several other daimyo lords."

Kaoru hissed her disapproval.

"When the original customer mounted an attack, he found his rival's palace already breached, the lord already defeated—using the secret entrance— the information he had paid for. He was rightfully angry. Jinnae's clan leader was labeled a cheat. His honor was called into question. Even when the truth was suspected, he was shamed for not instilling the proper code of honor in his men. It was a shame that no daimyo lord could bear. The leader was given the choice to give himself an honorable death by ritual suicide, or to be killed. "

"Fuma Jinnae didn't try to stop it?" I asked.

"No, Jinnae fled rather than admit to his guilt, but his tribe knew. The new leader, son of the slain man, swore to avenge his father. Over many months he hunted Jinnae down. When he caught him at last, he had a witch curse the traitor's soul before he was executed."

I stood still, absorbing all of this. My enemy had a name and a history as evil as his twisted form.

"He has only grown more greedy and prideful," Kaoru warned.

Hayate nodded. "If you have eluded him, he will take it as a slap to his pride. He will not stop in his efforts to find and defeat you." He shook his head and stretched out a hand. "I will do what little I can to help you." He took my hand in his. "I give you my chi, Starry-Eyed Girl."

I stared down at him as his eyes closed. I waited, surprised that I couldn't feel the transfer of life energy. But perhaps that was another aspect of the ring's power—and likely a useful one.

"That is unusual." Hayate frowned.

I began to grow a little nervous. Furrows creased the little creature's brow.

"It does not work." He looked up at me, puzzled. "I cannot give you my chi. The ring's power does not work on you."

"Let me try," Kaoru offered.

But the process did not work for her either.

I shook my head. "Truly, it does not matter. You've given me knowledge of my enemy—and I have been searching for that for years."

"Let me try something different," Hayate said. He took my hand again. "I'm not giving you chi this time."

I jumped as I felt a shock of . . . something more than just energy . . . transfer between us.

"Ah, that worked. This is very curious."

"What did you do?" Ken asked.

Hayate watched me carefully. "I have planted a gift in your subconscious. Close your eyes. Look inward. Can you see it?"

I did as he said—and after a moment I did see it—a green-tinged bubble in the corner of my inner landscape.

"It is the ability to breathe underwater. It will only last for a half of an hour and will only work once. Choose carefully before you burst that bubble—but I hope it will be of use to you."

My lip trembled a little as I bowed to him with the same reverence he'd shown me. "I'm honored by your gift."

"As we are by yours." He nodded and patted my hand. "Go now, and be as safe as you can."

Chapter Nine

We gathered our stuff and set out right away.

"Where are we heading?" I asked Ken as we left the park. "Where is Ryu?"

He watched me carefully. "We keep heading west. We need to head for Asheville."

I refused to react, but it took all of my discipline. His answer set my gut swirling into instant turmoil. The cabin where my father and I had hidden away had been located deep in the forests of the North Carolina mountains. We'd lived isolated and off the grid, but Asheville had been the closest town of any size. The suspicions that had sprang up last night—the painful thought that my dad had secretly been in contact with someone, that *someone* must have known where we were—grew suddenly stronger—and so did my unease.

"Okay, then." I kept my tone even. "Let's go."

"Should we head back to Greensboro and get a bus ticket? Surely between us, we have enough money for that."

I shook my head. "I don't know how, but the demon . . ." I paused. I knew his name now, and it was one that was associated with disgrace. I would use it. "Fuma Jinnae has a method of watching the major transportation hubs. Whenever I approach one, especially in a bigger town or city, the faint taste of him taints the air."

"He has hirelings, then, most likely." Ken sighed. "That's not really good news, is it?" He frowned. "I have plenty of energy now, but what of you? Will you be too tired?"

I shrugged. "No. I slept on the train and I have protein bars in my pack. We'd do better to keep to the smallest roads. If we are not going to blend in with a crowded city, then we should make sure we are where he will be least likely to look."

"Well, there are plenty of small, country roads in this part of the Piedmont. We just have to keep our heading and we'll be fine."

I nodded. "Let's go."

The light held until we hit the city limits. We continued on, then, with a beautiful sunset fading in the sky ahead.

"Can you make it seventeen miles or so?" Ken asked suddenly.

I shot him a look of scorn. "I already said I was fine."

He just grinned. "It's the weekend, right?"

I considered. "Yes. It's Friday night."

"Good. Then we'll take this back road until we hit Route 150." His mouth quirked. "Your hidey hole back in Raleigh has inspired me. I think I know a place we'll be able to rest."

I nodded and we walked without further discussion. I was thankful for the silence. I had a lot to process. I thought about Fuma Jinnae and the choices that had led him to a disgraceful and petty death. But I also thought about how grateful I felt for the chance to know the Kappa a little, to see that *yokai* might be different, but not necessarily evil.

It was reassuring, considering how out of step I nearly always felt.

When Ken said back roads, he meant it. Few cars traveled our way, and we'd been trudging for several hours with just the shrill drone of the cicadas and the incessant thrum of the frogs, when Ken suddenly stopped.

"Is it just me?" he asked. "Or did Hayate's transfer have an unintended effect?"

I paused, alarmed, and tried to peer at him in the

thin moonlight. "What? What effect?"

"Listen to the frogs."

I did, staring out into the dark woods. The nightly chorus was loud, but not unusual.

"Is the sound of them making you . . . hungry?"

I choked a little. "Hungry?"

Suddenly my stomach let out a loud, rolling growl. I glared at him. "Not until now, thank you very much!"

It wasn't even really funny. But just like that, we started to laugh. And laugh. Until my eyes watered and my knees grew weak and I sank down in the middle of that deserted country road and howled.

Ken drifted down too, and then lay back, beating the pavement as he laughed. I was caught in a loop—several times I started to wind down, but then I'd glance over, see his shadowy form convulsed, listen to his throaty laugh go on—and I'd be off again.

Gradually, though, the hilarity faded and we began to calm. I lay still for a moment on the center line, gazing up at the stars and the few wispy clouds trying to obscure them. I felt better. Lighter. Ken got to his feet and reached down a hand to help me up and I took it without hesitation.

"A couple of more miles should do it," he said. I couldn't see the smile still on his face, but I knew it was there, because mine matched it.

We walked on until we reached the outskirts of a small town. Ken had obviously been here before. He led us through a maze of neighborhood streets. The sky was just turning grey when he took a tree-lined avenue and stopped at a gated entrance.

"Bratwaite Academy?" I could just make out the engraved sign in the growing light.

"Yes. I can get us in. Since it's Saturday now, we should be able to rest undisturbed." He leaned in and waggled his brows. "I'll even let you have the bed in the nurse's office."

"I'll take it. How do we get in?"

He hitched his head to the right. "This way."

I followed him until the fancy bricked fencing turned to plain wooden slats at the back of the school. Ken stopped just past the corner and moved aside two boards that had been loosened at the bottom. They shifted easily, making a space big enough for us to slip through, then fell back into place.

"You must have hung out here a while, huh?" I asked as I straightened. The brick building stood large and stately before us. "It looks pretty high tone."

"Oh, it is. I was here a couple of months. I came because I heard there was a reclusive Asian girl here, who took most of her classes privately."

I stopped in the midst of pulling my pack back on. "You thought it was me?"

"I thought it might be." He shrugged. "Turns out it was only a violin prodigy with a rich dad and a tiger mother."

I laughed—and then I tried to imagine what that life might be like.

"But it wasn't wasted effort, now that we're getting a good sleep out of it."

I yawned. "Sounds good to me."

In the end, I claimed the sofa in the principal's office while Ken took the gurney masquerading as a bed in the nurse's suite. I slept deeply, but I came quickly awake early in the afternoon—well before I had planned to get up.

Instantly alert, I made my cautious way out of the office. Something had awakened me. Something loud. Keeping low, I crept to the nurse's station. "Ken!" I said, low. "Up! Now!"

"I should have known." He groaned and rolled

over. "You are one of those."

I kept going, heading for the administrative suite's hall entrance. "One of what?"

The cover went back over his head. "A morning person," he moaned.

I rolled my eyes. "Get used to it."

Crouching so that I could not be seen through the windows that made up the top half of the wall, I turned the knob on the door and eased it open.

The sound of voices echoed down the hallway. "There are a lot of them," I whispered.

Despite his earlier grumbling, Ken was suddenly beside me, wide-awake. "It sounds like kids. Students."

He swung the door open a bit further and peered out. After a moment he laughed. "Look out there," he invited.

I peeked out, but didn't see anyone.

"The banner," he said.

I looked up. A sheet of paper stretched all the way across the hall. In large, dark letters it read; **Murder Mystery and Dinner, Saturday Night!**

"Theatre group," Ken whispered. "Mostly students. We should be able to sneak out, no problem."

We grabbed our packs and met back at the doorway. "They're all gathered at the end of the hall, near the auditorium. When I say go, just stand up and stroll out the front doors. No one will bother us."

I admit, I gawked while we waited. I'd never actually been inside a high school. Staring around at the painted cinderblock walls and the brightly colored posters and notices hanging about, I realized it looked just like it did in all the videos.

Suddenly a rumble sounded at the front of the school.

"There's the truck," somebody called out.

"Let's get those chairs off and set up," another voice ordered. "Everyone pitch in."

The entire laughing, chattering group started toward us.

"Whoops," Ken said. "Change of plan." He watched, one hand on the door, then stood suddenly. "Let's go. Mingle in until we make it to the front door."

He pushed me and I was suddenly engulfed in the boisterous crowd. The pull of their tide was taking me right toward the glass entrance doors.

We were almost there when a voice rang out above the chatter. "Ken-sei!"

I paused, resisting the pull as a tall, grinning young male greeted Ken with a complicated mix of bumping fists and forearms. "Hey, Dylan!"

"I didn't know you were in theatre."

"I'm not, man. Just here to show my cousin around." Ken nodded in my direction and I looked down. "Newb," he said only mildly derisively.

The other guy tossed me a cursory glance, then dismissed me, as he'd been meant to. "I haven't seen you around! Where you been?"

"Ah, you know, family stuff."

Dylan nodded in sympathy. "Well, this will keep me busy all day and into the night, but ping me sometime, man! We need to hang."

Ken nodded. "Will do."

Someone shouted out a question about the chairs and Dylan turned away. "See you," he called.

Ken waved and we slipped out of the doors and through the opened front gates. The warm afternoon air felt good as we slunk away from the group and set out again, heading west.

I waited until we were a couple of blocks away

and then I raised a brow. "Ken-sei?"

He looked a little sheepish. "It's not the stupidest nickname I've heard, but it's close."

"Huh. Better than freak or *kawad* any day." I raised a shoulder. "I think it's nice."

I wanted the ease we'd achieved last night to hold.

His mouth quirked, but he didn't say anything else. We were on the main drag of the town now, and we stopped in at one of those mega pump and charge stations. They were my favorite because the facilities were often so nice. We bought cheap breakfast burritos and ate them as we walked. My mind kept drifting back to the loud, carefree teenagers we'd left behind.

"What are you thinking about?" Ken asked eventually. "I can almost see the wheels turning in there."

"Those kids."

"What about them?"

I thought a moment. "They seemed so . . . happy. So . . . free." I frowned. Maybe he would think I was criticizing. "Never mind—"

"No—I get it." A bus stop loomed ahead, with a bench and a nearby trash can. Ken tossed his sandwich wrapper and took a seat.

My heart beating just a little faster, I perched near him, trying not to notice the strands of his hair moving in the breeze. That hair, cut just a tad too long, had been distracting me for weeks.

"When I left Ryu," he said quietly, "I was a trainee. The experienced scouts would take on an apprentice and teach us to get along in the outside world. To blend in and look like we belonged, to observe, to gather information and report it as necessary and to act on it when it was called for. By the time I was ready to start out, our duties were twofold—we were to watch for signs of *yokai* activity, and we were to search out signs of you." He watched the traffic pass by before us with a slight grin. "I gawked at first. It was all so different. So fast. Loud." He glanced over at me. "It was fifteen years after the Rift when I first began scouting. Hardly anyone wore masks anymore. The new filters were mostly installed. People were moving freely again. They were reaching for normal lives, adapting to the new coastline, the refugees, all the new realities."

"Except for the *Kawaridane*," I said bitterly. "All these years later and we still haven't made that adjustment."

He sighed. "No. It's a shame that we are still fighting that battle."

I sighed, too.

"Anyway, they were getting back to normal—but it didn't look normal to me. I mixed in with one group of kids after another and I was amazed at how they were so similar to each other—but so different from the kids I'd grown up with. They weren't . . . busy. They had access to such knowledge, but didn't seem to want to use it. They had so many opportunities that so many of them ignored. They focused on clothes and objects and small dramas that they tried to make bigger." He shuddered. "I was appalled."

He glanced at me, but looked quickly away. "I grew a little resentful. I wanted to shake them awake. Show them the danger that we could all be in, the danger I'd trained my whole life to face."

"Did you?" I was fascinated. "Did you tell anyone?" I had never dared to.

"No." He didn't say anything more for a long moment.

"Did it make you . . . bitter, at all?" I asked the question gingerly.

"I let it make me angry for a while—but then I got over it."

"How?"

He shrugged. "Well, at first, I thought everything was so much easier for them."

"Yes." I'd harbored that resentment myself. "But it isn't. Not always."

He looked surprised. "No, it's not. I figured it out myself after I started to really get to know some of them. I would have thought it would be harder for you, not being able to truly connect with anyone."

"I know how to watch. And to really see."

"I'll bet you do." He nodded—as if he understood the difference, and I believed that he did. "I finally realized that their lives are different, that's all. They deal with hardships I've never had to face— and I have advantages that many of them do not."

"Your *minding*, you mean?"

He frowned. "No. Actually, I meant that I grew up in a close-knit community, with a shared goal and sense of purpose. Everyone in Ryu knows me. They are all interested in me and my family, in my well-being and in my fate." He made a face. "One way or another."

Longing surged in my chest. There was such simple certainty in his tone. I'd give a lot to possess such a sure state of belonging—to someone or somewhere. It was part of my early resentment of other, normal kids—the knowledge that I could never just be one of them, the endless, hopeless wish that I could. But I had quickly learned to squelch such thoughts. Life was hard enough without setting myself up for disappointment.

"Come on." He stood. "Here's the bus. It

should take us to the edge of town. Then if we hoof it, we should be able to make it to Winston Salem tonight."

He was right, we did make it, but by the time we arrived I was hungry and my feet ached.

Ken glanced at me. If he felt the rigors of the road, it didn't show. "There's a decent hostel on the west side of town," Ken said. "If we go the direct route we can be there just before sunset, I'd say."

I heard a question that he wasn't asking. "Is there something wrong with the direct route?"

"It's not the safest of neighborhoods."

I looked around. Winston Salem had gone through several revitalizing campaigns. I hadn't been downtown, but I knew there were some very modern buildings there and industries that had moved into the old factories. But there were still plenty of places around that had never recovered from the devastation of the tobacco industry. After the Rift, when the air was suspect on its own, the desire to pollute it further before you breathed it had died off. The loss of that main industry had hit the city hard. There were probably some pretty dicey spots still around.

I didn't care. I was starting to get impatient with our slow progress. I wanted to get to Ken's home, find the answers that I needed and be done with this thing once and for all. I let my urgency—and my feet—dictate my answer. "Let's go direct."

Maybe because we were travel worn, we passed through the worst neighborhoods without trouble. We must not have presented much of a temptation. Whatever the reason, I was grateful when Ken indicated a narrow side street and said, "It's down here."

"I didn't know there were any hostels in Winston Salem," I mused. I'd stayed in a hostel or two in my time alone. I'd learned where the good ones were—and learned to favor the ones that were often empty.

"It's sort of a . . . private establishment." Ken's gaze shifted. "I was thinking . . . maybe we should get a ride to Asheville. Between us, we should have enough to get bus or train tickets."

He must be growing impatient, like me. I nodded. "But not here. It's too big, too busy. It's probably being watched."

"Okay. Maybe in one of the next few small towns, then." He gestured. "But right now, here we are. It's just ahead."

The buildings were tall here, blocking off the last of the light that I could see above the rooftops. I followed along as Ken crossed the street and pointed to a narrow building. It bore a faded sign in a window next to a red door.

"See the pavilion with the dragon perched atop?" he asked, pointing to the sign.

I nodded.

"Remember it. Anytime you see it, you can find safe haven inside. Just tell them that you are a friend to Ryu."

I wondered if that would be true. The way Ken spoke of his home made me hope so.

A gang of young men loitered near the red door, lounging against the wall of the building or sitting on overturned boxes. They split apart as we approached on the sidewalk, but didn't really give way. They forced us to push our way through the pack. Ken didn't hesitate and I kept my gaze fixed on the ground as we made our way past them. I could hear them muttering to each other as Ken pulled the door open.

I forgot them, though, as I stepped inside—into a bamboo forest.

Truly. I caught my breath. We'd entered a
small square of a foyer—whose walls were mostly
hidden by stalks of living bamboo. The vast number
of trees grew from large troughs of earth that framed
the walls and looked as if they continued down past
the floors. I looked up. The walls of the room
extended all the way up—four stories high to a
skylight still lit with the fading day. Some of the
bamboo climbed nearly that high. Soft light filtered
down through narrow leaves, casting a green glow
over us, and over the wizened old woman sitting
across the small space, at a battered desk.

"Ken Sato," she said without looking up. Her
fingers were busily wrapping dough around a meaty
filling. "You want a private room or a bunk?"

I watched Ken's color rise. "Good evening to
you, Oba. The public bunk, please."

She nodded, still forming dumplings and lining
them up on a sheet before her. "You the last two for
today. Dinner's over." She nodded toward her
handiwork. "Dumplings for breakfast." She waved a
hand. "Go in, then."

I looked in the direction she indicated and saw
only more bamboo. Ken squeezed past the desk,
however and reached through the foliage to turn a
hidden door handle.

"Come on," he said over his shoulder. "Just
push through."

Still gazing over my shoulder at the indoor
grove, I followed him into more familiar environs.
Nearly every hostel I'd been in had a variation of this
common room—large, with an old TV, worn furniture,
a faded rug and a bookshelf full of old, dog-eared
paperbacks. This one also had bamboo in big pots,
none as large and mature as the ones in the foyer,
though.

"The private rooms are on the right. Public bunks are here." Ken entered the first room on the left. On his heels, I found a room filled with three sets of bunk beds. One of the bottom beds held stacks of folded clothes, another had a pack leaning against the pillow.

"So, a private room?" I teased. "I guess the scouts from Ryu live a little when they are away from home."

He blushed. A full-blown, actual blush. "Some do," he muttered.

A shuffling step sounded behind us. I turned away, tossing my pack to a top bunk and fiddling with the straps as an excuse to keep my face turned.

"Vouchers," the old woman said. Paper rustled. "For the sandwich shop down the block."

"Thank you, Oba," Ken said respectfully.

"You go out the back. Kids out front, some *kawad*, some not." I heard her slow footsteps begin to move from the room again. "All bad. You keep away."

"Thank you, Oba," Ken repeated.

"Breakfast early." She said, her voice fading as she moved away.

"Thank you," I called after her. My stomach rumbled at the mention of food. I managed not to wince. At least it was sandwiches instead of frogs.

"Showers or food first?" Ken asked.

"Food. I'm hungry—and then I can enjoy a long, hot shower."

"Sounds good to me."

"I'll just pop in the bathroom before we go. Will you watch my pack?"

He waved me on and I found the facilities easily enough. I stared in the mirror when I'd finished. It was still the same, the same long face, high cheekbones and freakish eyes. Yet nothing on the inside felt the same as it had two days ago.

I left, but listened to the urging inside of me and crossed back to the entrance hall.

Entrance forest, I should say. I wandered in, glad to see that the desk was empty and I could sit in the fading green light in peace. I touched the thick stalk of one of the larger bamboo trees and let out a sigh. Things might be changing, but I hoped it would be for the better. I wasn't alone anymore. I had the prospect of learning something new about my enemy, and the company of a . . . nice . . . guy.

I got the feeling that it hadn't been easy for Ken to share his own experiences, his own doubts—and I both understood his reluctance and appreciated his generosity. I appreciated his expressive green eyes and that just-a-tad-too-long hair too, but I pushed that thought away. I wasn't at all ready to go there. I'd found Ken interesting since before all this mess blew up, but he was the only person I'd spent a significant amount of time with in a long time. I had to move slowly—and I had to see what awaited me in Ryu.

I sat there a few minutes, drinking in the peace of growing things, then stood and made my way back to the bunkroom—but stopped, surprised to find the door shut and locked.

"Ken?" I knocked.

Urgent muttering sounded through the cheap wood.

"Are you still in there?" I asked.

Silence. And then he answered. "Yes. Be ready in a second."

I hesitated. My pack was in there. Who was he talking to?

More harsh whispering. It sounded like an argument. The hairs on the back of my neck rose up. I wanted my pack—and I wanted to know who Ken was fighting with.

I reached for the knob. As if he sensed it, Ken called out, "Be right out."

No way. Something wasn't right. His voice sounded . . . tense. I took the knob and jiggled as I twisted it. The cheap lock gave way and the door swung open.

Ken stood there. Alone.

I scanned the room, but there was nobody there. Just him, standing before a mirror, with one hand resting on a side table with a water basin. His eyes were huge as he turned my way.

I started to step in—and then froze.

For a moment, I locked eyes with the reflection in the mirror.

The reflection that did not belong to Ken. It was a woman, with proud features and a mass of dark hair pulled back and held loosely.

Even as I watched, she made a motion with one hand and the image faded.

In shock, I turned to Ken.

"I'm starving too," he said casually. "Ready to go?"

Chapter Ten

I sat quietly through dinner. Ken acted completely normal, as if he hadn't just been talking to someone else's image in a mirror. Perhaps he thought I hadn't seen—but I suspected he knew. By the not-quite-so-easy vibe between us, I thought we both knew.

I was probably over-reacting. It could have been nothing, a report to his superiors at Ryu. But why not say so?

I'd trusted Ken, fallen right in with his plans—and I still couldn't believe that my instincts had led me wrong. I was going to hang in. My gut had got me this far. And the prospect of information, of finding a path to freedom, held too strong a pull for me to back out now.

But I was going to be careful, too. I didn't have a lot of experience with people. I didn't think I was naive—more the opposite. Necessity often forced me to be distrustful and closed off. But the possibility existed that I might be missing something, some cue that would warn a regular girl off.

Shards, but I was tired of obsessing about it all.

"Finished?" I asked. "Let's head back, I'd like to get started early tomorrow."

Ken stood as I hefted my pack. I'd silently retrieved it as we left and Ken had shrugged and brought his along too. We stepped out, back into the street, and I deliberately let go of my worry. Better to focus on our surroundings as we walked back through the dark.

"Wait," I suddenly whispered as we left behind the bright rectangle of the lighted shop. Most of the storefronts had closed for the night, but still— "It's *too* dark."

He stopped. "Someone's taken out all the street lights. Get down," he whispered. "Move forward, away from the light from the store."

We crouched low and moved in close to the wall of the building.

"I can hear some of them ahead," he breathed.

I was impressed, my senses were pretty keenly developed and I hadn't heard anything yet. I turned to look behind us and caught a movement in the shadows just beyond the lit store window. "They're behind us too."

"Can you be quiet? I mean *really* quiet?" he said in my ear.

I nodded. He had no idea.

"Then keep down and let's move ahead. Don't make a sound. Do you remember the next building? It's apartments."

I nodded again, thinking fast. "The entry way?"
"Yes."

I recalled the short set of stairs leading into the old, converted building. It had a railing attached, and led to an overhang with pediments and a small, slightly curved roof.

"You take one side and I'll take another. Try to make it up onto the top of the overhang, but keep absolutely quiet."

I wasn't worried about myself. Stealth was one of my greatest skills, thanks to countless hours of my Dad's endless training. I could move over a leaf covered forest floor without alerting the local wildlife. A city street presented no challenge at all.

It didn't challenge Ken either. I was impressed all over again as he moved silently ahead. We reached the stairs and he leaned in again. "Not for long. Just until they pass. Hopefully they'll move on and we can make for the alley."

We never got the chance.

Out of the darkness, someone hit me, pushing me into the corner between the wall and the steps. The iron of the railing dug into my side. It was so dark that I could barely see my attacker, but I could feel that he grabbed the open edges of my jacket to push me upright.

"It's too dark," he complained over his shoulder. "I can't see her damned eyes."

I remembered how I'd slipped out of my pack straps to escape the Tengu. If these bad guys worked together, they didn't communicate. I didn't hesitate. I pulled the same move, sliding down, crouching even as I slid my arms from the coat. He was left holding the empty garment—but only until I braced myself back on my hands, raised my foot and kicked him hard where he was most vulnerable—and then he was on the ground, moaning.

I popped up and almost into a sweeping blow from another kid—yes, I'd recognized them—the gang who'd been hanging in front of the hostel. Ducking, I stared. Long, pointed talons reached for me again. From beneath his hood I caught a flare of red eyes and the quick flick of a forked tongue.

Kawaridane. And his mutation looked to be even more off-putting than mine.

I'd hesitated too long. I saw another flash of red and the stretch of thin lips into a smile. "It's her," he called, his voice rough-edged. "I see her eyes."

He rushed me.

I darted to the side, avoided his grab, rolled away and came up running. A quick dodge saved me from another thug's blow and suddenly I was past the surging, struggling crowd and running free. I picked up speed and was nearly half a block away before I pulled up.

Run and hide. Survive! My father's voice howled at me.

But—Ken.

Run!

I could hear the continued sounds of struggle behind me. The old instinct was strong. I wanted to listen to it. But I wasn't alone any more. Run and hide could not be my sole, prime directive.

I ducked suddenly—and the thug who'd launched himself at me flew over my head to land in a heap in front of me.

His hood had slipped forward. Only a faint red glow showed from inside it. He climbed to his hands and knees and I aimed my boot at that glow and kicked again, this time connecting with his chin. With a groan he sank back and the glow faded.

I turned. Ken hadn't broken away. He must be in trouble.

I sprinted back. I couldn't see a thing until I was nearly on top of them. Ken struggled with two figures at once. They each held a side, keeping him from bringing his hands together. Together, they pushed him back into a light pole.

A trash bin fashioned from flat rod iron bars stood before it. Without pausing I leaped for it, kicked off it in mid-air and launched myself at Ken's closest attacker. My weight and momentum carried him away, but not far. His weight brought us both down. I leaped up, but he reached out and grabbed my arm.

His hand was huge, his grip tight. I pulled, but he merely used my resistance as leverage to help hoist his bulk up.

I tried again to wriggle away. He was human, but large and strong as an ox. Reeling me in, he tried to wrap his arms around me.

I shocked him by stepping in closer until we

stood chest to chest. He stared down at me, then
pinned my arms to my sides.

I grinned and relished the surprise on his face as
I lifted a shoulder and pulled an elbow high and back.
Using the 'swimming' technique my father had taught
me, I slid my hand between the oaf's elbow and his
side. Quick as thought, I repeated the maneuver on the
other side until I held him clasped tight against me,
with my elbows bent under his arms and my forearms
pressing him towards me.

Before he even realized his predicament I
grasped his shirt and pulled it back until the edge of it
dug into his throat, cutting off his air. He gasped and
tried to fight, but I had him. When he at last stepped
back to escape, I let go of the shirt and pushed him
hard away.

He staggered back, but was too solid to go
down again. I turned and leaped to the top of the trash
bin. Crouching, I readied myself as he regained his
footing, growled and headed for me again.

He was stopped by a mighty gust of air. He
fought it, but even his density was no match for Ken's
relentless gale. Ken's hair blew about him while he
gripped his forearm tight and blasted the big ox with a
powerful, steady stream. Step by step it pushed the
thug back until he caught up against the stair rail.

"The rope." Ken's voice strained with effort.

Glancing around, I saw the first guy who'd hit
me, still bent over in the corner, had dropped a length
of nylon rope. I leaped down, grabbed it up and snared
first one meaty hand, then the other. I used the big
oaf's bulk as shelter while I tied his hands to the
railing. For good measure, I anchored it through the
thick wooden scrollwork supporting the entryway's
roof. Even if he did pull the railing up, he'd be hard
pressed to do the same to those.

Ken let go and the wind died away. I looked around. Besides the ox, I could just barely make out four other bodies littering the ground—in various states of consciousness, from the sound of it.

"Let's go." Now that we were both free, I was ready to get away, to run.

Ken took a deep breath, grabbed up his pack and we headed for the alley.

Unfortunately, it was already occupied.

"Change in plans," a voice rang out as a new trio stepped out from the darkness. "I'm sorry, but you'll be going with us."

I didn't wait to find out who they were, merely turned, pulling Ken with me.

Another group approached from behind.

We were trapped.

Chapter Eleven

"Bring the girl. I don't care what you do with him—just make sure he won't follow."

I turned my head back towards the speaker. He hung back, staying hidden in the shadows of the alley, but his voice held a curious resonance. I felt it like an itch deep inside my ears. Was he *kawaridane*?

His companions weren't so shy. They moved toward us, one staring intently at me, the other grinning and looking back and forth between Ken and me.

I crouched into a ready stance.

"Listen." Ken spoke low. "You are the one who has to get away."

I shook my head.

"No. You have to get away from them. They're probably working with that demon or for whoever *he* is working for."

I shivered suddenly. I hated the thought that I might have more than one enemy out there.

Ken looked up. "I'll lift you to the fire escape. You run, fast and far. Get yourself to Asheville. Find the Dragon's Eye. I'll meet you there." He paused. "Or someone will."

"No," I protested. "We stay together." My eye was on the intense one of the approaching pair.

The creep stared back at me—but lost his focus as a short figure stepped in from the darkness, inserting itself between our two groups.

"I'm tired of you hanging outside my place," it said in a flat voice. "Now you harass my guests?"

"Oba!" Ken gasped.

"They learn their lesson now," the diminutive woman insisted. "And you not come back here again," she told the others.

She gestured. After a moment, a rustling sound
filled the air, sounding ominous and seemingly coming
from every direction in the surrounding shadows.

"What is it?" The smiling thug had lost his grin.
"Rats? Birds?"

The little woman turned to face us. She
looked at Ken. "My bamboo trees have grown ten feet
higher. Get her to Ryu."

Ken nodded. I frowned. What was she talking
about? And what was making that noise?

One of the creeps made a choked sound and
pointed down. I followed his gaze and saw something
creeping along the ground, aiming for his feet. Peering
closer, I saw that they were plants—tendrils of weeds
that had grown long vine-like limbs that reached for
our opponents.

The other one yelped and shook off a long,
questing trail of petunia that reached down from the
balcony of an apartment above. Oba concentrated
fiercely, her hands held slightly out before her, her
fingers twitching. As she pointed, the petunia snagged
onto the thug's shirt and quickly wrapped around his
arm. His partner was standing on one foot and trying
to shake off a shock of weedy vines tangled around the
other.

"Now," Ken said grimly. He pressed his
fingers against his scar and a breeze began to blow
down the alley.

'No!" I said.

He didn't listen. The wind whistled, coming
stronger now, stirring up dust and trash and beginning
to coalesce into a swirl of air at my feet.

I stomped, then stepped back, trying to escape
it. "No, Ken!" I insisted.

He just shook his head. A funnel formed
around my ankles and began to climb higher up my

legs.

Suddenly the temperature plummeted. Goose bumps erupted on all of my exposed skin and abruptly my breath—and everyone else's—drifted like mist in the cold air.

"What did you do?" I turned to Ken.

"It's not him," Oba said quietly. She began to scan the heights of the buildings around us.

The funnel, which had faltered, picked up speed and began to grow again.

"Ken! Stop!" I hissed.

"Yes, do stop. In fact, don't worry yourself, old boy." It was yet another new voice, coming from somewhere above us. "I've got this."

With a thump a figure dropped in to land just in front of Oba.

I stared. The light was dim, but I could see that the stranger was tall. Not thin, but rangy with lean muscles that showed to advantage beneath worn jeans and a blue t-shirt. His hair was a shocking white and rumpled in a spiky fashion.

He stood perpendicular to our position. With a glance to the left, he grinned at Ken and me. His smile actually grew wider as he turned away to look to his right—at the still-struggling thugs. He pointed a finger at them and suddenly they were trapped chest deep in a huge, ragged chunk of ice.

I sucked in a breath even as the deep voiced leader of the gang called for a retreat. But it came too late for the group behind us. The stranger pointed at them next. A rush of arctic air, so cold it felt like it burned as it went past, hit all three of them and they were abruptly encased just like their friends.

I rushed past Oba and the stranger, intent on seeing if I could catch a glimpse of the leader, but he was gone.

"Well then," the newcomer stated. "That's done." He glanced from Oba to me and to Ken. "Shall we go, then? I believe we have an appointment to keep."

Chapter Twelve

Mei had finally succumbed to the drone of the tires on the road—and to the inevitable adrenaline crash that followed our . . . adventure. Relief made Ken slump a little further down into the back seat, but he was still too wound up to sleep.

Reik grew quiet once Mei dropped off, not bothering to waste his vaunted charm on Ken.

He shrugged. They were wary with each other. Distant. Exactly how he preferred it too.

Reaching into his backpack, Ken surreptitiously drew out a small blade. Lovingly, he stroked the edge, caressed the familiar grip. It was a prized possession, this small, wickedly sharp throwing knife given to him by Brian Barrett himself. He wasn't sure just why he hadn't told Mei about it. Maybe because she'd seemed so . . . protective of the memory of her father. He hadn't wanted to upset her further.

He didn't want to upset her at all, but he was walking a delicate line, balancing her needs and Ryu's. He glanced up into the front seat again. Having Reik around was only going to make things harder.

Nothing new there. He looked back to his knife. Since they were small, Reik had always made things more difficult.

Case in point: Mei's reaction to meeting the other scout. She'd stared, eying Reik's distinctive hair, the markings that framed his face, responding to his intensity, and in general acting as intrigued with the damned village favorite as every other girl Ken knew.

With a curse, he called up a soft cushion of air and let the knife go. He kept his hands clenched at his sides. The blade rested there in mid-air while he concentrated on supporting it with just his *minding* ability. It was considered an advanced technique to *mind* without using your trigger. It had been a sore point—one of many—that Reik had never seemed to need his trigger to call up his power. Ken had only just begun to explore the skill when he'd been chosen to go out as a scout. He'd had little enough chance to practice since then.

He frowned and set the knife to spinning. A sudden thought struck him and he paused it. "Whose car is this, anyway?" he asked Reik. Maybe he shouldn't risk the nice leather interior.

His old nemesis shot him a smirk in the rear view mirror. "Mine."

His? How had that come about? Scouts didn't own cars. The entire village itself only owned a couple of old trucks for transportation of supplies.

Shrugging, Ken set the knife to spinning again.

"So, you found her," Reik said, glancing back again.

Ken added another current of air, making the knife twirl in alternating directions.

"She's not like Akemi."

No. Mei was nothing like the other girl. Thank all the gods and ancestors.

"She's not what I expected." Reik watched for his reaction in the mirror.

Ken kept his expression perfectly blank. "No."

He turned to watch the dense tree line as they whizzed past it. The Elders had talked to him of Masuyo Barrett before he left. They'd had several theories on what she might be like, what her ordeal might have done to her—and she resembled none of them. She was so much more than anything he'd been led to expect. And if half of his suspicions were correct, then the Council, and Akemi, and the entire village were all about to get their expectations—and maybe their lives—turned upside down.

I find myself back in the garden, dreaming again. The stone path is familiar, the blooms as lush as ever—but something is different this time. I cannot quite put my finger on what it is.

I wander my usual path and the beautiful lady appears ahead of me, as always. She is wearing the same gorgeous pink robe. I notice that the jewelry hanging in her hair is adorned with tiny noisemakers. She chimes softly as she walks.

And I realize—that's it. Usually I can feel the breeze carrying petals as it brushes my cheek and smell the incense that the lady inevitably lights at the end—brief, fleeting flashes of sensation. But this time my senses are fully engaged. As if I were really there, I can hear the cheerful babble of the stream, feel the brush of a branch on my arm as I pass. As I step onto the first rungs of the bridge, they shift. My footsteps sound loud on the wood. It's all so real—including my urgency, my need to speak to the unknown woman. I pound again on the invisible barrier, more desperate than ever. Like the last time, she appears to hear me. She straightens and turns around.

And I gasp and stumble back.

Her eyes look like mine.

I jerk awake and realize that Ken is leaning over the car seat from the back, touching my shoulder.

"Awake?" he asks. "We're here."

I glance over at the new guy, Reik. He's giving me a strange, assessing look. Had I said something in my sleep?

"Here?" I ask.

"Asheville," Reik answers. They open their respective doors and climb out. I follow, peering about, just able to make out the narrow confines of an alley.

"Already?"

It's still dark. We were surrounded by quiet, and by the still, intense blackness that only occurs in the middle of the night. Reik shushes me, although I've only uttered the one word.

I still didn't know how to feel about him. He was good looking, without doubt, almost in an anime-character-come-to-life way. That shocking white hair looked incredible next to his slightly olive skin. He was obviously of blood as mixed as mine, but he looked more European than I did. He had a mark on his forearm like Ken, easily visible since he wore only snug jeans and a dusky blue t-shirt that highlighted the brilliant color of his eyes. Also comprised of thin, raised white lines, it depicted a feathered crystal, like the frost that forms on the window in winter.

Fascinatingly, he had a series of similar, varied versions of the mark lining both sides of his face as well, trailing from his temple and dipping below his jaw. Colored a faint, icy blue, they contrasted with his hair and added to his exotic look.

More than his look drew me, though. There was something—a distant intensity that called to me. He covered it with a flippant charm that made me want to push past it to the truth below. He awakened all sorts of twitching, jumping, interested urges in my gut—but I couldn't help wondering if all of it—the looks, the distance, the banter—was calculated to do exactly that.

We started down the dark alley, and all in all, I was glad that Reik led. I followed him, and felt safer knowing that Ken was at my back.

Reik stopped before a door, lit from above by a single, bare bulb. On the door was painted a symbol, an eye. Narrow slitted pupil, heavy scaled brow, brilliant red color.

"The Dragon's Eye," I breathed, remembering Ken's whispered instructions, earlier.

Reik entered without knocking. I pulled on my cap and followed. We passed through a crowded storeroom and into . . . magic.

It was the first word that popped in my head, and although part of me shrank away from the squealing-teenage-girl reaction, another part knew the place deserved a high-pitched squeak or two. It was a market, slightly rustic, brightly lit, neat as a pin—and filled with wonders. High ceilings, curved arches, natural wood, and gorgeous stone accents...it felt like a cross between a theme park and a high budget fantasy movie.

It invited me in. I stepped further into the warmth of the place. My jaw slackened as I stared around me. It was as if someone had peeked through my memories, read my mind and gathered every comfort into one place.

I blinked at Ken. "It's amazing."

He grinned. "I know. And it's different every time."

I frowned at that. What did he mean? But I forgot to worry about it as we moved in further. Strangely, we were not the only customers. The street outside the storefront windows looked as deserted as the alley had been, but there were people here, filling chunky baskets with a wild assortment of products.

The section we'd entered looked like some sort of organic produce market. I could see my favorites; cherries, strawberries and muskmelons. Ken stopped at a rack whose layers were covered with different types of mushrooms. An older gentleman in short pants and a long, ragged coat stopped next to him. Marveling, he picked up a Portobello as large and round as a dinner plate.

"One thing that never changes about this place," he remarked. "They always have the best mushrooms. The biggest and most flavorful I've ever seen!"

I raised a questioning brow at Ken and he nodded, a small, secret smile on his face. His father's work, then. Neither of us said a thing, but it felt good, sharing the secret.

Reik had moved past the produce. I saw him stop at a shelf on the wall. Trinkets and knick-knacks crowded together, making a colorful hodge-podge. I moved closer. He was staring at a snow globe resting between a smiling Buddha and porcelain cat. He must have just given it a shake, for the snow fell inside of it, around a figure of a woman whose hair floated about her.

I started toward him, but something brightly colored distracted my eye. I paused and looked—and my jaw dropped.

Talk about a flash from my past. It was a circular rack, filled with the Japanese snacks that I'd loved as a kid. When we lived in JanFran, my dad had taken me to the corner store every Saturday. They'd had a rack just like this, filled with many of the same goodies. I stepped toward it, glimpsing Pocky Sticks and banana flavored milk powders, candy ice cream cones and Cherry Blossom flavored Kit Kats.

I took a step toward it, but was distracted again. A tiered shelf of greeting cards stood nearby. They all looked handmade. I sucked in a breath. A layered rack of gorgeous washi paper stood next to it.

"Would you like a sample?"

I turned, finding a corner nook I hadn't noticed before. Floor to ceiling shelves were lined with marked tins and a counter stretched across, lined with beautiful teapots. A man smiled at me from behind the counter, and shocked, I looked down, pulling my hat brim lower. I'd been so caught up in the place; I'd forgotten to be careful.

"I've got some delicious cinnamon ginger tea all ready," he coaxed. I checked him out with my usual quick, careful glances. He was in his late thirties, perhaps. He had a kind smile, but I caught an air of alert tension coming from him too.

He picked up a lovely cast iron teapot, squat and decorated with carved twigs and blossoms. "Or perhaps you'd prefer Jasmine?"

I sniffed appreciatively. "I love Jasmine."

"Well, then." He poured a bit into a paper sample cup. "This is Silver Jasmine. Very special."

I stepped closer and took up the sample. I inhaled and then tasted, smiling down at my boots as the bright taste somehow flooded all of my senses.

"It's okay, you know. Here, you don't have to hide."

I set down the sample and took a step back.

"Here, why don't you have a full cup? You look like you could use it." He poured and slid the small, pottery cup my way. "Is it your eyes?" he asked casually. "It's okay. There really aren't any secrets here, in any case."

"Thanks for the tea." I turned to go.

"They can't be worse than mine."

I paused. I was danged good at quickly sizing up all the details of a scene with my quick, sure glances. I'd seen him. Nothing out of the ordinary had registered, save for that almost . . . predatory alertness.

"Go ahead, have a look."

It could be a trick. But Ken stood, relaxed and chatting to someone not far away, and the undeniably powerful Reik had moved nearer to the front windows, but still stood close enough.

I gave in to my curiosity. I looked up.

The same glance looked back at me—but with very different eyes. Bright green, with a vertical, reptilian pupil, they blinked at me. Tiny green scales had erupted around them. Past his brow and the corner of his eye they began to grow larger as they stretched to his hairline and crossed his cheekbones below, to frame and disappear behind his ears.

I stared and stared—and forgot that I was giving him the same chance.

"Ah," he said slowly. "Yours are beautiful."

"So are yours," I blurted.

He grinned. "Not many think so." He looked again at my eyes, then frowned and glanced around at the market. "So, are you Masuyo?"

I started. Would I ever get used to a stranger knowing my name? It still triggered an urge to turn and run. Finally, I nodded.

"I'm Neil." He glanced around the store again, his eye pausing on the rack of retro-Japanese junk food—and then on something else. "You like those sugar-bombed slushy drinks?"

I lit up. "Yes! Do you have those?"

"It appears that we do," he said with a shrug.

I turned searching. "The cola flavored one is my favorite, but cherry will do in a pinch." He made a noise and I glanced back. "You don't like them?"

"I prefer tea." He poured himself a cup of the Cinnamon Ginger.

"I like both," I replied firmly.

"You can have both."

There. I saw the drink machine near the front door. And score! They had cola-flavor!

"Wait. I'd like to show you something first."

He sounded serious. I turned back.

"Watch. Right here." He pointed at his face. Yes, it was different, but it truly was beautiful too. He blinked—and abruptly, everything that made it different disappeared. He stared at me now from the completely ordinary face that I'd thought I'd seen at first.

Excitement and an intense, jealous burn flared high. "How? How did you do that?"

"It's a simple charm. I'd lay odds you can do it." He looked over my shoulder at Ken. "Are you traveling with Kenshin? To his home?"

Kenshin? I blinked. "Yes."

"Good. You can learn it there, and more." Suddenly he reached across the counter and took my hand. "But remember, Masuyo, you don't really need such tricks. There is nothing you need to hide, inside or out."

I stood uncertainly, but I didn't pull my hand away. I didn't know what he meant.

"Mei!" Ken's call came from behind me. "There you are. I wondered where you'd got to."

I stepped back then, and turned to raise a brow. "I've been right here, in plain sight."

"Neil!" Ken crossed over and clasped hands with the other man.

"It's been too long." Neil glanced at me. "Nice job, finding our girl, here."

Ken colored slightly. "We've got to get back— as soon as we can."

Neil nodded. "It's the third gate today." He grasped Ken's shoulder and his voice lowered. "But be careful, okay?" He glanced across the store, in the direction of the darkened street outside. "Something's up. There's something stirring out there, but I can't quite get a grasp on what it is."

"We'll be careful."

Neil relaxed then. "Before you go, you'll have to see Tomoe first. She'll have something special for you, I'm sure." He pointed a finger. "Look for her over there."

Stepping out from behind the counter, he gave me a formal bow. "It's been an honor to meet you, Masuyo. Remember what I said." He grinned. "And go with Kenshin. My wife will have something for you, too, I suspect."

"Thank you." I said it quietly. I felt oddly reluctant to leave him, but he waved me on.

Ken stepped away, maneuvering around a stack of crates holding gorgeous oranges. I followed him— and gasped in delight.

"Dorayaki!" I rushed up to the sizzling griddle where a pretty woman presided, a little boy at her side. He stood on a crate and mixed a bowl of batter. Forgetting to hide my eyes, I smiled at the woman. "Those are my favorite."

She smiled back. "Mine too. My mother used to make them for me."

A pang thronged in my chest, like the strum of a bow. My father had been the one to indulge me with junk food, but one of my few memories of my mother was of helping her to make the small pancakes filled with sweet red bean paste. I used to eat them until my stomach ached.

"These are nearly ready." She smiled warmly at Ken. "And welcome back to you! I knew you must be coming, for we have takoyaki today!"

"And they are always best here at the Dragon." Ken smiled back at her and gave the boy a mock frown. "Excuse me? Who is this? You there—do you know where Tai is? It couldn't be you—you are surely too big to be him."

The boy, who looked about four years old, kept

stirring. "I am just the right size to be Tai." He
grinned, then. "And I am learning to make takoyaki!"

"You are indeed," his mother said, handing him
a small wooden tool. "Now spin the little balls around
a bit, so that they cook on all sides."

He bent over a special pan set right into the hot
griddle. It's many little round indentations held savory
dough mixed with vegetables and meat.

"Learn well, young Tai, so that you can teach
me," Ken told him. "Because these are my favorites!"

Suddenly Reik was looming close behind us.
"And thank your mother, young man, for being so
good as to teach you such a useful skill. You don't
know how lucky you are." He gave Tomoe a big smile
and a bow. "They smell delicious."

Ken must have caught my dubious expression.
"What?" He acted shocked. "You don't like
tokoyaki?"

Grimacing, I shook my head. "Octopus has
never been my favorite."

"You'll like Tamoe's," he insisted. He sobered
a little. "We'll take enough for three, if you have
them, Tamoe, but we'll need them to go."

"I'm already prepared for you." She began
pulling out take out containers. "But next time, come
when you can stay and visit a bit." She glanced at me
and I saw her hesitate a fraction of a second when she
met my eyes again. "And bring your friend."

He was right, these were better than any other
octopus balls I'd had, but they didn't compare to the
dorayaki. A few minutes later I grinned like an idiot,
climbing into the front seat, clutching my bag of little,
warm pancakes and a big thirty-two ounce cola slushy.

I was slurping happily as I waited for the other
two to load up—but suddenly I stopped stone-still—
and not because I had brain freeze from the cold drink.

My neck tingled. The hair on my arms rose. I rolled down the window and looked out, up and down. Something was watching us.

I saw it then—a pair of eyes shining close to the ground at the mouth of the alley. They met mine and didn't look away.

"Mei?" Ken had noticed my tension.

The eyes blinked. The car lights turned on and I caught a glimpse of large ears, then the flash of a red tail as the animal turned away. I relaxed a little.

"What is it?" Ken asked, low.

"Nothing." I pulled my head back in. "Just an animal."

But a lingering alarm stayed with me as we pulled away and I watched the winding streets of Asheville fade into lonely mountain roads.

And later, when I slept again, I didn't dream of the mysterious lady, but of slanted eyes glowing in the night.

Chapter Thirteen

I awoke to find the scenery the same; winding, unlit roads and the darkness of the forest surrounding us. Reik obviously knew where he was going, though, and he handled the car and the narrow lanes with ease.

Ken slept in the back seat. When Reik noticed I was awake, he smiled over at me. "Feel better?"

I nodded. This guy was not at all like Ken. Not to say this was a bad thing, except that there was . . . something about him. I couldn't quite get my finger on it, but I also couldn't dismiss the thought that the problem might just be my own inexperience with smooth, bad-boy charm and startling blue eyes.

We spoke a little. I asked him about life as a Scout and he happily told me a couple of stories about his encounters with *yokai*, but he mostly talked about the people he'd befriended and some of the shenanigans he'd resorted to in order to hide the truth from them.

I could empathize, a bit. He was smart, funny and quick-witted. He'd glance at me with that small, shared smirk, and my pulse would ratchet a bit. But I wasn't comfortable. And I grew less so when, after a little silence, he asked about Fuma Jinnae.

"Ken described what he saw, the tall column of air, like a standing tornado. But that's not really what he looks like, is it?"

I kept my gaze fixed on the passing darkness. "No."

"He said he thought there was an indistinct form hidden in there."

I didn't respond.

"What did you see?" he asked, low and urgent. "What does this demon's true form look like?"

I turned. "Why do you want to know?"

His face looked set and hard. "Because I think we'll be facing him, before this is over—and I'd like to know what I'm up against." He shrugged. "You know, I'm hunting a demon too. He's a *yurei,* like yours."

"He's not mine," I protested.

"Whatever. Mine was a sorcerer in life, which makes him a particularly nasty spirit. He's as much animal as man, now, though. He sometimes wears white fur and fangs. He's gets mistaken for a Yeti." He glanced over at me. "Ever seen or heard of one like that?"

"No, but then again, I thought there was only one supernatural being in the world just a few days ago." I returned the look. "What did that Yeti-man do to you?"

His face set. "Not to me. He hurt someone I . . . love." He sighed. "Now, I told you about mine, you tell me about yours."

A fair request. Yet I didn't want to speak of that day. I never had.

"Tell us, Mei." It was Ken. He'd awakened and sat, poised and waiting. Reaching over the seat, he gave my shoulder a squeeze. "You might feel better."

"I doubt it," I snapped. But we were all in this mess together, at least for now. And if I wanted to learn what they knew—what their people knew— about Fuma Jinnae, then I was going to have to share my knowledge, too.

It took me a few minutes to gather the strength I needed to relive my father's last moments.

"I was out in the gardens that morning, while my dad worked in his forge. I'd spent hours weeding and watering. I'd gathered a basket full of zucchini to bring back." I let out a sharp bark of something that might have passed for laughter. "I hate zucchini."

I swallowed and forced myself to continue. "I stopped at the forge because the old fashioned water pump there brought up the coldest, best-tasting water and I was tired, dirty and thirsty. My dad wasn't there. I didn't think too much of it. The fires were still burning." I hitched a shoulder. "I figured he'd gone to the barn for a tool or a measurement. We had a new kid goat that kept jumping on high things and getting stuck—he might have gone to help her. I washed up, cleaned the veggies and headed for the house."

I had to stop here, and both of the guys waited, respectfully silent. Outside, the dark forest passed.

"I knew something was wrong as soon as I got close to the cabin. The goat's lead was snapped, she and her baby were gone. I couldn't see or hear the chickens. I could hear a strange roaring sound, but I didn't know what it was. It was coming from the house."

I cleared my throat. "The door was open. I picked up a staff from our rack of training weapons and approached slowly, carefully, like I'd been taught to do."

I began to talk faster, hoping to get it over with. "My father was inside—but he was hanging suspended in the air. The demon stood before him, laughing."

Reik shot me a quick glance. "What did he look like?"

"Evil." I shivered. "Ken knows. He gives off an aura of hate."

Ken made a noise of agreement, but Reik just looked impatient.

"He hovered in mid-air too. His robes were long and shabby, the sleeves were overlong, reaching the hem and all the edges were jagged and worn. He wore an enormous *sugegasa*—those conical hats made of bamboo—it came down low over his face and was trimmed in a dark veil that dipped lower still."

"You couldn't see his face?" Reik asked.

"No—just the white glow of large, angry eyes.
Those swirling columns of air came from his sleeves.
That's what the sound was. He uses them as hands, as
weapons, as sensors, although I didn't know all of that
then. He was screaming at my dad in this strange,
resonant voice. 'Where? 'Where?' It echoed in the
small rooms, all while he tossed him about with one
hand and knocked furniture aside and cupboards open
with the other."

"What did you do?" Ken whispered.

"I ducked back to the side of the door and tried
to *think*, but somehow my dad knew I was there. 'You
know what to do!' That thing had spirals twisted
around his chest and his arms and legs. One squeezed
around his throat and pushed his head back, but he
gasped the words out."

"Did you?" Ken asked. "Know what to do?"

"I knew what he wanted me to do," I bit out.
"The cabin was small, but it was well furnished, well
supplied—and airtight." My fists tightened. "You
know how it was back then. Airtight windows and
sealed doorways—everyone had oxygen and filters at
home. We were all ready for the next cataclysm, the
next blast of poison to hit the atmosphere. Dad had
insisted on making the cabin airtight, so not a molecule
could get in. We did regular tests."

"He was planning how to keep it out," Reik
said.

"And now he wanted you to lock him in there
with it?" Ken breathed.

"The control panel was right by the door. I
could have hit the button and run. Survived. It was
the mantra he gave me. It's what he had prepared me
for, what he had drilled into me a thousand times

over."

"But you didn't," Ken said with certainty—and sympathy.

"It had my dad—of course I didn't! But I had no inkling that this was what I'd been preparing to fight all this time. For the first time it all made sense. I knew exactly what we'd been hiding from, but I didn't know what to *do*!" I let the anger I still felt spill out. It had only multiplied as time passed. All of these years and I still didn't know how to defeat my enemy.

"What else could I do? I wasn't leaving him, not in a million years. I stepped out into the doorway and told that thing to let my dad go. It laughed and its eyes flashed. 'Here you are,' it said. 'At last.'"

It hit me again, hard and swift in the gut, the other reason why I never relived this day. The sick certainty that *I* was the cause—of all of it. The running, the hiding, the solitude, maybe even my mom's death. It was all because that thing had wanted *me*.

I didn't have to share that. "It snatched the staff from my hand, tossed it across the room. It started toward me."

I don't think either of them was breathing now.

"My dad shouted at me to run, to hide. The demon stopped. It glanced at him, almost as if it had forgotten it had a hold of him. It looked back at me and without hesitation, without another thought or a threat or an attempt at negotiation, it tightened his coils and snapped my dad in six places." I fought back a sob. "Like it didn't matter. It didn't even look—just cracked him as easily as a porcelain doll and dropped him on the floor like garbage."

Silence reigned in the car.

"What did you do?" Ken asked quietly after a

few minutes.

"I hit the button," I said bitterly, " and I took off."

"Obviously the place couldn't hold the demon," Reik said.

"No, but it slowed it down. It must have taken it a while to summon up enough power to blast its way out, and by then I was long gone."

We all fell silent when I had finished. Exhausted again, I curled up in the seat and faced the window. Ken sat back and Reik gripped the wheel with restless fingers, but we kept our thoughts to ourselves. I slept again, only waking as Reik pulled the car onto a slight shoulder on a curve that looked like a hundred others we had already left behind.

"We walk from here," he said briskly, and winked at me. "Hope you got enough rest."

I was perfectly willing to go back to our previous banter, to pretend like my confession had never happened—until it was time to get some answers of my own.

I didn't answer his question, but I did think about it. He might be worried about my energy level, but Reik didn't appear to need any rest. He was just as sardonically chipper now as he'd been when he'd dropped into that alley in Winston Salem.

"What about your car?" I asked, stomping my feet and hefting my pack.

"It'll be taken care of," he replied, nonchalant.

I lifted a brow, but quickly ceased to care as we set off—and despite myself, my mood began to improve. We left the car and the road behind, moving deeper into the woods and my heart lifted right along with the dawning of the sun.

Bright, new leaves were bursting on red oaks, hickory and sugar maple trees. Dogwoods were still blooming and mountain laurels were pushing out buds. The smell of Fraser firs hung in the fresh morning air and at our feet, the surprisingly abundant number of wildflowers that thrived here were getting ready to put on their springtime display. All of this, and the slight breeze and the dappled sun—it meant home to me.

I'd grown up here. Yes, my worst moment had happened here, but so had many good ones. I'd lived and trained in these mountains with my dad. I'd missed my mom. I'd wondered at and nagged my dad about our solitude. But I'd been happy. And it felt good to be back. Our cabin, our home territory, had been located elsewhere in the thousands of acres of this old wood forest, but the sound of the awakening cardinals, chickadees and warblers was as familiar as the feel of needles and old leaves under my feet.

And significantly, I didn't feel resentful, sharing the experience with my two companions. Damn Ken, but he'd been right. I did feel a little better for having shared my story. Lighter. And conversely, it hadn't appeared to weigh the other two down any. They treated me the same and they moved as easily through the terrain as I did. As the light grew, our pace picked up a bit. There was no discernible trail, but both of them moved as if they knew where we were going. I didn't question it. I just breathed in the scent of home and followed along.

At mid-morning we reached a fast-moving stream. Stopping to rest, we spread out, each of us claiming a sun-warmed boulder. Reik dozed. Ken sat cross-legged, his hands folded peculiarly before him. I eyed the water with longing. Being on the run did not leave a girl as fresh as a daisy. Understandably, I had a thing about smells—I'd been on the road for a month before and still had never gone this long without a shower—and then I hadn't been keeping company with two exotically hot guys.

Ah, well, we'd had no hint of pursuit, by Fuma Jinnae or anyone—or anything—else, and I was sure those two were as smelly as I was.

Ken suggested we finish off the last of the goodies we'd brought from the Dragon's Eye. I nodded and gave him my last Cherry Blossom Kit Kat. "It's a little mushy. I had it in my jacket pocket," I said, grimacing an apology.

"I don't care," he said reverently. "I've only had a bite of one of these a couple of times. My mom talks about them, though." He shoved a piece of chocolate in his mouth and sighed in happiness. "I should save her half of this."

Reik didn't comment.

"You okay?" I asked. The further we'd come into the mountains, the happier I'd grown—and the quieter he'd become. He looked downright grumpy now. "Sorry. Did you want some chocolate? That was the last of it, but I do have some little pancakes left." I held out the bag.

"No, thank you," he said with a shudder. "None of that junk for me."

"Oh? What's your poison, then?"

He shrugged. "Rice is good enough for me."

"Reik never did eat much," Ken remarked. "But me? I could eat my weight in my mom's omurice." He grinned. "The food is one of the best parts of coming home."

"How long has it been?"

He thought about it. "About six months, I guess."

"How about for you, Reik?" He didn't look like he wanted to be included in the conversation, which perversely, goaded me into drawing him in.

"A long time."

Ken narrowed his gaze at him. "We were apprenticed together. It seems like I've run into all the regional scouts back at home at one time or another, but not you." He waited, but Reik said nothing. "You haven't been home since we were first sent out, have you?"

Reik just looked away.

"Have you?" Ken repeated.

I didn't know why this was significant, but it appeared to be.

Reik pressed his lips together and shook his head.

"Why not?" I asked, giving him another metaphorical poke and enjoying the annoyed look he shot me.

"I prefer the outside world." His usual grin was half-hearted.

"Which part of it do you prefer?" I was genuinely curious. His answer might tell me something about the place we were heading for.

He sat up straighter on his rock. "The crowds. The opportunities." He paused. "The anonymity."

I laughed outright. "I'm having trouble picturing you as anonymous—in any situation."

The practiced flirtation made its reappearance. "You'd be surprised. I have many talents."

I opened my mouth to make a smart-mouthed retort—but forgot it as something moved in the brush just beyond his rock. I clamped my mouth shut and waited, watching.

"Mei?" Ken said.

As if responding to the sound of my name, a narrow snout peeked out from beneath a hearty rhododendron. Unblinking eyes darted between the three of us.

"That's funny," I said slowly.

"What is?" Ken sat up.

"I thought I saw a fox at the end of the alley in Asheville—and now there's one here." I pointed.

The slender face had disappeared. Not even the slightest movement showed that it had been there.

But Ken and Reik were exchanging glances. "Are you sure they were both foxes? They aren't that common around here, although coyote are, and the occasional bobcat."

"I think I know the difference. Low to the ground, long snout, big ears, red fur. I even saw the tail of the first one."

"Huh. Weird." Ken said nothing more, but silent messages were flying between him and Reik.

Ken sat up, yawned and stretched. "Well, we'd better get moving again before I fall asleep in the sun." He came over to give me a hand up. "Go along with whatever we say," he whispered. "Be ready to move."

My sun-drowsed calm disappeared. I stood, trying to follow their lead and act casual instead of instantly alert.

"I'll bet I can beat you both to the falls," Reik challenged. He waggled his brows at me. "I hope you packed a bikini."

"Don't be a perv," I said without heat. I had to fight to keep from searching the bush all around us. And I realized what I was doing and wondered at the urgency of it all. Foxes were small. Even a couple of them should be easy enough for the three of us to handle.

"I gotta get something for dragging you all the way out here for the day," he retorted.

"Ignore him," Ken advised. He was already starting out. I moved in behind him.

"No, ignore *him*," Reik said with a laugh. "Pay attention to me." He brought up the rear and I realized that Ken was setting a faster pace than before. I grew warm as we covered a good deal of ground in a short time, but then were forced to slow when we hit a thick patch of birch trees. It lasted for half a mile or so, and when we finally left the closely situated trees behind, we emerged before a suddenly vertical ridge.

Vertical, but not too high—maybe ten feet. Reik surged ahead suddenly, whooping. He hit the base running and scrambled up. When he reached the top he jumped up and threw his hands in the air. "I'm the king of the mountain!"

"Not for long," Ken scoffed. He ran for it and I followed. It wasn't a difficult climb. The slope tilted forward a bit, which helped, and it was thick with grasses and growth so my feet always had a good purchase.

When I crawled over the edge, I paused and knelt as the guys made to move on. "Gotta tie my shoe," I explained and waved them on.

I took my time, staying low and facing back the way we'd come. I didn't like running without knowing what I was running from. It took me a moment to identify the vulpine heads of two foxes, poking from beneath underbrush. After a moment I caught sight of another, slinking along the base of the ridge, but it was the figure leaning against a narrow birch that froze the blood in my veins and gave me a hint of what they knew that I didn't—a human figure, naked, with a narrow nose and shaggy red hair. It stared at me, intent. After a moment, it wiped its chin with the back of a crudely formed hand.

As if it had been drooling.

Almost involuntarily, I glanced back to see how far the boys had gone—and when I looked back the figure had gone and another fox stood at the base of the same tree.

A shiver ran down my spine. I stood, and had
to force myself not to hurry off, but to stretch a bit
before turning to go.

I wasted no time sprinting after the others,
though.

"Reik says there are several of them ahead of
us," Ken said quietly as I drew abreast of him.

"These are not just normal forest animals, are
they?"

"Why?" he asked sharply.

I told him what I had seen. He looked grim
when I finished. "Well, it's what we had suspected,"
he sighed.

"What?"

"Spirit animals."

I merely raised a brow and waited.

"Nature spirits. They are usually benign
enough, but the fox can be mischievous and sometimes
sly. They've been known to take on a task if the
persuader is slick enough—and the reward great
enough."

I didn't think I wanted to know what their
reward might be—the look on that strange figure's
face . . .

"Yes, you get the idea. I've heard they are
particularly fond of livers."

I shivered.

We've got to move quickly," Ken urged. "And
you have to be ready to fight—both forms."

"Okay." I veered off suddenly, and swooped
past an elm tree. A pine had fallen and knocked a few
of the elm's branches off. One of them, a slender,
good-sized limb, still stood leaning up against the
trunk. I broke it off, then tested it. It was still tough
enough, not rotten. I trimmed off a few twigs and
cracked the end off over my knee—and held up a

pretty serviceable staff.

Ken nodded in approval. "It won't be long before they make their move. This slight valley—see where it curves ahead? We'll be leaving it and taking the higher ground heading west. They'll come for us soon after."

"How do you know?"

"Because until then the doubt remains—we could be any kids out for a day at the remote waterfall that lies not far to the east. When we head west, we'll be going the wrong way, to their thinking. Toward Ryu."

"Are we close, then?"

"Not close enough." He frowned. "Be ready."

He was right. We had gone a mere quarter of a mile beyond the valley when the attack came. And not from just the dozen or so animals that I'd thought we'd have to contend with. Suddenly a swarm of them was closing in behind us, a hundred or more of the sleek bodies moving quickly and looking like converging streams of dusky red water. A few came from ahead of us too, as Reik had suspected.

"Keep going!" Reik called. "Don't stop!"

I had no plans to stop. The trees were sparser here, mostly cedars and a few young maples or elms. No good opportunities to climb up and away from our pursuers.

"Come on!"

I followed Ken, sprinting ahead. I braced my staff on a shoulder, holding on with one hand as I concentrated on running.

I didn't falter until I saw one of the creatures . . . morph. Right before Reik it transformed, rising up as it shifted into a variation somewhere between the animal and human forms I'd already seen. It growled and snapped at him with a mouth full of razor sharp teeth.

Reik didn't even pause. He spread his fingers wide, palm facing out and the hybrid animal suddenly hit a transparent wall of ice. As we watched, walls sprouted to join the first, and a ceiling and floor too, until the thing found itself encased in a clear box of ice, like one of those glass phone booths you see in old movies.

"Nice," I called as Ken and I reached his side.

He grinned. "You can't kill them. It's contain them, delay them, or lose them."

I wondered how we were going to be able to do any of those in this situation. We were still running and I noticed that he hadn't included 'outrun them' in his list of escapes.

Crap.

He caught two more of the creatures in the same fashion, catching them together in one enclosure and then the way before us lay clear. We raced ahead, until suddenly the rocky ridge we'd been following curved around and flattened out—into a narrow ledge. It led between a steep fall into a ravine on one side and an equally steep wall rising on the other. We had about fifty feet before we hit another blind curve to the right—which meant we could not see what might be lurking around the corner.

Twenty feet in, Ken reached out to grab my arm. "Wait." Pulling me to a halt, he whirled and faced the narrowing pack of silently bristling creatures behind us. With a defiant shout he clasped his arm and let out a mighty blast of air.

The creatures stopped and crouched, eyes closed against the current and the leaves, dust and debris that washed over them, but Ken didn't let up. He leaned in and sent forth a sweeping current that sent a good number of them tumbling over the edge into the ravine.

"Now, we climb!" Reik urged. He turned to face the vertical wall. "Watch where I put my hands and feet."

I watched him start up. "Let's go," he called, but I waited for Ken, using my staff to sweep from one side of the ledge to the other, holding off the next wave while he fell back.

"We have to go up," he said. "They'll be a few waiting around that corner—and it'll be easy for them to pick us off one by one."

"Let's go, then."

I didn't waste any more time, just stared grimly at the nearly vertical wall, covered with loose soil and leaves. Not ideal, but Reik was doing okay and I could see scattered rock outcroppings that might be useful. Ken stepped up and onto a protruding root and I slid the staff into a loop so that it hung crossways across my pack, then hugged my body in close to the rock and tried to follow the path that he and Reik were blazing.

It proved easier than I had anticipated. In fact, as we climbed steadily higher I began to suspect that some of these convenient hand and footholds were not accidentally placed.

Below us, the foxes in animal form paced restlessly or planted their front feet on the wall while they whined in frustration. A few had shifted to humanoid form and were trying to follow us, but their coordination did not seem to be developed enough for them to climb easily. We left them behind before long. Back down on the ledge, the rest of them gave up pacing and moved to continue further on the trail.

I looked questioningly down at Ken. His head was at my shoulder's height as he waited for me to give up a prime handhold and climb on.

"It does switch back to the trail above, though it loops around a bit and will take them a while," he said.

I looked up in horror, tossing the hair out of my face. "You mean eventually they'll be up there, above us?"

"Yep. So get moving, will you? I don't want to still be here when they get there."

"They are not stupid," Reik called. "They'll have a few advance guards up there already."

I hoped he was wrong.

He wasn't. As we began to near the top, a red snout poked over the edge. Then another and another, until three of the creatures peered down at us.

"Advance guard," Reik announced. "First to die."

One of them tried to reach us, snapping and making an odd barking sound. It put its feet over the edge, bracing itself and growling at us as we inched closer.

"Heads up," Reik called. He pointed a finger at the fox and abruptly a collar of ice snaked around its neck and began to grow. The weight of it unbalanced the animal until it suddenly fell, yipping as it traveled past us.

Another one shifted form, then lay down along the edge, reaching a hand towards us, grabbing blindly, hoping to catch hold of one of us. This time Reik wrapped a large cuff around its arm. A thin, icy column, like a rope, attached to the cuff and dangled between us.

"Grab on and pull," Reik ordered.

I could reach it. I steadied my feet and held tight to a rocky outcropping with my right hand, then reached for the ice rope with my left.

"One . . . two . . . PULL!" Reik ordered.

I yanked hard and we caught the creature by

surprise. It was still trying to knock the ice off when our united effort overbalanced it. It too, went bouncing downward. We leaned away as it went past, but it smacked into one of the other transformed creatures still trying vainly to climb up after us and they both fell to the ledge below.

That left one lone fox above us. It kept to its vulpine form and raced about up there, leaning over to snarl at one of us then another. Reik climbed higher and it leaned out, snapping at his hands. He shot sharp, icy shards at it as it dashed from one position to the other, but it darted in and out, avoiding them.

"I've got this one," I said grimly. My arms were getting tired, holding on so long, my pack was starting to feel heavier and heavier—and I couldn't shake the vision of the other, larger group of them reaching that point of the trail up there and stranding us here.

Moving carefully, I inched upward before once more making sure I had good sturdy positions for both feet. Reaching back, I slid the staff free. I watched the animal, gauging the timing and rhythm of its attacks and retreats.

There. I poked upward with the staff, catching it on the chest—and swung the pole outward, sending the creature spiraling into empty space. It fell a long way, its yelps echoing back up to us, before it hit the bottom of the ravine.

All three of us scrambled up and over the side to solid ground. I lay there a moment, face down into the lovely, solid ground, shaking out my arms and listening. I could hear the yips and barks of the larger pack. They were still a fair distance off, and I wasn't familiar with the trail, but I knew it wouldn't be long before they were surging up the hill toward us.

I got to my feet just as Reik waved us on.

"Let's go," he called out.

The trail hugged the edge of the drop we'd just climbed up for a bit before it hit a wider spot over rocky ground. We followed it, being careful as we hit the rough terrain. All too easy to turn an ankle or twist a knee over ground like this—and then we'd be toast.

"Look," Reik said. He pointed ahead, to where the rocky ground ended at an up-thrust section of bald stone. Gravel and larger rocks littered the base of it. "See the two large boulders? That's where we're heading."

I glanced back to say something. Ken was bringing up the rear and I wanted to make sure he wasn't fatigued.

"Behind you!" I shouted instead. One of the little monsters was creeping in behind him. It reared up, changing even as I yelled, "Duck!"

I planted my stick, braced myself and grabbed a hold with two hands, then swung out with my feet, passing over Ken and knocking the half-morphed spirit animal in the chest. It fell back and I looked beyond it to see the crude hands of another patting and searching the ground, straining to find a purchase so it could pull itself over the edge of the cliff.

"Come on." I pulled Ken along and we hurried as best we could, still being careful of our footing.

But the cursed little critters could move faster over this terrain in their natural forms. One slid past us and rose up again, reaching for Ken. "Watch out!" He moved aside, but stumbled on some rocks, landing heavily. He didn't make a sound, but I saw his face as he grabbed his ankle.

Cover him.

I didn't need to hear it in my Dad's voice or to wait to assess the damage, I moved between him and the creature and settled into bo stance.

Stay nimble.

It jumped at me. I brought up the stick and chucked it hard under the chin, knocking it on its backside.

This time it paused, blinking craftily up at me. So quick I could barely register it, it switched back to a fox and darted at my feet.

I swept the staff low, catching it across the midsection and pushing it back, away from Ken.

It transformed again and I was ready. I thrust the small end of the staff forward, striking it in the abdomen. With a whoosh of spent breath, it bent over the stick. I pulled back and thrust again. It scrambled away; retreating further, back the way we had come. I followed, staff whirling. It shifted back and forth rapidly and I adjusted just as quickly, always pushing it back, back, away from where Ken limped to his feet. We were nearly back over the rocky patch at this point, nearing the cliff again. I made to thrust again and it morphed, snapping at me. I struck it hard on the snout.

"Mei—get it up—in the air!" Ken called.

I understood. Increasing the speed of my circling staff, I advanced and it retreated. The other one, the one that had finally made it over the edge of the cliff, crowded in behind it. I shifted my grip and struck the growling, first creature on the sensitive nose once, twice, three times. Mad as fury, it fought back, snarling and rising up on its hind feet to jump at the stick and smack it away.

That's what I was waiting for. I pushed the tip of the staff between its legs and further back to its belly, then I used my knee for a fulcrum and pushed down, launching the spirit animal a couple of feet in the air.

"Down!" Ken shouted. I flattened myself against the ground as he let loose a fierce gale that caught the creature and sent it tumbling back over the cliff.

"One more!" I shouted. I hopped to my feet to confront the last animal, but clearly it decided that retreat was the better part of valor and backed away. I swung the staff and advanced on it and it turned tail and ran.

I followed suit, racing back to find Ken moving, but favoring one foot. "It's not bad," he insisted. "I'll walk it off."

"Good," I said with a grin, "because I believe I just saved *your* Shitake Mushroom at last—and I'd hate to have to do it twice in one day."

"I did help at the end," he protested.

I shook my head and let him lean on my shoulder. "You couldn't just give me one, could you?"

He laughed, but it died away as we struggled closer to the pair of huge boulders. The area was littered with half a dozen or so foxes, their front ends all encased in solid ice, their back legs scrambling in vain.

Reik was sitting perched atop one of the big rocks.

"What in the world?" I asked, gesturing toward his odd victims.

He shrugged. "I don't know why, but this seems to keep them from transforming."

My mouth dropped. "How did you figure that out?"

"Trial and error." He hopped down, smirking, but whatever smart remark he meant to make died away as he stared over our shoulders. "Here come the rest of them. Let's move!"

I didn't even stop to look back, just followed as he and Ken dashed through the open space between the largest rocks. It wasn't a crevice or a cave, as I'd expected, but a path, hewn right out of the stone monolith. The sky, dwindled to a narrow strip at the top, felt far away. Behind us the noise of the advancing horde sounded louder by the second.

Thankfully the lane was short. It opened up and we spilled out into a tiny, perfect valley.

I gasped at the beauty of it. A meadow of grasses, larkspur and dainty pink trillium. A wall of profusely blooming rhododendron, spindly dogwood and hardy pines. Near the back, off to the left, a pond stretched out, reflecting the brilliant blue sky and near the edge of it, it's feet planted in the water, stood a Japanese torii gate of rough-hewn logs. It bore a plaque with an Asian inscription and on top perched a magnificently carved dragon.

I stumbled to a halt.

"Don't stop!" Ken pushed me from behind as he emerged. "Get through the gate, quick!"

"Go! Go! What are you waiting for?" Reik pushed me forward.

I obeyed, but paused at the edge of the water. I was struck by the gate, which looked like a rough replica of the infamous floating gate at Miyajima—and weren't there rules about approaching such places?

Seeing my hesitation, both boys yelled at me. "It's not deep," Ken said. "Go! Through the gate!"

I stepped into the water, wincing as it rushed to fill my boots. My steps slowed as I sloshed through the water, my companions on my heels. I stared upward as I approached. There were no walls, no fencing, just the gate standing alone in the water in a remote part of the Appalachian forest—and yet I felt . . . something . . . as I passed through.

Ken and Reik followed—but instead of running further they turned to face the passage we'd just come through.

I sucked in a breath as multitudes of the red-pelted little demons poured out. They were piled upon each other, fighting to get through. The first ones ran up to form a line at the edge of the water. They all stopped though, as they caught sight of us, just standing there on the other side of the gate.

For a long moment we all stared at each other. And then, without a sound, they all faded away to nothing. We stood alone, our feet wet in the shallow water of the pond, the meadow gorgeous around us. Above, the late afternoon sun picked out the inscription on the plaque.

"We made it," Ken said with relief. He waded out to sink down upon the turf and shot me a grin. "We did it, Mei." He held up a hand. "Welcome to Ryu."

Chapter Fourteen

We left the gate behind and traveled on—with some differences. There was a definite trail here, for one. We moved more slowly along it. Ken's ankle clearly needed attention. Truth be told—I needed rest. A real rest. I was hot and sweaty and utterly wiped from the repeated adrenaline highs over the last few days. My pack felt as if it had doubled in size. Even Reik's stride had shortened, as if he too had begun to feel the strain.

Another difference lay in the land itself. We'd left the foothills behind and entered mid-elevation territory. There was more scrub here and the trees tended to grow in clumps rather than great swaths.

But that wasn't the biggest change, either. I'd felt it as soon as we'd crossed through that gate. The land here—it breathed.

I didn't know how else to explain it. But there was a definite . . . presence. I could feel a sense of calm alertness, an underlying level of contentment— and a definite taste of anticipation.

I stopped worrying about it, though, as we made our way around a large outcropping—and exhaled a sigh of pleasure instead.

We stood at the lip of a valley, ringed with green, lined with freshly plowed fields. Figures moved in the neatly furrowed lines. At the center of the valley sat a cluster of barns, storage silos and farmhouses. It looked calm, orderly and very Asian.

"The houses are built in the traditional *gassho* style," Ken said after a moment. He was happy to be home—it nearly lit him from within. "The steep roofs are meant to represent hands in prayer."

"And to keep the snow off," Reik added.

"That, too." Ken grinned.

"Which one is your family home?" I asked with
interest.

"None. This is just one of the farming
settlements. My family lives in the one north of the
village."

We started down into the valley. Men waved
from the fields. When we reached the group of
buildings, people came out to greet us.

Ken was obviously popular. He was welcomed
with warmth and good-natured banter. Reik was met
with surprise and distant respect. And I—for the first
time I encountered a group of people and was met with
smiles and bows and a sort of polite awe.

I relished it—and I remembered Neil's words
about not having to hide anymore. So I met their
gazes openly and returned their smiles. I enjoyed the
freedom of it immensely, until a door opened and a
group of little kids tumbled out. They crowded around
us, chattering, staring and I suddenly blushed crimson
when I remembered what Ken had said about me being
the topic of bedtime stories.

But my discomfort faded as we moved on and
the children followed. They ambled a few feet behind
us like a pack of puppies. I laughed as, every now and
then, one would dart forward and touch my leg or
pack. One brave little girl in braids caught up and
offered me a flower. I took it with a bow of
gratitude—then reached out to pull her in for a quick
hug. She grinned, then dropped back to be
congratulated by her friends.

In this fashion we crossed the rest of the valley.
The trail followed through a gap in the valley wall,
made by a stream. It changed on the other side. We
stepped from packed earth to thick, round-edged
paving stones—and into a very different sort of
garden.

I gazed in wonder. Here was a more formal landscape. It closely resembled the luxurious Japanese garden I traveled in my recurring dream. Graceful willows trailed their branches in the stream. Finely graveled beds, mounding bushes, tall orchids and little stone temples graced the sides of the walkway. I felt transported, and a little apprehensive.

"These are the temple gardens," Ken told me. "They stretch further than we'll see now and contain some amazing spots."

"They are beautiful," I whispered.

"That's just it, Mei. It's all beautiful."

I knew he was talking about more than the landscaping. It meant something to him, sharing his home with me. I had to admit—standing there, meeting his gaze and forcing myself not to push back the stray strand of hair blowing in his face—it meant something to me, too.

"Let's get there today, people," Reik called— and the spell was broken. But my heart felt a little lighter and I let myself drink in the beauty as we made our way along the path.

Eventually it led us onto a little bridge—a smaller version of the one in my dream. Our footsteps echoed as we crossed, and at the end we stepped off into a cobbled courtyard. A wizened man moved about it, lighting the lanterns that ringed the spot. Small, graceful trees helped to outline three sides of the space. Beyond them I could just glimpse other buildings and wide streets or pathways. The fourth side faced a lovely temple.

I stopped to look again. It was a large building, with beautifully curved roofs, gorgeous etchings, stone stairs that led to a wide, spacious gallery running around all sides and that air of fragile beauty that only graced buildings built hundreds of years ago.

I frowned. "Wait—"

"Shhh." Reik motioned toward the temple.

Doors opened. Two columns of people filed out, men and women, some dressed in traditional Japanese and others in modern clothing. They took up positions lining the stairs and the wide gallery.

Then from the edges of the courtyard, a crowd came spilling in. Old and young, smiling and serious, but all silent, they gathered in around us. A large group of them surrounded Ken, all smiles and patting hands. Reik was quickly surrounded by a gaggle of grinning young girls.

The press of people shifted me toward the middle of the courtyard. I suffered a moment of brief longing for the makeshift staff I'd left behind at the gate—clearly these people had no familiarity with the concept of personal space—but though they pressed too close and no one spoke, they seemed pleasant enough.

Suddenly, as one, they all turned to face the temple.

Heavy wooden doors, heavily carved, split open. A woman strode out, tall and imposing. She stopped at the top of the stairs and I recognized her.

The woman from Ken's mirror.

Rigid. Sternly beautiful. Her face was still unsmiling, though her hair had been tightly braided today, into one thick strand that swept forward over her shoulder. She bowed to the people in the courtyard and said something I didn't understand. As one, everyone else returned the gesture and the words.

Our eyes met and held as we stood there, for a moment, the only two people upright.

"I know rumors are circulating," she told the waiting people. "And it is true that some strange things are afoot." She tilted her head. "But there's nothing new about that, is there? And we are doing what we do best, what we've always done: gathering information and making plans to adjust."

Suddenly, she threw out her hands. "But today? Today is a good day." She peered out into the crowd. "Kenshin."

Did the imposing look on her face soften just a bit?

He bowed.

"We are glad to see you—and very proud of you, too." Her mouth quirked. "I believe your mother started cooking yesterday."

She arched a brow at Reik. "And Reik Hama. I look forward to hearing a long overdue report from you." She ran an eye over the girls gathered around him. "Although it can wait until you've greeted your admirers."

Finally, she turned a dispassionate eye toward me. After the shy warmth and approval of the others, her formality felt . . . significant. "Masuyo Barret?"

I nodded.

"I am General Rin. We have waited a long time to meet you."

She took a step back and swept a hand to encompass the surrounding village. "Welcome to Ryu, our honored guests. We are very glad to have you."

The crowed erupted then, all eager to talk to one or more of the three of us. Over and over again, I was welcomed to the village. My eyes were remarked upon and complimented—complimented! My health was asked after.

A girl, about my age, stepped in close. She had the upswept hair and heavy make up of a mid-twentieth century pin up girl, but wore the conservative, tight sleeved tunic associated with Manchu fashion. Her expression sparkled as she

looked me over and then grinned at me. "Your eyes
are pretty," she said, agreeing with the consensus, "but
those jeans are kicking!"

Startled, I looked down. My pants were dark
and form fitting, perfect for hiding and fighting. They
were also very much the worse for wear, at the
moment. But I looked up into her hopeful face and
returned her grin. "Thanks."

"I knew Ken would be the one to find you. We
are all glad you are here at last."

Her expression dimmed just a bit as she looked
over my shoulder. I followed her gaze towards the
temple.

The general had disappeared from the temple
stairs, but another figure hung back there, above the
crowd, near one of the engraved posts. Another girl, I
thought. Although much of her was hidden in the
shadows, I did see a swath of long hair. I felt the
intensity of her gaze upon me and I got the impression
that she frowned at me from her solitary position.
When she noticed my attention, she stiffened and
whirled away, melting into the depths of the gallery.

So. Not universally welcomed, then.

I shrugged. Nothing new there.

"Oh, don't mind *her*." The girl in front of me
waved a hand.

Ken's name rang out nearby. I glanced over to
see a teary-eyed woman laughing and hanging on his
shoulder. Others hovered in his proximity, spilling
stories and sharing news. He met my eye over the
intervening crowd and beckoned.

Before I could respond or take my leave of the
girl still watching me closely, General Rin stepped
through the throng and stopped in front of me. "You
truly are welcome here, Masuyo," she said without
preamble.

"Thank you," I answered.

"I understand that there is much we have to discuss." She spared Ken a glance. "I believe we can help each other. But first, after your ordeals, you need to rest and recoup."

"And eat." A wrinkled older woman scowled as she pinched my bare arm.

Everyone laughed. General Rin gestured and two women pushed forward. They looked remarkably similar. Twins? They both greeted me kindly, their words soft and welcoming to the ear.

"Tak and Noff have invited you to their home. They often look after the village's guests. They'll know just how to see to your needs."

I blinked. "Thank you." Somehow I hadn't anticipated being separated from Ken. I glanced his way again, to find him pushing his way over.

"General." He bowed, then looked between us. "I'd thought—" he began.

Something stopped him. General Rin's raised eyebrow, perhaps.

He turned to me and nodded. "It will be fine, Mei. Go. Let them pamper you a bit. You deserve it."

I stared and he nodded, encouraging. So I turned and offered thanks to the two older women for their hospitality. Thoughtful, and a bit uneasy, I made my goodbyes and allowed them to lead me away.

Tak and Noff were indeed twins, I discovered. They were also everything gracious, but I was so tired I kept nodding over the dinner they offered. Shaking their heads in sympathy, they sent me off to bed. I went gratefully—and didn't awaken until the following afternoon.

The village boasted another bit of Asian

tradition, I discovered. Public baths. Tak took me off
to the women's bathhouse, where I wallowed in
scented waters and scrubbed my hair until my scalp
tingled. When I finally finished, I was given a soft
tunic and plain pants—very gender neutral but
extremely comfortable. I put them on and followed
Tak back home, where Noff had dinner waiting.

I did justice to her efforts this time—although
anyone would have, so delicious was the deep rich
broth of the ramen dish with curly noodles, pork, egg,
nori and scallions.

"Thank you so much," I said, refraining from
picking up the bowl to drain the last of the broth. "I
haven't had ramen like that since I was a girl—and
never so wonderfully delicious."

"Thank you, dear," Noff said with a nod.
"Cooking is like chemistry, it's all about knowing how
the ingredients are going to mix."

"And no one knows either like Noff," Tak said.
"Now, leave that for a moment and I'll show you
around the house."

It was a warm and comfortable home, if a bit on
the sparse side. It had many touches of old Japanese
homes, like rice paper sliding doors in the interior and
a central fire pit in the main room, although this one
was decorative instead of functional. "We don't like
clutter," they said together.

But they did like art. Their walls held some
strikingly beautiful calligraphy pieces.

"It is Tak's work," her sister told me when I
admired a breathtaking sketch of a bird poised amidst
fern fronds. "She's just one of the artists and
craftspeople we have here in Ryu."

"It is wonderful." I almost couldn't look away.
"I feel as if the bird is just about to take off—and I
wouldn't be surprised if it did."

"I'd be happy to show you my studio," Tak offered, "but it's better seen in the daylight. Evening's coming now." She moved to start taking up dishes. "We'll take care of this. Why don't you sit out and watch the night come in?"

The house, situated just a few doors beyond the temple, boasted a porch that over looked the temple gardens. I took a seat there and let my head fall back, enjoying the scents, the sleepy evening sounds and the beauty that faded with the light.

Until I heard a soft footstep and the small crunch of shifting gravel.

I was up and out of my seat before I even consciously registered the sound.

"Hi!"

I glanced wildly about, but it took me a second, with the coming dark, to locate the girl standing on the curve of a path in the garden.

She waved. "It's just me. Hitomi. We spoke yesterday. Do you remember?"

"Oh." I relaxed and tried not to look sheepish. "Yes. Hello."

"I don't mean to disturb you, but . . . I thought . . . Well . . ." She sucked in a breath. "I'd love to talk to you, and my mother agreed, so I thought . . . I'd invite you over to my house. You know? To hang out?"

I valiantly tried to hide my surprise. It was such a normal thing to hear from a teenaged girl, but no one had ever said it to me.

"Oh, well, I'd love to." I paused then, struck by the notion that I had yet to talk to any of the village officials. "But I wonder if I need to be here in case General Rin—"

"Don't worry. She and the Council spent the day grilling Ken and Reik. They're holed up strategizing now. I know, because my father's on the council."

"Oh." I glanced back towards the house.

"Mother's already cleared it with Tak and Noff." Her shoulder lifted. "But if you'd rather not . . ."

"No! I'd love to. Thank you. I'll just tell them I'm going, then."

Moments later I was walking slowly along the village street, but answering questions at a breakneck pace. Hitomi was bouncy, full of energy and even more full of questions about life outside of Ryu. She wanted to know everything about clothes, food, music, and movies. I did my best to explain what I could.

"You don't have implants?" she asked, peering at my temples.

"No. Too easy to be tracked that way."

"Makes sense." We turned in at the gate to a house, but she paused with her hand resting on the sliding door. "I feel as if I should warn you . . ."

The door opened from within and we were hit by a blast of light, sound—and spit balls.

I froze, but Hitomi squealed in fury. "Nordu! You are a dead fish if I catch you!"

She pulled me inside—and thus began one of the strangest and most wonderful evenings I'd ever spent.

Hitomi had five siblings, all younger than she. They were engaged in various activities as we arrived. Two chased each other through the house. One scrubbed the kitchen floor while another looked to be doing homework. The last was just a baby—and Hitomi's mother handed him over to us as she corralled and wrestled the running pair into their pajamas.

Somehow I ended up ensconced on a pillow in

the open family space, with the baby on my lap, feeding him bits of dry cereal while trying to explain to Hitomi the appeal of high-priced lattes.

"But doesn't everyone make coffee at home? That's how it looks in the vids. Why go out and pay so much more?"

I laughed. "You're asking the wrong person. I'm a tea girl, myself."

"Yeah. I tried coffee at the Dragon's Eye." She made a face. "I don't get it." She bit her lip suddenly. "Listen, I'm sorry if I'm being obnoxious. There's just so much—and I want to know *everything*." She noticed I was out of cereal and replenished my supply. "You're the best source of information I've ever got a hold of."

"But what about the scouts? They come back, at least occasionally, right?" I remembered Ken's indignation that Reik had not. "Why not pick their brains?"

"Oh, them." She rolled her eyes. "They report to the Council. And frankly, I suspect that they are under orders not to pass on too much information. Either that, or they just don't have time for a *girl* like me."

"Are there no girls in the scouts?"

"There are, but they are few and far between— and mostly those with elemental *minding*, like the general."

"You should talk to Ken. I can't imagine him blowing you off."

She sighed. "No, Ken's a good guy. But I swear, all he does is train when he's here."

I laughed. "And eat, I hear."

"Yes. His mom *is* a great cook, though." She grinned.

Suddenly it occurred to me that I had a great

resource in her as well. "You mentioned the Dragon's Eye. So it's not like you are trapped up here, right?"

"No, we're not that medieval." She sighed. "I've been to Asheville, but only on short visits. And there's only so much you can learn online."

Online. And she did know a bit about vids and movies. Hoisting the baby a little straighter, I took a look around. I saw books and papers aplenty. Calligraphy supplies in one corner. But no monitors. Thinking back, I hadn't noticed any in Tak and Noff's home, either.

Hitomi realized what I was thinking. "We do have access to the net—but all of the screens are in the Council's building. Which means you have to share them with everyone else—and someone always knows what you are doing." She sighed again. "It must be one of the best things about being out in the world. You can do, eat, watch, learn what you want. Whenever you want to do it. So many choices. And the ability to make them without the comment and opinions of everyone around you."

I privately thought that I might not mind a little of that sort of attention, but I could understand that too much of it could quickly become a pain. "Are you still in school, Hitomi?"

"Just out." Her expression took on a stubborn cast. "And I will take the scout's trials, despite what my father thinks. I may not be able to fight like Ken Sato, but I've done well in most aspects of training, and my skills could be just as valuable out in the field." She frowned. "There are lots of ways to dig out information—and many ways to fight *yokai*. There can be more than one sort of scout," she finished fiercely.

Her passionate rant raised more questions than it answered, but I focused on the one that interested me the most. "Training? What sort of training?"

She lifted a shoulder. "Oh, you know. Various martial arts. Strategy. Fighting alone and in teams. And all the ninja skills."

I sat a little straighter and the baby, who'd been gradually relaxing into sleep against me, made a sound of protest. "All the ninja skills?"

"Yeah. Sword, archery, balance, agility, adaptability, hiding, blah, blah, blah."

All the skills I'd been trained in. I blinked.

She raised a brow at me. "Did Ken tell you nothing of our life here?"

"No." I responded slowly. "Not a thing."

She frowned, but just then her mother returned. Offering her thanks, she took the baby from my arms. "They are asking for a story, Hitomi." She nodded towards me. "And I imagine that Masuyo would enjoy seeing your talents as well."

"Talents?" I wondered if she meant Hitomi's *minding* skills.

Her new friend shot her mother a dark look. "Well, one aspect of it, anyway." She slumped forward. "Oh, come on, then. They'll never be quiet if I don't do it."

I piled on a sleeping mat with the older children while Hitomi took a seat nearby with a book. She touched her inner arm and closed her eyes for a moment. Her hands folded, her fingers interlaced in a complex arrangement, then she began to read. My jaw dropped and my awe grew as the old tale of *The Bamboo Princess* began to unfold.

Because Hitomi did not just *read* the fairy tale. Somehow, she *became* it.

I watched, agog, as the changes happened. When she read the part of the old bamboo-cutter, she transformed. Her smooth cheeks sunk in, her shoulders widened and rounded. Wrinkles appeared across her face as her nose elongated. Even her hands changed, spouting age spots and ropy veins.

It happened again with each character she voiced. She became the calm and beautiful, serene Princess, complete with ripe lips and heavy-lidded eyes. She grew shifty, like the lazy princes, rough like the seamen and sturdy like the shining army of moon soldiers. It was like nothing I'd ever seen. Mesmerizing. I had to remind myself to shut my gaping mouth several times, and when she was done, I joined her brothers and sisters in loud and vigorous applause.

"That was amazing!"

She flushed a little. "It's just illusion, but . . . thank you." She rolled her eyes. "Father calls it sideshow tricks, but I *know* it can be useful."

"Of course it can." I thought of just how many times I might have made good use of such a talent.

Her gaze grew a little misty as she ignored the kids hanging on her. "Thanks."

"For what?" She'd reached out to touch my wrist, and I didn't pull away as I normally would have.

"For believing that, when you said it."

I shrugged. "Sure."

"Time for bed!" Her mother came in, clapping her hands. "Hitomi, why don't you show Masuyo the way back to Tak and Noff's?"

I shook my head. "No need. I can find my way."

"Sure?" Hitomi asked.

I nodded.

"Okay. See you tomorrow, then?" she asked shyly.

"I hope so." And it was true.

I said my goodbyes and left and wondered when

I felt suddenly bereft at the quiet, instead of relief.

Tak and Noff were retiring when I arrived. They bid me goodnight and I went to the room they'd lent me, but it was no use going to bed myself. I'd slept most of the day—and now my mind was full of the things I'd learned—and of those I hadn't.

Restlessness built. My clothes had been washed and returned to me. I restored order in my pack. I paced a bit. I stood at the door that led onto the porch. I breathed in the scents of the garden—and then I gave up the fight and stepped out.

I didn't venture further into the gardens. Instead I circled around and took to the deserted streets again.

I was unsettled once again, though the village was not. Many of the homes were of traditional Japanese architecture, timbered with many gabled, tiled roofs. They'd been altered to suit the harsher weather, I noticed. But soft light shone from the windows. I smelled dinners cooking, heard the sounds of talking, laughter, music and squabbling little ones.

Wasn't this the sort of thing I'd always dreamed of? Staying in one place. Making friends. Becoming part of a community. Making myself a place to belong. But part of me wondered if I could really adapt, after being on my own for so long. Would I chafe as Hitomi did?

And really—there was no use worrying about it until I finally defeated my enemy. But could these people really help me? They seemed so . . . normal. And yet their children trained 'in all the ninja skills.' Hitomi talked of fighting *yokai* as if it were just another thing adults got to do that kids didn't.

And for the first time, I worried that I might be bringing danger here along with me. It hadn't seemed such an issue when I was alone with Ken and Reik—

they were experienced fighters and clearly knew what they were doing—even more than I did. But the weight of that baby in my lap suddenly haunted me. Older people like Tak and Noff, women, children— what if they were put at risk because that damned wind demon followed me here? Those fox spirits might have been blocked at the gate, but Fuma Jinnae was another thing altogether.

It was likely too late to worry, in any case. The demon always seemed to find me, in the end. And that just allowed the anxiety in my gut to roll over into guilt.

I stopped walking; realizing that I'd reached the edge of the village. The northern edge.

I scoffed at myself. What was I going to do? Press my nose against Ken Sato's window like some hungry street urchin at a bakery?

Yet I didn't turn back.

After a few moments, I realized I recognized the configuration of the building ahead. I started forward and before I reached it, the smell hit me—that singular odor of heavy coal, hot metal, smoky residue and animals.

The smithy.

A wave of longing hit me hard. I remembered what Ken had said about my father living and working here. Surely he must have used this forge. I missed him so much in that moment—his casual affection, his sooty smiles, even his relentless training demands. Most of all I missed the utter certainty that he always exuded, his rock hard faith that what he—we—were doing was the right thing.

Why couldn't I ever feel that way?

I walked beneath the high roof, held my hands out to the residual heat of the forge. I tasted the water from the nearby pump and then I wandered around to the paddock on the other side of the wall.

Fresh straw was piled in a covered corner, as I'd thought it would be. I sat down in it, and after a few moments, I snuggled in deep enough to keep myself warm. Folding my jacket into a makeshift pillow, I closed my eyes, sucked in a breath full of old, familiar smells, and drifted off.

Chapter Fifteen

Something struck me on the forehead, waking me up. Something tiny, stinging, and *cold.*

I opened my eyes to meet Reik's brilliant blue gaze.

He peered down at me, morning sunlight making a halo of his striking white hair and picking out the chiseled highlights of his fabulous cheekbones and strong jaw.

"You really are ridiculously good looking," I said, sitting up.

His jaw dropped. Clearly that was not what he'd expected me to say. If I wasn't mistaken, there was a hint of pleasure mixed in with the surprise, too.

"It hardly seems fair," I continued, yawning.

His expression abruptly shuttered. "Nobody ever said life was fair, minx." He pulled back a bit, then lounged in the straw beside me.

I frowned and rubbed my forehead. "Ice pellets? Really? Couldn't you have sprinkled me with a nice, gentle spritz of rain?"

"Nope. Sorry." He waggled his fingers at me. "No gentle rains here. Only ice in all of its myriad of forms."

"Hmmm." I brushed straw from my hair.

"You know, you're not so bad yourself," he said casually. "In the looks department."

"Thanks," I said sourly. Not so bad sounded a long way from ridiculously good looking.

"Something we have in common. In fact, I think we are alike in a lot of ways."

"Really?" I drew up my knees and rested my chin there while I blinked sleepily at him. "How so?"

He sat up again. "Well, here you are, for one thing. Not where you are supposed to be. Getting

everyone riled up." He waved me back down as I
started to rise. "Eh, let them go a bit. They need to be
riled more often." He tilted his head at me. "I saw
you fight a bit, back there in Winston Salem."

I frowned. "Did you?"

"You know how to get mad."

Was that where his edge came from? Anger? I
didn't think that was the whole explanation.

"You know how to fight, too," he continued.
"And none of it looks like *minding*. Which means you
also know how to work."

"Is that what you do? Work?" Because he did
a very good job of making every word, every
movement, look easy and smooth.

"Every. Single. Day." He bit out the answer.

My breath caught as he reached for me, but he
only plucked a few more straws from my hair. Just as
I was relaxing, though, he slid both hands down to cup
my face. He leaned in close. My heart pounded and I
wanted to jerk away because I knew he could feel it.

But I wanted to lean in, too. I wanted to touch
him the way he touched me, feel the hard angles of his
face beneath my fingers.

He stared at my mouth and I returned the favor,
watching his lips curve and wondering how they might
feel against mine.

What was wrong with me? I snapped back,
away from his grip. Seriously, my head and my social
skills were royally screwed up. Hadn't I just hours ago
contemplated embarrassing myself for just a glimpse
of Ken Sato?

Reik shook his head. "Now see, a hundred
other girls would have rushed in the other direction."

I rolled my eyes. "A hundred other girls would
gag hearing you say that. The next time you are
working, try to drum up a little modesty."

He laughed. "I like you, Mei." Getting to his feet, he stared down at me, suddenly serious. "Rin wants to see you. Listen, you should stand firm in there with her and the Council. Don't let them make you do anything you don't want to."

I stood, trying not to feel disappointed that I'd shut him down so easily. That urge to flirt must just be automatic with him, pure instinct. Brushing myself off, I decided not to hold it against him. "Okay. Thanks for the advice." He followed as I hoisted my pack and headed around the paddock wall. "They're looking for me?" I asked over my shoulder.

I stopped suddenly, at the corner of the smithy. "Oh." I blinked back sudden tears and reached out to touch the thickly blooming vine that climbed the wall. "He really was here, wasn't he?"

Reik looked around at the forge and all of its accompaniments. "Your father?"

I nodded. "Ken mentioned that he lived here for a time. Now I know it must be true. He loved these flowers." I stroked one of the scarlet, trumpet-shaped blooms. "He always said that they reminded him of my mother, because they were beautiful and exotic, and also strong enough to stand the heat of the forge."

Something crossed over Reik's expression. Something dark and . . . yearning. "Do you remember your mother?"

"Yes, a little."

"What was she like?"

"Soft. She always felt so soft when she held me. And she smelled good." I thought back. "She liked to sing. She always sang to me at night, and she sang while she worked." I hesitated to share anything more concrete when I still didn't know how I felt about Reik. "It's just impressions, mostly, I guess."

He looked like he was going to say something, but he turned to the climbing vine and frowned at it instead. "So, you think your father planted this?"

I plucked one of the blooms and tested the softness of it against my cheek. "He planted one just like it at our home, in just the same place. Where he could see it while he worked."

"Yes, but there's something funny . . ." He stared at me oddly. "I don't remember this vine."

I scoffed. "From your last visit, years ago? I'm sure it's grown since then."

"No. I passed this way yesterday—and I don't remember this vine."

I stared at the plant, sure my skepticism showed clear. It was huge and gorgeous, an eye-catcher. "Well, you must have been particularly self-absorbed." The corner of my mouth twisted. "Even for you."

"Maybe." He sounded thoughtful.

"Well, I'd better head out, if they are looking for me."

He leaned a shoulder against the wall. "Yes, you freaked them out when they found you weren't tucked in bed where they left you."

I started to go, but then stopped. "So, Reik, if they are all still looking, how did you know where to find me?"

"I didn't know." Reaching out, he plucked the blossom from my hand and tucked it behind his ear. "I just had a hunch."

I nodded. "I guess it was a good one."

With Reik's advice in mind, I stopped back at Tak and Noff's house. I apologized for alarming them, and insisted on changing into my own clothes before being escorted to meet the Council.

"Hurry," Tak urged. I nodded as I tucked my

knife into my boot. It was a good move. I felt more like myself as I followed the twins into the Temple building.

It truly was a remarkable sight. The ancient lines of the building were gracious and welcoming. The aged wood shone with polish and care. One thing, though, set my nerves on edge. The feeling that I'd first noticed on crossing the gate into Ryu? That sensation of awareness and expectation that emanated from the land itself and tingled like a whisper along my spine? It grew much stronger in here—and I discovered why when we made our way into the temple's heart.

"Oh, my." I stopped in my tracks.

The center of the temple was an open-air chamber. Fine lattice covered the openings in the roof, running between sturdy, old beams. An actual moat circled the room, the waters still and dark. In the middle sat an island—and on that small, green piece of land grew a wonderful, twisted, magnificent weeping cherry tree.

Here. This is where it came from, that living, breathing awareness. It was beautiful. Fragile and precious. All the hairs on my head, all the soft down on my neck, it stood at attention. Excitement, some sort of elemental recognition, raced along my nerve endings. It called to me.

At my side, Tak bowed. I didn't have to be urged to do the same. It came as naturally as breathing, as easily as the whisper that beckoned me toward it.

"Masuyo Barrett." General Rin had entered from another passageway.

I straightened and turned her way.

"Please come with me."

I did, but I craned my neck over my shoulder as

I went, staring at the tree. It looked ancient. But there was something . . . just the slightest droop to the leaves, perhaps? I ached to turn back and look closer, but the general opened an ornate door and we went through.

The Council room was bright, but bare, with only a low table in the center of the room. Two other women and three men waited there. I took the offered seat across from them and waited.

"We're pleased to have you in Ryu, Masuyo." General Rin took her seat at the table.

"Please, call me Mei."

Her eyebrows rose. "Very well." She gave me a grim smile. "We've been looking for you for a very long time."

"So I've come to understand." I swept my gaze across the lot of them. "Why?"

The question appeared to have taken them all by surprise. The general spoke for them. "Why, to welcome you, of course. To offer you friendship and comfort."

Despite Reik's warning and my own cynicism, something inside of me softened at the words. "Thank you."

"Did your father tell you nothing of us?"

I shook my head. "Nothing at all."

She sighed. "I knew Brian was being careful, but . . . Never mind. We'll speak of that later." She waved an encompassing hand. "We are all glad you had the chance to rest yesterday. We spent the time hearing the reports of Ken Sato and Reik Hama. We hoped to hear a similar accounting from you."

"I would be happy to *trade* information." I paused for emphasis.

"Yes, of course." As one, they all nodded. "Our scouts have told of us of your . . . predicament.

We will help you all that we can, of course."

Hearing the words said out loud lifted a tremendous weight. They would help. I didn't have to fight alone anymore. "Thank you," I repeated in a whisper.

General Rin's expression softened. "I know it might be painful, but we'd like to hear your story— from the time of your father's death."

Breathing deep, I agreed. I started out haltingly, but it actually grew easier as I talked. I felt grateful that I had shared it once with Ken and Reik. It made it easier this time and I knew to brace myself against the wave of accompanying guilt. I talked for a long time, describing how I'd hid from my enemy, recounting the few really close calls I'd had. They listened politely, breaking in occasionally with questions. They appeared especially curious about the Tengu and Ken's interactions with it, and about the *kawad* we fought in Winston Salem, too.

When I finished at last, General Rin called for pots of tea to be brought in. I sat, sipping mine while the Council talked amongst themselves. I was able to follow most of it, although I didn't completely understand it when they fiercely debated defective squares and ineffective casts.

When they'd finished, all the members of the Council stood and thanked me. They began to drift away, still talking in small groups. I stood too, as General Rin approached.

"Thank you for answering our many questions, Mei. As promised, I will do the same for you. But I thought you might like to walk as we talk?"

"I would like that," I said with relief. Beyond stretching my legs, I thought it might be useful, as I got answers, to also see how the village reacted to their leader.

"Ken told us that he never got the chance to tell you much about us, either."

"Next to nothing."

"Then I'll return your favor and start at the beginning—although ours goes back quite a bit further." With a wry smile she led me over to one end of the narrow room, where a beautiful rendition of old Japan took up most of the wall.

"Our story begins centuries ago, in the mountains of the Iga Province of Japan. Ryu was a small village, out of the way, but rich in history and tradition. She turned to look at me, watched me closely as she spoke again. "We are Ninja, Mei. As are you."

"Me?" I stared at her.

"Of course. You are Ninja, as your parents were before you."

My skepticism must have shown in my face, for she laughed. "Oh, Brian Barrett was Ninja in heart and deed, even if he was European by descent. And your mother was Ninja by blood."

I frowned. "My mother is of the Oshuni family."

"Yes. We did occasionally intermingle with neighboring villages. Throughout the centuries there have been others that mixed with the Oshuni paper makers."

There was nothing I could say to that.

"I heard that you managed to keep your mother's *sugeta*."

"How did you—" I stopped myself. Tak and Noff had taken my soiled clothing from my pack while I slept.

"It speaks well of you that you managed to keep it intact all this while—and that you would want to." She stepped away from the map suddenly and

motioned for me to follow her toward a door at the
back of the room. "Come. Enough about that. I
promised to tell you about Ryu."

"Yes. I don't understand how all of this," I
waved my hand, "how all of that," I pointed back
towards the map, "ended up *here*."

"Indulge me, will you? The tale truly does
begin centuries ago. Many would dismiss it as pure
fantasy, but you have seen—and lived—enough to
know better."

We passed through several administrative-
looking rooms, then stepped out into the street. She
led the way in a direction I had not traveled before. It
looked like the craftsmen's section of the village.

"I used to be a scout myself, you know," she
said as we passed a workshop set up with several
looms. I could see the outlines of several different
sized frames and hear the clack of shuttle and reed.

"Hitomi mentioned it. She hinted that you
might have an elemental *minding* talent?"

A small quirk disrupted the general's normally
solemn visage and her eyes lit up. She came to a stop.
Loud pounding sounded from inside the nearest shop.
Grinning at me, she checked ahead of and behind us,
then spun around and shot a tongue of flame down the
empty center of the street.

The pounding stopped and men gathered in the
doorway. They subjected her to some good-natured
cat calling and teased for a bigger show. Across the
street several children spilled out onto the porch. The
youngest, little more than a toddler, shouted, "Boom!
Rin—boom!"

She flung her hands towards the sky. A small
burst of multi-colored fireworks went off above our
heads. The kids cheered. She blew them a kiss full of
sparkles and we moved on.

And I guess that answered my question. General Rin might be serious and direct, but her people liked her.

"I never fought a Tengu," she said. "Although I did once help take down a mountain troll. And the kitsune you fought off—I've never heard of so many banded together like that."

"Kitsune—the foxes?"

"Yes. I exposed a mature one, once. The ones you faced must have been young. They grow wily and more skilled at transformation as they age. The one I fought had grown into her nine tails. She developed the ability to become a most seductive young woman and had attached herself to an up-and-coming young physicist. I had to set her skirts on fire to get her to expose her tails before he would believe me."

We passed a building set off away from the others—and I found why when the fumes of a tannery hit us. We moved quickly past and reached a fast-moving stream with a working mill wheel turning. From inside came the buzz of large saws. We left the road and paced along the stream until we found a bench a bit past the mill. We took a seat and she gazed back the way we'd come with pride shining clear.

"So. The history of Ryu." Bending forward, she sifted through some gravel and chose a smooth, flat rock. Standing again, she rubbed the stone between her hands and then whispered something over it inside her cupped hands. She tossed it then, sending it skipping across the slight bend in the stream before us.

I stared. The water where the stone had touched began to change. It became reflective at first, then an image shimmered across it. I could see a picture, a pretty little village, smaller and more primitive than the Ryu we currently inhabited.

"A simple scrying spell," she said. She waved her hand and the picture came to life. I could see small forms planting rice, others moving along the trails. "Our clan was one of several prominent Ninja families back then. We kept largely to ourselves, except when we were hired by one daimyo lord or another to perform a service. But that changed when a special child was born to us. A girl—Rialka."

The picture changed focus. I could see a pretty, laughing toddler. A running girl. A group of young men gawking as a young woman passed by.

"She was beautiful beyond words. Intelligent and kind. She could make flowers bloom and vegetables grow to a substantial size. As she grew older, she became beloved by the whole village—and then tales of her beauty began to spread. Visitors began to come to us, just to see if such beauty truly did exist. It grew out of hand—until one day she was kidnapped by the son of a daimyo lord."

The image pulled away, showing dark figures carrying a struggling form out into the night.

"For himself?" I asked.

"No. His father was out of favor with the Shogun. The son presented Rialka as a gift from their family."

I made a sound of disapproval.

"Things were different back then." She frowned. "The Shogun was enchanted. She was as clever as she was pretty and she quickly became his favorite concubine."

The picture shifted to something out of a movie. An oriental palace. Sumptuous rooms decorated with gorgeous screens and priceless pottery. Beautiful gardens. And in them—I gasped. I couldn't breathe.

It was her. The woman from my dreams. She moved through the shifting scenes with the same grace. In one, she even wore the same dangling hairpiece. My chest tightened and my fists clenched. What did it mean?

"He treated her well, saw her educated, gave her rich clothes and presents, and he also kept her close, allowing her to interact with his warriors and advisors, even asked her opinions."

"How forward thinking of him." Maybe sarcasm would disguise just how freaked out I was. I still couldn't wrap my brain about the image of my dream figure moving before me.

"You scoff, but it was. But like most courts of power, his was full of intrigue. People began to resent Rialka—or to covet her. One of the latter was Lord Inaba." The general's expression hardened. Her voice changed, roughened, even just saying the name.

"He was a small man, not in stature, but in character. Full of jealousy and hate. He was thirsty for knowledge and for power. He made allies of other discontented men, and of scholars and magicians. He dabbled in dark magic and darker schemes. It was said that he kept a man of learning as a slave. He was a healer and a sorcerer of earth magic, bound to Inaba against his will by some evil trick. Inaba sought out other men of letters and magic as well, and associated with witches, doing all he could to learn or steal their abilities."

The hate in her tone only seemed to grow as she talked further. The shimmering image in the water showed a man in rich robes and a samurai's distinctive top knot. Shadows and smoke shifted around him.

"In those days, the daimyo lords were at times required to live in the Shogun's city, away from their homes. It was during one of those times that Inaba met Rialka. He quickly became taken with her. Loudly he praised her grace and beauty, her poetry.

Always he would manage to be near her in her public appearances. And then strange things began to happen. Rialka felt eyes on her even when she was alone. She heard strange whispers in her ear. Her things went missing, and then she would find odd bits and bundles of herbs hidden amongst her clothes and possessions."

"It was Inaba?" The beautiful face in the water had become furrowed with worry and unease.

"Of course. He went a little mad with lust and jealousy. He'd long been obsessed with the idea of immortality and ultimate power. Now he was convinced that Rialka was the women meant to share both with him. Already knee deep in schemes to steal the Shogun's influence, he merely added her into the mix. Back then, it was a crime merely to leave the Shogun's city without his permission. Inaba not only left, he stole Rialka away with him. And he managed to make it look like a rival daimyo lord had taken her."

"So, he was freaky and insane—and good at both."

"Unfortunately so. It was tantamount to a declaration of war. He raced for home while the Shogun's men wasted time chasing the wrong man. But he'd forgotten one important thing. Rialka was Ninja. There'd been no chance of escape from the palace, with its many watching servants and officials and warriors, but it was another story, being on the road with Inaba and his men. On the second night she slipped her bonds and stole away in the night—and she freed the earth sorcerer too. Together they headed back towards the mountains and her clan."

"She didn't make it, I gather."

"No. Inaba used his dark magic to track her down. They found them in an old mountain temple, run down, with only one monk to help defend them.

The three of them were easily defeated."

It was the same temple, in the watery image. Looking more tired and worn then than it did now, but it was the same building. My head was beginning to ache. "Did he kill her?"

"No. The chase and the delay had hurt Inaba, though. The Shogun's warriors were closing in, as was a group of Ninja dispatched from our village, sent to help her escape. The rival daimyo had also dispatched his oldest son and a group of his samurai to avenge his family's honor. They all approached the deserted mountain temple."

"But he wasn't captured."

"No. He prepared feverishly for his final stand. He threw up wards—magical barriers around the temple. And he began casting spell after spell, using his own magic and the earth sorcerer's—trying to make himself immortal and all-powerful."

"What of Rialka?" I asked quietly.

"He performed the spells on her too. Again and again, he tried. There were changes. He grew taller, more physically powerful. He was marked too—a living flame roamed his body causing great pain.

I stilled, suddenly, sickly certain that I knew where this story was going.

"Yes." The general saw the realization in my face. "She was changed too."

"Her eyes?" I whispered.

"Yes. They were taken. Changed."

The same face stared out at me from the water. The same face that had at last turned to look at me in my dreams. And now her eyes were just like mine. I breathed deep, fighting back a sense of panic. No wonder these people told bedtime stories about me.

But I was not her.

The general continued. "The Shogun's men

arrived and the rival's son and his men. None of them could break through the magical barriers, though. Only our clan came prepared. They knew that only an object of power could take down the wards. They arrived with a dragon's scale, spelled and given to them by a friend."

"It worked?"

"Yes, the wards came down, but they were too late. Desperate, Inaba had struck on the idea of using his sorcerer to call upon the earth power of a fissure beneath the temple's hot spring. He forced the man to call it up, to channel it, as a last, desperate attempt at immortality."

Her shoulders drooped, making me nervous to hear the rest.

"The rival son challenged him even as they began, but Inaba's last gamble had worked. The earth's power, twisted and changed, was already growing in Inaba. Laughing, he disarmed the boy with a twist of his fingers, and defeated him as easily as a man steps on an insect."

In the wavering picture, I watched the Shogun's men, the tall, brash samurai warrior, even the Ninja, as they were all picked up and tossed away, forced back against the walls by the laughing Lord Inaba. The villain stood, bathed in a massive pulse of angry red energy that flowed from the fissure, through the earth-mage and into him. He chortled his delight as he gathered the power, absorbed it, and bent it to his will.

I saw the earth sorcerer, looking ill and frightened, meet Rialka's gaze.

"The earth mage looked to Rialka. He was held helpless, caught in the transfer, and he knew Inaba was going to succeed."

In the wavering image, Rialka nodded her understanding.

"In the crucial moment, she stepped forward, positioning herself between Inaba and his mage, interrupting the flow of energy."

I watched the pulsing light change as she took control, shifting into more soothing colors of blues and greens.

"She stole the energy for herself, then confronted Inaba, and drained him of the power he had absorbed, taking it all."

She did it by embracing him close, and kissing him soundly upon the mouth. I shivered even as I watched the villain diminish in her arms.

"But in that moment of pure and massive power, she saw the truth. Though she might defeat him now, Inaba had changed too much to die completely—not if he wanted to hold on. And he did."

The beautiful woman in the image turned to those who had come in an attempt to help her. Throwing back her head, she extended her arms and speared each of them with a blazing charge of her energy.

"All of them. She gave them all gifts—and a new destiny. She set them up as opposing forces—as her soldiers. For she'd seen that Inaba would never die. He would never give up, never stop trying to gain immortal life in this world and the rule of it all. She made them her warriors in the fight against his evil."

"And Inaba?" I asked hoarsely.

In the picture she held her tormentor tighter—and destroyed them both in an explosion that shattered Rin's scrying spell.

I watched the colors fade away and the normal blue and sunlight sparkle return to the water before us.

After several, long, silent moments, I spoke. "Ken said that you were given gifts, and that you carried a burden."

Chapter Sixteen

"That can't be true." I had to force the words out.

"It is," General Rin answered bitterly. "He's never stopped in his mad quest for power. Rialka's sacrifice trapped him in the spirit world, but he's never stopped trying to come back through. His obsessions have only grown over the centuries. And now, somehow, he's found a way to cross the plane from the spirit realm. We don't know all of the details, only that he is somehow combining magic and technology to merge spirit and flesh. Every time he does it, we have another disaster."

"But the scientists," I protested. "They say it's over. The fault lines, they are calm now. We're getting back to normal." I wanted to believe it as much as the rest of the world did.

"Until Inaba starts experimenting again." The general's tone hardened again. "We can't let that happen. We need your help."

"My help? I don't even know what any of this has to do with me, with my enemy."

"You're one of us, Mei. That should be obvious to you by now. And I believe that your wind demon is one of *his*."

I stared ahead, unseeing, for several long minutes. "I don't know what you want me to do," I said at last. "I don't have any *minding*—"

"You have skills aplenty," she interrupted. "That much is obvious. The rest, we hope, will become clearer. We'll see." She shrugged. "Will you be able to help? I don't know. But that Tengu was one of Inaba's creatures. He was looking for you. *Inaba* is looking for you. If nothing else, we must keep you out of his hands. And if there is even a chance that you can do more . . ." Somehow she managed to give me a look that was both determined and pleading. "Then we have to try."

I continued to sit, staring at her, trying to process how this changed everything.

"Excuse me, General!"

She turned to face the bridge across the stream. I followed her gaze to find Ken Sato standing there. "I don't mean to interrupt," he called. "But I thought I'd offer to take Mei to lunch."

General Rin glared at him for a moment, but when she turned to look at me, her face changed. "Oh. Perhaps she could use a reprieve."

I let annoyance sweep away the relief I felt. Annoyance at her, and at Ken too. I could not let myself fall into the habit of being rescued by Ken. From danger *or* discomfort.

I looked to the general. "We haven't even discussed the wind demon and what can be done—"

"No one in Ryu at the moment has any experience with such a creature," she interrupted.

"But you said . . . We agreed . . ."

"We will consult others. There are people who may know more. Experts in JanFran. And perhaps . . . closer to home."

"How long will that take? What will I do in the meantime?"

"Stay," the general answered simply. "Your father was one of us. Your mother was once an honored guest. Take your place here. Explore your heritage. See if you might fit in."

She must have seen the conflict in my face.

"At the very least you can continue your training here. Test your skills. You might even learn something." She started back toward the street. "I'll notify you as soon as we hear something. There should be some sort of development soon."

She turned back toward the Council building and was quickly gone. I was left alone with Ken—in what felt like the first time in a long time.

"You should have told me," I snapped at him as he approached across the grass.

"I don't even know what you are talking about, but I know you're right."

I folded my arms and glared at him.

"Which thing I should have told you, do you mean?"

"Rialka. About her. About her eyes. And mine."

"Oh, that." He grimaced. "Yes, well. It's not as huge a deal as you might think. There have been others, you see, through the ages."

I let out a huff.

"Truth? I was afraid you would freak out." He flourished a hand. "See? You *are* freaking out."

My frown deepened. "I'm not her."

"Nobody thinks you are."

I dropped my hands. "Listen, I appreciate the welcome I've received here. I'm truly enjoying feeling almost . . . normal. But I'm not her."

"I promise. Nobody wants you to be her. Least of all, me."

The look he gave me shorted out what was left of my brain. His dark gaze held mine intently—and something shifted. Something lived and breathed between us—where before it had only existed as potential.

Now it was alive, charging the air, creating a rising warmth in my chest.

That wayward lock of hair drifted across his face. For the first time, I gave in to temptation. I reached out, savored the softness on my fingertips as I brushed it back into place.

Like it was a signal, he smiled. "Come on. You really do look like you need a break. And I'm starving."

I drew my hand back and tucked it in my pocket. My heart lightened and my brain cleared a bit. I decided to give us both a break. "Okay. Let's eat."

He took me back the way I'd come, to the communal kitchen that sat across the courtyard from the Temple.

"Most people cook at home, but the kitchen is always open to anyone who needs it, or to those who just want to be social. And to our guests, of course."

"Do you get many guests, then?"

"Enough." He led the way up the stairs into the building. "Scouts, of course. We have a fair amount of visitors from JanFran, too."

"Hold up, you two!" Reik bounded up the steps behind us.

"Hey," Ken answered with a marked lack of enthusiasm. "What are you up to? Getting ready to take off again?"

Reik smirked. "Hate to disappoint, old boy, but I'm sticking around a while." He shot me a grin that sent a zing of nervous energy down my spine. "Survived the inquisition, did you?"

"Yep. Want to have lunch with us?" I strove to sound like my senses wouldn't be balancing on a knife's edge between the pair of them.

He shook his head. "Thanks, but I have people to see. Catch you tonight, maybe." He looked at Ken. "Give your mother my regards."

With a flourish, he was gone. His words triggered a question, though. "Ken, General Rin said that my mother was once an honored guest here. Do you know what she meant?"

He scowled, thinking. "Yes, at least I think so. I'd always heard that your father met your mother on one of his scouting missions. When they grew serious about each other, it's said he brought her here. Rin says it was because he wanted her to settle here, with him, after they were married."

"But she was apprenticed in JanFran." I knew that much, that she worked with her family, making beautiful washi, and had been working to master the skill. It's why we'd been living there when she was killed. Had my dad meant to return here to stay? Then why didn't he bring me here? Why did we live so isolated? I thought of Rin's remark about him being careful, and Ken's earlier musing that he hadn't trusted someone here.

I shook my head. It was too much to take in all at once. I let my gaze follow Reik instead as he moved quickly through the courtyard. People lounging at the benches in the shade of the trees waved at him. A lady called a greeting. He barely acknowledged them with a nod and hurried on. *People to see*, he'd said.

"Does Reik have a family, a mother?" I asked Ken, changing the subject abruptly. He'd seemed interested in mine.

"Yes, and no. He's an orphan. He was left at one of the gates when he was young, three or four."

"How awful." I had troubles enough, but I hadn't been abandoned.

"He clearly belonged here, though. His *minding* had manifested already, even at such a young age. Someone had already given him his mark. He was taken in, of course. He's one of the most powerful scouts we've ever had."

"But he doesn't have any family?"

"He has the older couple that raised him. They are frail now, but proud of him. And he is close to one person. Boru."

"I haven't met him."

"Her. No, she lives apart. Some people need seclusion, you know? But Reik has always visited with her often. I think they are fond of each other."

"I'm glad he has someone."

"Some people used to wonder if he is her child, but most don't believe it. They speculate that he must have been the child of a scout who became involved with someone from the outside." Ken looked at me in all seriousness. "But truly it doesn't matter. We're all his family. He's one of us, as we hope you will be."

Ducking my head, I didn't answer, and after a moment, he sighed and opened the door. As we entered the dining hall, I craned my neck, hoping to see what sort of visitors Ryu might get, but the place was empty except for a table of young kids and their teacher.

"Ken! Mei!" The children appeared to be equally delighted to see us both. They'd been having agility lessons, they said, and they were all eager to brag about their skills.

"I crossed the highest, springiest beam and I only fell once!" It was the girl who had offered me the flower—was it only two days ago? It felt like a lifetime. "I didn't even cry."

"It would have been okay if you had," I assured her. "Everybody cries sometimes."

"Not you!" she avowed.

"Yes, her. And me, too," Ken interrupted. "In fact, I'm so hungry I might cry now."

The kids found this hysterical.

"Go and eat," the young teacher urged him. "We are ready to head back."

I waved goodbye and followed Ken to the serving station. We took our seafood stew and crusty bread to a table and my own stomach started rumbling as we sat down. Deliberately, we kept the conversation light as we ate. I laughed as Ken told me stories of his brothers and sisters.

"Are you the eldest?" He did give off that confident, competent vibe.

"No. Second. My older brother is a farmer, like my dad."

"Ah, but does he have an affinity for mushrooms?"

"No, but he can call rain."

"Now that would be really useful in a farmer."

"Useful for all of us, really—"

"Ken!"

We stopped. A girl approached. A little younger than us, I judged. She carried a stack of bulky envelopes. When she set them down on our table I got a better look at her and my mouth dropped open in shock.

"General Rin asks if you would deliver these to Sho. When you are done eating, of course."

"Oh. Uh, sure."

She cast a cool glance my way. "She also suggested that you take along . . . our guest. That she might be interested in seeing some of our preservation efforts."

"Okay." He glanced between us. "Mei, this is Akemi."

"Hi." I couldn't stop staring at her. I knew I should. I knew such direct attention would likely make her uncomfortable. It always did me—and for a *very* similar reason.

She was another. Right here in front of me. Another girl with stars in her eyes.

Not the same as mine. Her eyes were dark. Black as night, with shining pin pricks of light scattered across them, instead of blue with one silver starburst like mine.

They narrowed at me now. "Hello."

Ah, there was the disdain I was used to encountering. Funny how quickly I'd gotten used to being treated politely.

She turned back to Ken. "These are likely wardrobe bits and fabrics for Sho's next production. You know how important costumes are to him." She smoothed her trendy, flowing dress, worn over colorful tights, then raised her brows as she gave me the once over. "You know what they say," she sniffed. "Clothes do tell you so much about a person."

I realized suddenly that this must be the girl who had glared at me from the Temple, that first night in the courtyard.

"Manners do too." Ken stood. "Please tell the general that we'll be happy to deliver these." He gathered up the packages. "Come on, Mei."

"Okay. Bye," I said to Akemi.

She reared back, nodded frostily, then flounced away.

"Don't mind her," he told me. "She's got an attitude."

The corner of my mouth twitched. "Yeah. Her and the rest of the world." But something worried me. "Ken, she's not . . . shunned or anything, is she? Because of her eyes?"

"What?" Surprise nearly choked him and that reassured me more than anything. "How could you say that, after the way you were welcomed? No," he said, suddenly fierce. "We do not discriminate like that. No one here will ever call you *kawad*, Mei."

"Okay," I said meekly. "Thanks."

We left the kitchens and set out, heading downhill on a well-won path instead of following one of the streets.

I was still thinking about the encounter with Akemi. "What did she mean about preservation?"

He squinted over at me. "Well, judging from how you looked when I came upon you and General Rin, I assume she told you about the quakes—and Inaba?"

"Yeah." I still wasn't sure I could believe such a thing. And suddenly that stew wasn't sitting on my stomach so well.

"You can understand, then, that there would be a great deal of sorrow and anger here. So many of us lost loved ones, homes, livelihoods, when the Rift destroyed so much of Japan. And there's a good deal of guilt mixed in with the despair."

"Guilt? Oh, because they feel as if they should have been able to stop . . . it?"

"Many feel that way. Others suffer from survivor's guilt, and some from just plain, debilitating grief." He sighed. "But there is a feeling of responsibility. So we do everything we can now, to remember, and to preserve the history, the heritage, the old ways. So that they don't disappear completely."

I understood that. My own mother had been expert in the ancient techniques of making paper. But something he said caught my attention. Survivor's guilt. It triggered some of my unanswered questions. "Yes, about that. I understand that a village can be rebuilt. But that Temple? That's the same—"

I paused. The path had wound to the bottom of a small hill. From beyond it came some very familiar sounds. "Is that—?"

A drift on the wind brought the clack of wooden sticks, the repeated thumps of arrows sinking into targets, the hard smack of flesh, shouts of encouragement, grunts of effort . . .

I raced to the top of the rise and stood, all agog.

Below me stretched the most perfect training ground I could ever have imagined.

Yes. There were the archers, and some surprisingly young children practicing with wooden swords. But there was also a warped wall. Mock ups of other walls, wooden, brick, stone, with gutters and without, with varied windows and topped with many different sorts of roofs. A complex system of training bars. Vaults, barrels and other obstacles to practice on. And the most elaborate, spreading obstacle course I'd ever seen.

My fingers twitched. I started to bounce. I practically drooled.

Ken came up beside me, still balancing packages. I glanced at him, wide-eyed before turning back to the wonderful spectacle before me.

He chuckled. "Yes. I thought you'd like this part of Ryu."

I glanced over again, and let the challenge show in my face. "Let's go," I said, low and urgent.

"We will, I promise. But first I have to deliver these."

Chapter Seventeen

Ken's spirits lifted a little, even as he shifted his load of packages yet again.

Mei had been entranced by the training ground. He'd known she would be, had counted on it, in fact. But her reaction had been even better than he'd hoped. He could barely wait to get her down there, to see her in her full glory—when neither of them were in danger from some bloodthirsty *yokai*.

She'd held up well through the morning's revelations. A relief, since there were more—and bigger ones—to come.

It all left him hopeful—and nervous. Overall, he thought she'd reacted pretty well to her introduction to Ryu. Thanks be to all the gods and ancestors— because he very much wanted her to like it here.

They reached the end of the trail and he wondered what Mei would think of the complex—one of the most recently completed in the village. A pretty little paved overhang stood before a much plainer building. Made up of two connected structures actually, they were constructed of simple stacked timbers, with only a few small windows up near the roofline.

It was different inside, though. He led the way through the brightly decorated foyer and past a set of double doors—and into the main auditorium of the theater. It really was so well done, with state of the art seating and a beautifully crafted stage. Uniquely, it also held a gracefully lined, roofed pagoda-type addition on the left side of the stage. It actually reached out into the audience. The whole thing was lit softly at the moment. Mei made a sound of appreciation as they marched down the center aisle.

"Sho!" Ken dumped his armful of envelopes on

the stage.

"What?" The irritated answer came from high above their heads. Craning his neck, he found his friend up on the scaffolding, squatted over a torn-apart spotlight.

"I've carried your pain-in-the-butt slippery mail this far," he returned. "The least you could do is come down and get it."

"Ken?" Sho peered over the railing. With a whoop he grabbed a nearby pole and slid down, landing offstage with a flourish. He hurried over, grinning. "I hoped you'd pop by, but I didn't expect you to be my errand boy."

"Just doing a favor for the general. And I brought someone for you to meet." He turned. "Sho, this is—"

"I know who she is!" His friend hopped down from the stage. He always looked a bit of a mess, with his constantly disheveled hair and his collection of ragged, vintage tees, but today he also had grease smeared on one high cheekbone and across his pointed chin.

"Well, that's no great feat, is it?" Mei asked with a grin. She held out a hand. "Nice to meet you, Sho."

He took it without hesitation of course, which made Mei's grin widen slightly. Ken felt a quick pang, but brushed it off. Girls loved Sho. He had a big personality, a quick, well-read mind and a never-ending run of smart jokes and pop-culture references. But his friend would never poach on a girl that Ken expressed interest in.

He frowned. Unlike Reik.

"No, no," Sho was saying to Mei. "I'm glad to meet *you*. I was hoping for the chance. I hear you know all about movies. I was wondering if you also had some experience with theatre?"

"Who told you—" She paused. "Hitomi?"

"Who else?" Sho hitched a thumb toward the backstage area. "She's been talking of nothing but you all morning."

"She's still here?"

"Yep. Back in the props, I think. Want to see her?"

"Please." Mei had lit up. Her eyes were always a little more silver than blue, when she was relaxed or happy. And Ken thought he'd seen the sparkle of other colors in the depths of that starburst pupil, too.

He jerked his attention back as the other two set off, taking the door just in front of the stage that led to the labyrinth of storage, dressing and prop rooms in the back. They found Hitomi amongst a collection of large set pieces, bent over a stage rock, her back to the door.

"Come here, Sho," she said, hearing the door. "I've almost got this down. What do you think? A little grey camouflage outfit and I'd be near invisible." She sighed. "Except for my hair, that is. I've got to figure that out."

"Shave it off," Sho suggested. "But not now. There's someone here to see you."

Hitomi whirled around. She broke into a big smile when she saw them. "Hey! What are you guys doing here?"

Sho held back as Mei went to exclaim over the complete transformation of Hitomi's hands. He met Ken's gaze. "I'm to do a reading on her, I suppose?"

Ken sighed. "That's the impression I got from Akemi."

Sho's gifts had never expressed themselves as an outwardly visible *minding* ability. Instead, they'd turned inward, and they'd discovered that he was

incredibly adept at the Kuji-in skill of Jin, one of nine
Kuji-in practices that centered and empowered a Ninja.
Jin was the skill that allowed a trained Ninja to harness
psychic energy and 'read' other people. Some could
actually read another person's thoughts, but Sho's gift
was more accurately described as being able to see into
someone's heart, to read their character. It had turned
into a valuable tool for an actor like Sho, helping him
to understand his roles and deliver some powerful
performances. But General Rin also occasionally
made use of his talent, too.

"I know the general is just being cautious, but I
also *know* that Mei is the one." Ken still had to tell
Mei about his suspicions, and about Rialka's warnings.
She needed to know. He gave his friend a pleading
look. "Will you let me know what you . . . see?"

"Sure." Sho nodded his sympathy. "Let me
spend a little time with her. Then why don't you offer
to give her a tour while I prepare for the reading?"

Ken agreed. He hovered in the background,
fighting off guilt, as Sho plunked down next to the
girls. "So, Mei. What of it? Have you seen any good
theatre?"

She grimaced. "Actually, I've seen some
surprisingly good high school productions." A little
sheepishly, she indicated her layered tees and black
jeans. "But I've never really had the wardrobe for Off-
Broadway."

"Ah, well. No matter." He settled back. "So,
tell me what struck you about the high school
productions."

They set off on a discussion of sets, adaptations,
props and directorial choices before Sho entered into a
lengthy description of the differences between Noh,
Kabuki and Bunraku theatre. Ken listened, silently
thrilled to see Mei connecting with his friends. He

didn't see how Sho could find anything but good in
her.

"You know so much, I'm amazed," Mei told
Sho eventually. "But, is there no one else to help you?
Aren't you young to be in charge of all of this
yourself?"

"I'm not alone when there is a production in
swing. Then I have a cast and crew around, all of us
pulling together. But I'm the theatre director for now.
It wasn't always this way, but it's my birthright. My
parents were in charge before me. My father designed
this building."

"It's beautiful."

"It is. But he's gone now. They both are."

"I'm so sorry," Mei whispered.

"They were in JanFran."

Ken was surprised when Sho continued. He
didn't often talk of his parents these days.

"They were consulting with several traditional
Japanese theaters out there. They were very passionate
about keeping the old forms alive." His tone grew
bleak. "Inaba controls a large section of the city.
Some of his spies discovered that they were from
Ryu."

He stopped, his lips pressed together.

Hitomi placed a hand over his. "They were
killed."

Mei paled.

"And here I sit, blocking movements for *The
Treasury of Loyal Retainers*," Sho said bitterly.
"When I should be out there, fighting, avenging their
deaths."

Familiar with his friend's frustration, Ken
touched his shoulder.

"At least you've passed the trials. There's a
chance you could go. I'll be lucky to get to take

them," Hitomi said with a frown.

"What good does it do, when the Council won't send me out?" He tossed a carved Noh mask onto a nearby table. "I know I perform a valuable service here. But I deserve the chance to fight back." He stood. "Well, it does no good to moan, does it? Why don't you two show Mei around the place while I put that spotlight back together?"

"Yes!" Hitomi pulled Mei to her feet. "Come on, we'll start in wardrobe and I'll show you the kimono I wore in *The Damask Drum*."

Ken followed and let Hitomi shoulder most of the role of tour guide. They reached the stage last. He could see Sho, sitting quietly in the roofed pagoda across the auditorium. His eyes were closed and his fingers interlocked with the fingers inside—in the traditional Jin hand seal.

Mei good-naturedly admired everything Hitomi showed her, but she grew quiet when they made their way out onto the stage. Her steps slowed. She looked around, ran a hand down the curtain, and then stopped when she caught sight of Sho.

Hitomi noticed him too—and turned to Ken, eyes wildly questioning. She'd realized what was going on.

He gave her slight nod.

Mei waited a long moment. Ken wondered if she could tell that Sho was 'reading' her?

"Sho," she said finally. "Are you okay?"

Sho's eyes popped open and unfolded his hands, and the rest of his body too. "Yep." He left the pagoda and joined them. "Sometimes it helps to drink it all in, to lose myself in the energy of this place." He lifted a shoulder. "Makes it easier, you know?"

"Well, that's everything here," Hitomi said hurriedly. "Mei, would you like to spend the afternoon at my house?"

Ken's heart revved a bit when Mei turned toward him, brightening. "Actually, what I'd really like to do is to hit that training ground."

"Oh, that's a great idea!" Hitomi was easily persuaded.

"Then let's do it." Ken turned to Sho. "Want to come along?"

"Are you kidding?" Sho shot Mei a challenging smirk. "I can't wait to see what she can do!"

"Let's go get my stuff." Hitomi dragged Mei backstage again.

Ken rounded on Sho as soon as the girls were gone. "Well?"

Sho looked . . . thoughtful. "She's good, man."

"Sho!" Ken seethed with impatience. "More?"

"I like her. Seriously, she's one of the good guys."

Ken slumped in relief. "Is she the one? Can you tell?"

"No. I can't see anything like that. But, Ken? There is something. It's dark, and it's buried deep." He sighed. "I couldn't get an eyeball on it, but it's . . . serious."

Ken stood stock-still, unbelieving.

Sho shook his head. "No, I don't want you to think badly of her. In fact, I'm not sure she even knows it's there. Whatever it is, it doesn't make her dangerous or evil. I think it makes her vulnerable."

Vulnerable. Ken knew she was vulnerable beneath that tough, distant, I-can-handle-what-you-throw-at-me exterior. But he was pretty sure he was one of the few people alive who had seen that side of her.

"Dude, you know you have to tell her everything you suspect. That's some heavy stuff. She deserves to know."

She did. But Ken wanted her to get a little more comfortable before he added to her burdens. Again.

The girls returned and Mei sought him out with that incredible gaze, just for a second. His pulse ratcheted again and a swift, fierce surge of determination swept through him. She was the one Rialka had told them to expect, and that meant that there was worse to come. But he was going to do whatever he could—anything at all—to make sure she wasn't *vulnerable* to the darkness coming.

He would protect her. With everything he had.

Chapter Eighteen

I deliberately let it all drop away. The worry, the shock of the morning's revelations, the added burden of confirming that I likely had more than just my wind demon to worry about. I banished it all to some back compartment of my mind. I'd take it out and deal with it later. Right now I was going to enjoy myself.

And shards, but did I live up to that promise. I couldn't ever remember having so much fun. I attacked every sort of wall they had, and happily let Ken show off a bit and teach me the best way to shimmy up a gutter and move soundlessly across a rooftop. I sincerely admired Hitomi's graceful fighting skills with her weapon of choice—the *nekote*, or steel claws worn on the fingers and associated, she told me, with ancient female Ninjas. I engaged in wooden sword fighting with Sho and lost handily— because he moved like lightning and because it had been too long since I had an opponent to work with.

One place I could not be beat, though, and that was on the obstacle course. I threw myself into it with joy and abandon. One after another I soldiered up net climbs and across rope swings. I threw myself up devil's ladders and wore out my shoulders and fingers crossing long gaps while hanging from the shallowest of finger grips.

Ken showed me a timed course through a challenging section and we raced it. I beat him easily, crushing his time. A crowd of kids and young adults gathered. They gave him a hard time and patted me on the back. It was so exhilarating I ran the course again, and then a third time.

Still sweating from the last run, I sat back against a post and stretched my feet out in front of me.

I was still breathing heavily when the crowd parted to let Akemi through.

"Not bad." She looked with disdain at the soaked tank top I'd stripped down to. In contrast, she looked like the Work-Out version of a kid's fashion doll in her coordinated tight nylon outfit. Her mouth turned down. "Still doesn't beat my time, though. I have the course record."

"Congrats." I grinned up at Ken as he offered me a water bottle.

"So, feel up to trying it against me?" Akemi arched one manicured brow. "Or are you too tired?"

I was tired. Pleasantly so. I could have happily been done for the day.

She sneered at my hesitation. "I figured you were all talk, no action."

"All talk?" I tried to keep my tone light. "We've hardly had a chance to speak to one another."

"Well, sometimes things do go as planned," she snarked.

Something rose in my gorge as I looked at her. So tidy. So superior. Suddenly the only thing I wanted was to wipe that smug look off of her face—as if this sneering girl was standing in for every person who'd ignored, taunted, chased or reviled me over the past four years.

I jumped up. "Let's do this."

We lined up at the start and I was on fire with excitement and resolve. I would not lose this time.

The timer sounded and we were off. I had done the course enough to know what to expect now, but I couldn't have the same sense of familiarity and rhythm that Akemi had. And I was right. The first obstacle was a large gap we had to cross by leaping from one tall, narrow pedestal to another. She fairly flew across, barely lighting on each step, or so it looked.

But I was right with her as we muscled up a pegboard. I marveled as she pulled ahead of me on a pipe slider. Her timing was exquisite as she jumped the long pipe from one level to another. She exhibited the same perfect precision as we moved through the swinging parts of the course. She always let go and grabbed on at exactly the most efficient moment—and made it all look as smooth and easy as a kid on the playground traversing the monkey bars.

It wasn't that easy. And I was tiring. But I dug deep and hung with her until at least we hit a narrow chimney climb. Here, all those hours of parkour paid off.

Push hard, use those thighs.

Not something every girl hears in her dad's voice, but I did, and it allowed me to pull ahead and I reached the top first. The next—and last—obstacle was one of the most difficult. A spider wall, where you had to leap from a platform and land spread out between two vertical walls, holding yourself aloft and making your way over a long gap to the end.

I didn't hesitate. I jumped—and winced when the landing strained my already tired thighs. But I'd landed high and that gave me a mental kick, for some reason, although it didn't change the extreme challenge of the obstacle. My legs and shoulders screamed as I spider-walked across the twenty-foot gap, and doubts rose up as I heard Akemi hit right behind me. But I clenched my jaw and kept going. I dug deep and increased my pace. I hit the end at last and barely paused as I braced myself and took the long drop to the mat on the platform below.

I'd won. I collapsed back onto the mat and rolled over into a ball. I was sore and exhausted and seriously oxygen deficient, but I'd won—and Shards, but it felt good.

Akemi came in about eight seconds after me.
She looked in far better shape than I did, and she
called for both our times as she landed.

The answer eased her scowl a little. "You beat
me this time, but you still didn't beat my record," she
snarked at me.

I rolled my eyes and sat up, facing away from
her—but she leaned in close behind me. "You'll never
beat that record—and you'll never have Reik Hama
panting after you like that lap dog, Ken Sato."

I jerked away and glared back at her. "Say
what you will to me," I bit out, "but keep your
poisonous darts away from my friends."

The crowd moved in and I was glad to let them
separate us. And I was glad to realize that I'd
achieved another first today—friends. Real friends I
wanted to spend time with—and defend from petty
attacks. I just hoped I never had to defend them from
real danger.

They crowded in around me now and I ignored
Akemi and accepted their congratulations.

"Akemi never's been a good sport," Hitomi
said, shooting the girl a dark look.

"What is her problem, anyway?" I asked. "I've
barely met her. How could she dislike me so much?"

The three of them exchanged looks.

"Don't mind her," Sho answered.

"Yes, that's what everyone keeps saying, but
she's making it progressively more difficult."

"She has an unfortunate mother," Ken said
seriously. "She's always puffed Akemi up,
encouraged her to regard herself as above most people.
In fact, why don't we take off and find a quiet place to
talk about—"

A shout from the hilltop, over by the trail,
interrupted him. A boy stood up there, whistling

loudly and shouting for attention.

"Come on!" His voice carried over the dying conversations around us. "There's been an attack!"

Noise erupted around us again as I got to my feet. An attack? I shared a worried glance with Ken. Was it Fuma Jinnea?

People were already moving, speculating as they headed toward the main village. We followed. I ignored my protesting muscles as we made our way to the courtyard before the Temple.

General Rin was there, speaking with several members of the Council at the top of the Temple steps. We all filed in, making room for everyone, and though the crowd wasn't silent this time, the talk was subdued, worried. After a moment, the general stepped forward.

"You've all heard by now. There's been an incident. Tangi Lim was found outside the second gate just an hour ago. He'd been returning from a supply run when he was attacked. We don't know who or what dared to harm him so close to our borders. The most disturbing element is that he appears to have been drained of both blood and chi."

The throng erupted in shocked gasps and angry mutters.

"We found him in time," the general said, "he will live."

"What sort of creature devours both blood and chi?" someone called out.

"We don't know. We don't know if it was one attacker or perhaps more."

The crowd grew louder.

General Rin raised her voice. "It appears as if we are entering a period of increased *yokai* activity. Reports from JanFran and from our own scouts confirm this." Her hand rose to stop another wave of comment. "It's not the first time we've faced this. We know what to do. We've sent out orders—all scouts will be working in pairs for a while."

"What about the gates? That's two incidents right outside them," a woman shouted.

"We are increasing patrols. We are also restricting trips outside Ryu. For now, anyone who wishes to leave must clear it with the Council first. Traffic into the village has always been watched closely, as you know. We'll continue our monitoring. We ask everyone to keep his or her eyes open and watch carefully. If you see or hear or even *feel* anything unusual, we want to hear of it."

My spine straightened abruptly as the general's gaze met mine. She looked flat and bleak.

"Everyone be careful. Help Tangi's family if you can. Take care of each other. We'll call you together again if we have any news."

She turned and moved away with the rest of the Council. The crowd began to disperse, but slowly. People were still talking in hushed, worried tones.

"Well, that put a damper on the day." Hitomi slumped over to a bench under one of the bordering trees.

Silently agreeing, I followed her. Ken and Sho came too. "Blood and chi?" I asked. "Has there ever been a *yokai* that fed off both?"

They all silently conferred. "Not that I've heard of," Ken said eventually.

"So all the rumors from JanFran must be true," Sho mused. "We're facing something new."

"Or something *changed*," Ken answered. "I told you guys, that Tengu did not act right."

The respite of the afternoon's play had gone. I had the sinking feeling that I was the reason for these attacks and wondered how many others were harboring the same thoughts. The weight of all my burdens rushed back, settling over my shoulders, pressing tight in my chest.

"It's getting late." All I wanted to was to be alone now, to process everything and try to think of what my next move should be. "I think I'll head back to Tak and Noff's now." I turned to Sho. "It was nice to meet you—and even to lose to you." I gave them all a stiff smile. "It really was a great afternoon. Thanks."

"I'll check in on you tomorrow," Hitomi offered.

"I'd like that." I waved. "Goodnight, all."

I headed off, shoulders bowed, gazed turned down again so I couldn't see the accusatory looks that were likely following me.

Dinner was delicious, just like last night, but this time the grilled fish and vegetables sat largely uneaten. The tea cooled in the pot. Even Tak and Noff sat largely silent. They seemed quite as disturbed by the turn of events as I was—and their solemn unease only added to the heavy guilt weighing on me.

"Mei, you're not eating."

I bit down on my lip, telling myself to toss off a standard answer. To not get too close, too transparent. It was the strategy that had served me well for so long.

But the polite, distant answer died away. Instead I blurted out exactly what I'd been feeling. "Neither are you. I'm sorry if you've changed your mind about hosting me."

And it was in that instant that I knew things had truly changed. *I* had changed.

Tak frowned. "Of course we haven't. Why would you think so?"

"Because I might be the reason that boy was hurt today? That's what everyone is thinking, isn't it?

Those creatures are looking for me—and I might have led them right here."

"No one is thinking any such thing," Noff answered firmly.

They were kind. Fondness rushed over me. And a fresh wave of despair. "I can't stand the thought of defenseless people here being in danger—because of me."

They blinked at me, a pair of identical, flanking owls. Then they both laughed. "I think she means that *we* are defenseless," Tak said to her sister.

Noff's eyes sparkled. "I got that impression." She pursed her lips. "You worry needlessly, dear. There are very few of us in Ryu who are truly defenseless."

"What do you mean?"

"Let's show her," Tak said. "The poor thing is distraught."

Her sister nodded and Tak rose. From a shelf in the living area, she brought back a sketchbook. "Do you remember when you complimented the picture of the bird amidst the fern fronds?"

"Yes." I watched her fingers fly over the page and wondered what this had to do with anything.

"You said you expected the bird to take off right from the image," Noff reminded me.

"Yes."

"Watch." Tak flipped the book around and I saw a very similar sketch—only without the ferns. She lifted the picture of the small bird and whispered something over it. She touched her wrist beneath her long sleeve, then touched the finger to the sketch.

I frowned at her air of expectation—until my attention was drawn back to the image.

My mouth dropped open. The bird was *moving*. The little head was turning from side to side. It's eyes blinked rapidly. As I stared, it poked its head right off of the page, color blossoming from its crown and on down as it literally hopped off the page—and into life.

I swallowed.

"Isn't my sister amazing?" Noff asked.

I bobbed my head vigorously. The bird pecked industriously at the table, bent to look under Tak's plate, then fluttered to the back of her chair. She stood and used the sketchbook to shoo the tiny thing to the window. Sliding it open, she motioned the bird out. "Go and enjoy yourself," she told it.

I watched it fly off. "I can't believe it." I sat, still dumbfounded. "Does that work with everything you draw?"

"No." Tak shook her head. "If that was true I would have populated the world with unicorns and dark-eyed, handsome sorcerers when I was a girl."

Noff laughed.

"I do best with animals. Smaller is better because they take less out of me. Also, they only exist for a few hours, and the bigger they are, the shorter the time span." She threw out her hands a little. "I can only do it with a subject I'm intimately familiar with. I have to have held them close, smelled them, peered into ears and between toes, felt their beating hearts." She gave a devilish smile. "But you'd better believe that I've visited nature reserves and zoos the world over. I have quite an arsenal in my fingers." She glanced askance at me. "I've even spent a good amount of time at the wild cat rescue that's located outside of Raleigh."

"Panthers," Noff said, leaning forward. "Lions. Tigers."

"Seriously?" I imagined the havoc she could cause—and how valuable such a gift could be.

"Yes, I see you understand the implications.

They will do their best to obey me, too, so it's quite a useful talent."

I nodded, still lost in imagination. A tiger? And I'd worried that the twins were helpless.

"My sister is no slouch, either. She is a chemist as well as a cook, you see. She has developed many interesting and useful items for us to use in our battles." Tak leaned forward. "Tell me, when Kenshin fought the Tengu, did you see it?"

"Yes."

"He used his *seihoukei*, didn't he?"

"The weapon that looked a bit like a ninja star? Yes." I thought back. "He used it twice, in different ways."

"Yes," Noff said with satisfaction. "We designed it that way, to conserve the weapons, as they are difficult to make. He used the powder first, right?"

"Yes, and it didn't work the way he expected it too."

"That's one of the most troubling developments we've encountered lately," Tak said. "Noff concocted that powder and came up with the way to coat the weapons with it."

"I make it using ground mushrooms—grown by Ken's father, in fact." Noff grinned. "I doctor it up a bit, enhancing the hallucinogenic properties, and I mix it with some of my own creations and a special powder that the witch makes me."

"The witch," I said dully. I wasn't sure my brain could take in any more shocks.

"Oh. Yes. We'll speak of that later." Noff waved the comment off. "When you invoke that powder with the right words and blow it at a *yokai*, it sends them hurtling back into the spirit realm. They cannot return right away, either."

"Why not?"

"The powder drains them of vital energy. All spirits and *yokai* need a deal of it to transfer between worlds." She frowned. "I have to discover why it didn't work on that Tengu. We'll lose a major advantage if the stuff is no longer effective." She trailed off, clearly thinking on the matter.

"There, you see, we are not so defenseless," Tak said. "So, why don't you eat your dinner?"

I tried. And I did feel a little better. I wondered what hidden talents the other seemingly simple people of Ryu were hiding.

Still, later, alone in my room, I found myself unable to sleep again. I'd learned so much today, and yet I had more questions than before. It all swirled and rushed about in my brain until I thought my head would explode. I tried to sit on the porch and let the nighttime calm me, but my thoughts still swam and my knee bounced like a jackhammer. Eventually, I gave up. I needed to move. Like the night before, I snuck out into the garden and on to the quiet village streets.

I wandered a bit. The road I traveled wended downhill and then curved around a pretty little pond. The edges were lined with aromatic herbs and the occasional solar light. Lily pads stretched across the surface and I saw a few froggy eyes reflecting back at me. They reminded me of Hayate and Kaoru. Smiling a little, I sank down, peeled off my jacket and dipped my hands in. I pressed the water to my brow and let the rest run down my arms. The coolness of it anchored me to this peaceful moment and kept the jumble of my wayward thoughts at bay.

I knelt there for a few long moments, then pinched off a piece of thyme to take with me and stood—and jumped a mile when Reik materialized out of the darkness right in front of me.

"Tsk, tsk." Even in the moonlight I could see

the hard glint of mischief in his face. "Wandering at
night is becoming a habit with you, minx. But it's a
bad habit. You never know what you might run into."

"Don't do that!" I scolded. Shrugging back into
my jacket, I frowned at him. "And why shouldn't I
wander? You and Ken were so insistent that I would
be safe here."

"Safe?" He laughed, but it was an ugly sound.
"You met me, didn't you?"

"Funny."

"Well it wasn't so safe for Tangi today, was it?"
he asked bitterly. "He's just a boy. And he almost
didn't make a man."

"I know, that was terrible. But isn't that why
the attacks are occurring outside the gates? I'd thought
. . . it seemed . . . I mean, I thought we were protected,
once we passed the gates?"

He eyed me speculatively. "So, you did feel it?
I wondered." He moved closer and it wasn't until I
felt his breath stir the tendrils at my temple that I
remembered that my hair was down. It made me feel
suddenly vulnerable.

"In fact," he said, his tone rumbling and setting
off vibrations low in my belly, "I wonder if all they
say about you isn't true?"

I glared at him. "I don't know what you are
talking about."

"Don't you?" he smirked. "I watched you
today. Have they seduced you so easily, with just a
fairy tale and an elaborate playground?" He moved
closer still. Reaching out, he touched my hair,
stroking it softly, then digging his fingers in and
following a long strand to the end.

I should have retreated. I knew it. But it felt
good. It had been a long time since anyone had
touched me with any thought but violence.

"Nobody's seducing me," I insisted, raising my chin.

"Is that so?"

He slipped an arm around my waist and fit his body against mine. His head tipped down and I realized our lips were mere inches apart.

I wanted him to kiss me. And I didn't. Confusion sang through my veins. He was incredibly attractive and my body recognized it. My mind knew that he was dangerous, and for some reason liked it. But it was my heart that made the decision at last.

Shaking my head, I stepped away.

"Damn it." He reached for me again and this time I saw that his hard edge had dropped away. "Listen, Mei, I have it. Why don't we just leave?" Even his voice sounded different. He sounded . . . hopeful. And a little desperate. "The two of us? Together and on our own. We'll just go and leave all of this. Let them fight their own battles. We'll be fine, we can handle anything together—and I'll help you find a way to kill that wind demon. You'll have your revenge at last."

For a heartbeat I was tempted—and then I was ashamed.

"No. I'm done running, Reik." Sudden resolution traveled up my spine and lifted some of the weight from my shoulders. "It's time I take a stand. And everything that I've seen and heard tells me I should stand here, with these people."

He turned away. "Yes, well you haven't seen and heard everything yet, minx."

"Why do you talk as if you are not one of them? I don't understand. I heard they took you in when you were alone. I'd think you'd be grateful."

"Is that what you are? Grateful?" He exhaled and spun back around. "Maybe you are right, I suppose I should be, but you know what? They took me in, but they never really made me one of them. They don't even really know me."

"They know you as well as you'll let them," I hazarded. "And what they know, they seem to like well enough. They are proud of you."

"Yes, I'm good at hunting *monsters,*" he said bitterly. "That makes them happy."

"Well, the girls seem to like you for other reasons." I grinned, trying to lighten his mood. "Akemi certainly hopes to capture your attention. Maybe you should give her a chance."

"Yes, because that's what I need. Another female manipulating me for her own ends."

Before I could ask what he meant, he swooped close again and took both of my hands. "Go back to your bed, Mei. And stay there. Ryu isn't safe. Not for me. And not for you."

He let go and backed away. Stiff and rigid, he melted into the darkness.

Chapter Nineteen

I did not listen to Reik. He'd only unsettled me further. Instead, I hurried back the way I'd come, because suddenly I knew where I'd wanted to be all along.

The heavy Temple doors were unlocked. I didn't make a sound as I slipped through and made my way to the center. When I stood at last at the edge of the moat, I heaved a sigh. Both in relief to be here and longing to get closer.

I squinted, straining to see the beautiful weeping cherry in the thin moonlight. Eventually, though, I just closed my eyes. I don't know how long I stood there, basking in the warm feeling of welcome wafting over me. I only knew I suddenly opened my eyes to see that three stepping-stones had appeared in the moat, calling me to cross.

They startled me. There was no one else here. Not a ripple showed in the smooth moat water. Had they been there all along?

And did I dare use them?

My feet were on the first step before I'd even finished posing the question. My brain caught up, however, and played back a dozen hair-raising scenes from the adventure movies I'd loved as a kid. I paused, but the stone didn't sink. No one shot poisoned darts at me. No ancient stone guardian rumbled to life to run me off. I forged ahead.

As soon as I set foot on the island I was glad I had. I felt good. Really good. Warmth and comfort settled over me like a blanket. Had I ever felt this cared for? This safe? Yes. I recognized the feeling. I'd felt the same in the past, when my dad would return to our cabin after being gone for several days. I'd rush to him and he would always sweep me up into a huge bear hug—and I'd feel like this.

I stumbled forward and sank to my knees. I leaned up against the gnarled trunk and closed my eyes. I must have slept. I definitely dreamed. The old dream. The garden. The island. Only this time I was standing on the edge of the bridge and the lady saw me. She stood on her side of the bridge, smiling at me with her matching eyes. I reached for her—

And startled awake. Someone else was in the Temple, after all. A woman, walking toward me, not pausing at the stepping-stones, but crossing to me without hesitation.

Not the woman from my dream. *Rialka*. I said her name silently, hoping it would bring me strength, for I suspected the figure before me might be a spirit.

Everything about her was thin. Her narrow, pretty face. Her long, slender fingers. The gossamer gown of green that moved with the air and trailed long flowing sleeves. Only her eyebrows defied the trend. They stood out thick and black against her pale skin. Her hair too, shone ebony and reached below the length of her sleeves.

"Hello, Mei." She stopped before me. "I've been expecting you."

Why did everyone in Ryu greet me this way? It usually made me feel a bit behind, a little at a loss. Strangely, with this odd figure, I didn't feel that way. Something inside of me knew I'd been waiting for this, too.

"I'm Boru," she said simply.

"Hello." I waited.

"Has no one told you about me?" she asked with a grin.

"I don't think so." I tried to say it politely.

"Well." She sat back. "I'm the Witch of Ryu."

"Ooohh," I breathed. "Noff did mention a

witch." I cast my eyes skyward. "It figures."

She looked amused. "What figures?"

"You know. Water sprites, wind demons, shifting foxes. Why wouldn't a witch be real too?" My mouth quirked. "Next it will be dragons."

"Oh, I think you already know that dragons are real." Without pausing to explain that cryptic remark, she glanced up at the tree above us and bowed.

I had so many questions. I decided to go with the easiest one first. "How did you know I was here?"

"You have a connection to Rialka. So do I." Gracefully, she sank down beside me. "So. You truly do have the eyes. And your connection is strong. I felt it the minute you crossed through the gate."

I sat up a little. "How?"

She raised a brow. "Didn't you feel something when you passed through?"

"Yes. Was that you? I felt like someone had been expecting me. And a little like I was being watched." I glanced up. "I thought it was . . ."

She smiled in approval. "You have good instincts. And both answers are right. You see, I am the keeper of the wards. I created and maintain the magical barriers that surround our village and lands."

"Oh. Well, that makes sense, then." Curious, I asked the next question that popped up. "Are you doing it now?"

"Holding the wards?" She laughed. "Yes. Always. It's sort of like auto-pilot, I guess." She folded her knees and made herself more comfortable. "Actually, it's one of the earliest skills I learned. I had to, you see. A large part of my gifts come from my ability to commune with spirits."

"*Yokai*? Or the spirits of humans?"

"Both. And they can be rather an insistent lot, as a whole. I had to learn how to protect myself or be driven mad. So the wards protecting the village are just a larger, sturdier version, with some very specific tweaks. For example, no one can cross into Ryu without my permission."

I frowned. "But how did I do it, then?"

"You went to the Dragon's Eye. Neil is our gatekeeper. We have a rotating system. Only one gate is open at a time, and you have to talk to Neil to discover which one on any given day. He evaluates all requests and lets me know who is coming. And I give my blessing. Or not."

"Well, then, thank you. You saved our lives."

"You did it yourselves, actually, but you're welcome." She looked upward into the trailing branches. "And though it was me, it was also Rialka that you felt when you entered. That you feel now."

"Rialka is the tree, isn't she?" I'd suspected, but that dream had confirmed it.

"Partially." She heaved a sigh. "You spoke with Rin, who shared with you some of our history. She told you of Rialka and Inaba—and how she thwarted him?"

I shuddered, thinking of that explosion, and nodded.

"This is the very spot where it happened. Here, on this island. And when the confusion and the dust and the debris cleared—there was a sapling. This tree. It contains a piece of her spirit."

"So, it *is* the same Temple!" I exclaimed. "It feels so old and it looks just like the one in Rin's images. And yet, how could it be? How is it *here*?"

Boru gave a little laugh that transformed her. "Well, I'm afraid I'm responsible. Though, of course I could never have done it without Rialka's help."

I merely gaped at her.

"After that first battle with Inaba, the first

village of Ryu did migrate from the high mountains to this Temple--where Rialka made her sacrifice. We wanted to be near her. And we wanted to always remember how she died and why she set us on our path."

"Us?" It was hard enough to imagine Inaba still living on. Surely Boru wasn't—

"No, I'm older than I look, but not so old as that. I am descended from the Earth Mage in the story, in fact. Inaba's servant, who helped Rialka save us, in the end. Throughout the centuries, the sorcerer's gifts have been handed down in my family—and longevity seems to go with it."

I refrained from asking how old she was. Barely.

"There have always been others with a connection to Rialka since then, too. A girl in most generations. Some have the eyes. Others do not."

"How often do they combine in the same person—the connection to both the sorcerer and Rialka?"

"Only in me." Her brow furrowed. "And when the Rift hit, I discovered why I was made this way."

She sat silently for a moment, then turned to me. "Do you ever dream of her?"

I started. "Yes. In the garden?"

She looked almost relieved. "It is the same for me. But she touched us all that day. The rumbles hadn't even started and she was there, in our minds, calling us all to the Temple, to gather in the courtyard."

Boru's gaze drifted. "For me, it was like being trapped in a waking dream. I was there, in the garden with her, but I was also in the Temple. She told me what I had to do—create the strongest, largest, most impenetrable ward I could imagine. It wasn't easy. I could barely think. Japan was dying around us. The skies were black and the ground heaved. I couldn't tell where one began and the other ended. The air was choked with dust and dirt. It felt like it was on fire. There *were* fires and explosions everywhere. People screaming and crying. Dying. And yet I had to block it all out."

The memory had distressed her. Her eyes looked huge and her skin had paled further.

"I don't know how she did it. There was a flash, as bright as a hundred bolts of lightning. And then—all was calm. We were here. The Temple, the courtyard, a few bits of the gardens, and nearly two hundred people."

She fell silent again, and I imagined she was thinking of those friends and relatives who had not made it. Who were left behind and likely died in the cataclysm.

"We had no idea where we were. It took us days to discover we were half a world away. To hear what had happened to Japan."

She painted such a vivid picture in my head— and still I could barely conceive of such a thing.

Yet here they were.

"And so here we are," she said, echoing my thoughts. "It nearly killed me, and it drained Rialka horribly as well. The tree was in a dismal state, so dry and withered. But we recovered, rebuilt, and she has strengthened too." She glanced over at me. "And now you are here as well."

I sighed. "Yes, although nothing here is like what I expected." And everyone seemed to expect so much more of me.

Maybe she read my face, or perhaps her talents extended to mind reading, but she seemed to hear what I did not say. "You've been alone a long time. This can't be easy for you—but it is necessary. And we can help you. I can help you."

I sat straighter. "How?"

The corners of her eyes crinkled. "Weren't you listening? I can talk to spirits."

Alarm erupted and blazed through me. "No! Please don't try to talk to Fuma Jinnae!" I shuddered. "I'm afraid of what he would do to you."

She stroked my hand soothingly. "No. No. Don't worry. There's no use in me contacting your wind demon, or any of Inaba's creatures. I learned that long ago. But the spirit world is large and well populated. There are those who work with us against Inaba. And there are many more he's made enemies of, or who just don't want to see him succeed. I have sent out a few messages. I can contact more." She placed her hand over mine and left it. "Rin will talk to our contacts on the mortal plane and I will speak with the spirit realm. Someone will have answers."

"Thank you," I whispered.

"Rin says you have not fully accepted that you are one of us." She ducked her head to look me full in the face. "You cannot deny it to me, sitting here in the warmth of Rialka's regard. Can you?"

"No. I knew it for sure the moment I stepped onto the island."

"Good. You need only be patient and give us a chance."

I agreed, even though I was inwardly cringing. These last few days of waiting, of hoping, felt more miserable and fraught with danger than all the years of running, hiding and not knowing. It hardly felt fair.

Don't ever expect a fight to be fair.

It was just one more thing my father had been right about.

Chapter Twenty

I spent the next few days trying to absorb everything I'd seen and heard—and admitted to. A good bit of time I also dedicated to trying to discover just why I wasn't adjusting more happily to the idea of realizing one of my most cherished dreams.

A place to belong. It was what I'd hoped for, planned for. And now, as both Rin and Boru insisted—I belonged in Ryu.

Part of me did feel good about it. Most people were kind and I had the sort of acceptance of my differences that I'd always imagined. But I couldn't help but feel that something was not quite right. Like there was an axe about to fall. I told myself it was just lingering paranoia, but truthfully—being here *was* an adjustment. I'd been alone a long time. The constant buzz of people grew wearing at times. More than that though, I had to adjust the mental picture I'd nurtured for so long.

In my head I'd always imagined my first step would be to free myself. I'd defeat Fuma Jinnea and then I'd be free to choose the life I wanted.

Yet I wasn't free. I wasn't running any longer, but I wasn't free. Truthfully, I felt a little . . . trapped. By both circumstances and expectations. But I tried to be fair. After all, who was to say that I wouldn't have chosen Ryu if things had gone as I'd planned?

So I gave myself permission to learn all I could about the place—and my place in it.

I spent a good deal of time with Hitomi. She showed me around the rest of the village. We trained together. We spent a morning babysitting her siblings. And we spent a lot of time walking in the beautiful Temple gardens—especially when I felt the need to get away and find some peace.

We were sitting on a pair of thick, squared rocks at the side of a narrow stream one afternoon. There was a swath of gorgeous red flowers behind us and a gathering of big, colorful koi fish in the stream before us. They were jostling for position as Hitomi peeled a grapefruit and fed them halved sections.

"Hitomi," I began shyly. I hoped she wouldn't mind my asking. "Would you mind . . . that is . . . I'd wondered . . . about your scar?" She always wore those long, tight sleeves, so I'd never seen hers. "That is, do you have one? On your arm?"

"Oh. Yes. We all do—everyone with a *minding* ability. Of course you can see mine." She peeled back her sleeve and thrust out her arm.

It was a framed oval. Inside was a swirl of waving lines. I looked at her for permission, then ran a finger lightly over the thin, raised lines. "Did it hurt?"

"Just a little, and only at first. The lines are so thin that they heal quickly."

"How old were you?" I couldn't remember seeing a scar on any of the young kids I'd been around.

"I was twelve. We get them once our formal training in our *minding* begins. I was a little older than usual because there's never been a gift quite like mine. A special course of study had to be crafted for me."

I shot her a slightly mocking smile. "I knew you were special."

She rolled her eyes at me.

"Twelve was late?"

"Well, the first signs of my gift began to manifest at the usual time—eight or nine, I think I was." She laughed. "I remember the first. My mother had made me a nice dress. I liked it, but it was blue and I wanted it to be hot pink. She had the fabric already though, so it wasn't to be—until the first time I put it on. Somehow I changed the color." She sighed.

"My mother wasn't thrilled, but I loved that dress."

Brightening, she leaned forward. "In fact, it's a side effect, sort of, but I can still change fabric colors." Her brow raised and her finger hovered near my shoulder. "So. May I?"

"What?" I looked down at my black tank. "My shirt?"

"I've been dying to!"

"Oh. Uh . . . okay."

Just the lightest touch to the strap and my tank was now a deep, royal blue.

Hitomi sighed, almost in relief. "That's so much better! It brings out the color in your eyes. And unlike my usual illusions, that will be permanent."

"Oh? Thank you." I paused again. "Yes, well, actually, you've reminded me of something else I meant to ask you."

She waited.

"You've been to the Dragon's Eye, haven't you?"

"Of course! I love it there. Did you have the hamburgers when you stopped in?"

"I don't think they had them when I was there."

"Too bad. They are wonderful." She shrugged. "But then again, it's the only place I've ever had a hamburger, so you might know better."

"When I was there, Neil showed me a trick. A simple spell, he said. To hide his eyes?" I bit my lip. "He seemed to think that I could learn to do it, too."

"Wait," she interrupted. "You've seen Neil's eyes? His real eyes?"

"Yeah."

"Wow. He must really have liked you."

"I hope so. I liked him. Anyway, I wondered . . . General Rin performed that scrying spell and Noff does something magical to her food and you can

change fabrics . . . So, do you think I could learn a
magic spell, even if I don't have any *minding*?"

She glanced past me to the bank of flowers
behind us. "You know, I've never seen these flowers
bloom before." She tilted her head at me. "I really
think it's possible you do have a *minding* ability, Mei.
You just haven't found it yet."

I highly doubted it. Wouldn't my father have
trained me to use it, if I had had any such ability?
"Well, I don't have one now. But if it's true that I'm a
descendant of Ryu, do you think I could still be able to
perform . . . little magic? The way some of you do?"

"I don't see why not," she answered slowly.
"Lots of people have little side effects and abilities that
go along with their *minding*. Like how Ken can talk to
birds."

I blinked. "What did you say?"

"You didn't know?"

I shook my head.

"Oh. It was one of his early signs. Birds love
him. They gossip with him all the time."

I shook my head again, this time to clear it.
"Okay."

She wiped the last bits of peel from her lap and
stood up. "Let's try it!"

"Now?"

"Why not?" She'd turned around and was
rooting amidst the blossoms. "Here's a good one.
Now," she said, kneeling at my feet. "Changing the
color of something is not that unusual. Lots of times,
it's a first sign of ability. Simple magic. Lots of
people here can do it to varying degrees. Let's see if
you can." She placed the blossom in my hand. "Now,
close your eyes a moment. Lift the flower. Feel the
smooth petals, smell the fragrance. Hold it in your
mind."

I did as she instructed, smiling a little as the stems inside tickled my nose. I rubbed its softness against my cheek.

"Picture the red color."

I did. I imagined the red petals with the sun shining through them, pictured the cells stacked together and imagined further still, all the twisting strands of DNA. Somewhere in there existed the instructions that made the petals red.

"Now, change it to blue."

I tried to imagine shifting out that particular bit of instructional matter, and replacing it with just slightly altered coding. But the soft brush of the petal against my cheek made me think. It had taken this flower so long to get to just this state. Hundreds of thousands of years of evolution. It was Nature who worked with it, nurtured and shaped it. The flower merely adapted as needed. Why not ask if it should like to be blue?

Would you? I wondered. *If you could decide, would you like to be blue?*

I felt a surge, a zing of power somewhere deep in my core. It siphoned out of me like someone had opened a drain.

"Mei. Open your eyes." Hitomi's words came out on a whisper.

I did. I looked down to find the bloom was a vivid blue, just like my tank. "I did it!" I looked up at her in amazement. Or did I? Maybe I just lent the flower the energy it needed to do it itself. But still, something swelled inside of me. I felt incredible. Maybe I truly did belong here. I had just done *magic*.

"Look behind you," Hitomi said quietly.

I turned. The red carpet was gone. *All* of the flowers were blue.

"Holy—"

"Yeah." Her head was bobbing up and down. "Yeah. I'd say you could probably handle that simple illusion spell just fine."

"Let's do it!" I bounced on my rock. I felt giddy with excitement and hope.

"Okay. Oh, jeez. Okay. But we have to be careful. We don't want to actually change your eyes. We just want to create a mask, an illusion."

"How do you do it? Change your hair, your nose, all of it?"

"My gift is different, because I can actually change my own skin, my own coloring and shape, and then change it back again. At least, I can now that my gift is mature. I once spent a week with skin like the bark of a tree."

I couldn't help it, I laughed.

"Yeah, funny now, but my sister was afraid of trees for years." She frowned. "You might not be able to reverse something you try. And you could mess it up. So, you want to keep the idea of *temporary* firmly in your head. It's just a *mask*. Just creating an illusion for others to see. An illusion that exists on top of your real features."

"But what do you create it out of?" I was thinking of that DNA, wondering exactly how I'd done that trick. I didn't know what I was doing. I could seriously damage myself or someone else.

"Energy. Chi. Life force. Whatever you want to call it. We Ninja know that it connects us all, every living thing. It's inside you, but there's also a layer just outside you, around the surface of you, linking you to the rest of the world. You know what I'm talking about, right?"

"Yes." My father always spoke about chi when we trained. How to center it. Keep it balanced. How to open myself to the forces around me. Also, Ken and

Tak both spoke of theirs being drained when they used their *minding*. I'd watched Hayate transfer his chi to Ken and watched Rialka drain the engorged, powerful version from Inaba. This, I knew about.

"Good. Close your eyes again and imagine you can see it."

I could see it. Vibrant lines of energy that silently held the universe together. I'd spent years with my father's guidance, learning meditative techniques, learning how to see beyond the physical world. In my mind they were there, just as Hitomi said—and they were beautiful.

"Now, call up a bit of that energy and use it to make the mask you want. Picture your eyes the way you want the world to see them. Craft it. Create it out of the power you see and let it rest, hovering just over your real eyes. Remember! It's just a mask!"

I did as she said. I already knew just how I wanted them to look. How many nights had I lain and imagined it? The same vivid blue color, but *normal*. I knew just the shape and width I wanted. And lashes. Thick and dark. I mentally touched the energy lines over my face, imagined them separating from the rest, swirling them into just the image I'd pictured so many times. I wove the picture and imagined it fixed over my eyes, like a superhero's mask.

"Let me see." Hitomi said.

I opened my eyes and looked at her.

She gestured for me to look down at my reflection.

There they were. Exactly like I had always imagined them. I gasped. They were wonderfully, beautifully normal. I looked so different without that blaze of starburst and color. I looked . . . like any other girl.

Another reason to like this mask. I was

crying—and it didn't show.

"You did it." Hitomi said softly. She scrunched up her face. "I don't know. They're pretty and all . . . but kind of boring."

I thought of all the times that boring would have saved me from harsh words, from thrown objects, from rejection and isolation and misery. And I imagined going out into the world again, wearing this face, instead of my own. I turned and threw my arms around her. "Thank you so much."

"Sure thing." She patted me kindly as I clutched her. "And Mei, we'd better get you a real teacher. I really think that those are only the beginning."

It turned out, though, that I could only maintain the spell for short periods at first. I wasn't too dismayed. I practiced every moment I could. Now this was something I was familiar with—practice, repetition and drilling to perfect a new technique. Somehow, it actually reassured me. The thought of something so profound coming too easily made me nervous. Not to mention the thought that I could easily have been hiding all along might have driven me a bit batty.

Ken did not approve of my 'mask.' "You need to start thinking of those eyes as a badge of honor," he admonished. "It's what they are."

"So I'm learning. It's easier to do, here in Ryu. But it's a lifetime of thinking to change," I told him. "And nothing is changing out there. I can't hide here forever."

He looked pained at that statement.

"When I go out into the world again, this spell is going to save me a lot of grief."

He let it drop. And in actuality, I think I spent as much time with Ken as I did with Hitomi.

I even met his family. They were a large and friendly group, and all obviously proud of him. His father was amusing and his mother was very kind and indeed an excellent cook. His siblings all fought for the honor of sharing the most embarrassing Ken story.

"That's the second actual blush I've seen on you," I remarked, as his older brother finished telling how Ken refused to wear pants for most of his third year.

They all clamored to hear about the first blush, but I refused to jump on the Ken-shaming bandwagon. "That would be a poor way for me to repay your brother for all that he's done for me. And in any case, I owe him some Shitake Mushrooms. I have to stay on his good side until I pay my debt."

The younger ones clamored that they had all the mushrooms they ever wanted to see, but Ken gave me a private smile that sent a zing right up my spine.

I got to know some of the other folks in Ryu a little better, as well. I spent a morning with Sho, showing him how to make colored paper lanterns for one of his set pieces. The two of us trained together a good bit, too. Working with him, I regained some of my lost prowess with a sword. I showed him some bo techniques in exchange, and in general, I spent as much time training as I could.

I explored Tak's studio and marveled at Noff's lab and the inventive devices she spent her time concocting. She even gifted me with my own *seihoukei*. I spent some time fabricating a special cargo pocket into my jeans to hold it.

Because Tak and Noff were so busy, I began to take my breakfast in the public kitchens and began to enjoy meeting people on my own.

One morning I found Akemi there before me. She had a basket over one arm and I sighed when I realized she was giving one of the cooks a hard time.

"I distinctly asked for a selection of Wagashi," Akemi hissed. "I need something sweet to serve with the tea."

Kami, the cook, shook her head. "You'd do better with plain salted salmon rice balls with that one. Never saw him eat a sweet in my life."

"Oh, what would you know about it?" snapped Akemi.

"Actually, she's right—if you are speaking of Reik, that is." I gestured towards the basket. "Going on a picnic?"

"Yes." The girl tilted her nose up. "If you must know."

"Well, Reik told me himself that he prefers plain food. He might be impressed that you actually took his tastes into consideration." I shrugged. "That is, if you are interested in impressing him."

"I don't believe you," she sniffed. "You're just trying to make a fool of me."

"Why would I do that?"

"Why would you help me?" she countered.

"Why wouldn't I? I have no idea why you decided we cannot be friends, Akemi, but clearly you are interested in Reik. I'm not."

"*Everyone* is interested in Reik."

"Suit yourself, but I want you to know, I didn't come here to take away anything that is yours."

She sneered in response.

I shrugged and walked away.

"You'd better give her a little more than that," Kami called after me. "She needs all the help she can get."

I looked over my shoulder. "Tell him about your mother," I advised. "He seems to enjoy that."

A couple of hours later, I was returning from

the training ground when I saw Chou moving toward me on the trail. She was the wizened older lady who had pinched my arm that first day in Ryu. She took breakfast in the public kitchens too and we had taken to exchanging pleasantries and stories.

"Good afternoon," I called to her. "No lunch today? You are moving in the wrong direction."

She grinned and returned my bow. "No, no! I'm off to the orchards. My sister has a house near there. She's old now and doesn't get into the village much, so I'm going to share the news with her!" Her eyes shone bright from her wrinkled visage.

"News?"

"Yes, have you not heard? The weeping cherry—it has buds on it this morning!"

"Oh? It seems the right season for it."

"No, you do not understand. The tree has never bloomed. Not once in all these centuries."

"Oh." I thought about it. Wouldn't that mean that perhaps Rialka's spirit was growing stronger? "But if it did now—that would be good, wouldn't it?"

"Yes." She bowed again. "If the buds actually bloom—it will be a good sign. A very good sign." She looked like she meant to say more, but she pursed her lips and moved off. "I must tell my sister. A good day to you!"

"And to you, Chou."

I continued on my way. Those I passed did seem to be more animated than usual. People were gathered in small groups, all smiling and talking. Most nodded at me as I passed. As I emerged into the village proper, I saw Ken and General Rin ahead, engaged in earnest conversation—but there were no smiles there.

Rin caught sight of me as I approached. She broke off the discussion and beckoned me. "Mei, I wanted to talk to you. Boru is having no luck with her research in the spirit realm. It seems your demon is nearly as feared and disliked as his master." She held up a finger at my disappointed reaction. "But I have had an interesting talk with a friend in JanFran. He suggests taking a scientific approach, rather than supernatural."

I frowned. "What kind of science?"

"I didn't follow him completely. He spoke of something about a swirling column of air needing a cold downdraft and a warm updraft. Removing one could destroy the demon's ability to form and control those swirling appendages."

My mouth dropped in dismay. "How am I supposed to do that?"

"It's theory only at this point, but this gentleman is one of our top *yokai* investigators. He said he would work on it and send us a report." She raised a brow in warning. "It will take a few days at least, maybe a week."

My shoulders drooped at the thought of another delay. But it was something. "Please convey my thanks to him, General. I do appreciate all of your efforts."

Her face softened. "And we . . ." She paused. "We are very glad to have you here."

Morosely, I watched her go. Ken stayed back. "Actually, I wanted to find you. We really should talk, but first, I was wondering if I could show you something?"

"Sure."

"It's something I've been working on." He gestured back toward the training ground. "Back there—or did you need to do something in the village first?"

"Nope. Lead on." I followed him to the edge

of the fields, to an apparatus I'd never noticed before. It was made of several poles sunk close together. Each one was circled by several bands, while each band held two curved metal pieces sticking out from the pole. They were each about the size of a bucket, cut in half.

"Watch," Ken said. He took a ready stance and breathed deep. He folded his hands together for a moment, fingers steepled, in a move I recognized. I knew I'd seen him use it before.

Extending first one arm, then the other, he began to send swift, hard bursts of air at the curved metal pieces, setting them to spinning. He had to be careful of the order of it, to keep the different appendages from different poles from interfering with each other. It was quite elegant and beautiful, and when Ken began to move, stepping in time with his blasts, I suddenly felt as if the whole thing should have been set to music.

"It's like you are dancing with them," I exclaimed, but as he continued, I realized what I was seeing. Two hands. He was *minding* with both hands, without pressing upon his scar.

"Wait! How are you doing that? Both hands at once!"

He paused, flushing a little with pleasure. "I've been practicing." He ducked his head. "It's considered an advanced skill, *minding* without using your trigger."

"Is it?" I was delighted for him. "Congratulations." My mind was flashing back over what I'd seen over the last days. "Oh, yes. General Rin didn't press hers before she sent a blast of flame down the street. Although she did check to see if it was clear." I grinned. "Everyone else . . . No. Reik doesn't use his either, does he?" I grimaced. "I suppose I haven't been paying close enough attention."

"You're the only one who hasn't," Ken grumbled. "From early on we are taught to use our trigger. It helps us focus our will and energy. Many people never move beyond using it."

"It must take a lot of hard work to retrain yourself," I mused. "And mental strength."

"For most of us. Not for Reik. He was two-fisting icicles at us on the playground when we were kids."

I laughed. "Is that why you did it? Because all the girls were swooning over Reik's trigger-less *minding*?"

His expression grew serious. "No. He can have the attention of all the village girls. There's just one girl whose opinion matters to me." He took a step closer.

I didn't move back, although I considered it. Instead I kept my gaze fixed on his chest.

Another step and he was close enough to reach out and tilt my chin up, forcing me to look at him.

His touch was warm. A shiver ran through me, chased by the spread of a slow burn.

There was no doubt this time. I'd stolen long glances at him way back when he was just another guy in my parkour crew. Now I was remembering every single one, and every shared laugh, every casual touch, every kind moment and secret yearning. I wanted him to kiss me.

If a simple touch felt this good, I was imagining how the heat of his kiss would flow through me, heating up all the cold and lonely spaces.

But then something changed. The electricity dancing in the air between us faded. He looked away, his expression a mask of regret and frustration.

The back of my neck suddenly tingled with awareness. I turned to see Reik ambling towards us, eating up the ground with his long stride.

"The Council is asking for you, lover-boy. Better head on back." He grinned as he drew close. "Right away."

Ken nodded. "Come with me, Mei? We were going to talk."

"Better not," Reik counseled. "Akemi is in a tizzy. You don't want to subject Mei to that." He tilted his head. "Don't worry. *We'll* have a nice little talk."

Ken ignored him. "I'll come find you when I'm done."

"Okay. See you then."

Chapter Twenty-One

When Ken had gone, Reik turned to me, arms crossed. "I suppose I have you to thank for that . . . ambush today?"

"Ambush?" I laughed, then covered my mouth. "I assumed the two of you had a date!"

"We did not," he ground out.

"Oh, no. Well, I have to give her credit. She's determined." I scrunched my face in question. "Did you have a good time?"

He shot me an incredulous stare. "What do you think?"

"It couldn't have been that bad."

"At least there was some decent food. I understand I have you to thank for that." He shook his head. "Why on earth would you give her advice? Why help her?"

"Why not? And in any case, I suppose I was thinking more about helping you." I looked him over. "I think you could use a friend."

"Me? You wanted to help me?" Now he really looked disbelieving.

"Shocking, isn't it?"

"Yes. Stop it. Don't help me."

I tilted my head at him. "Why not?"

"It's not what people do. I don't know how to handle it."

I rolled my eyes. "Poor baby. Get used to it. I've had to."

He glared at me.

I moved off.

"I don't understand you," he called after me.

"Well, join the club. I don't understand me, either. And I certainly don't get you."

"Get used to it," he repeated mockingly. He'd

come up alongside me again. "What a joke. No one's helping you. Not really. Are they, Mei? Has anyone up and given you instructions on how to defeat your wind demon?"

"No, but people are working on it. They are trying to help me. Stop being so . . . you."

"Ha. *You* should be more like me. But you can't, because you have friends now and they are trying to help you." He halted. "Stop kidding yourself, Mei. They are not your friends here. They want something from you." He crossed his arms again. "Tell me, has any of them explained Kuji-in to you yet?"

I glared at him. "I don't think so. But neither have you. So does that mean that you're not my friend, either?"

"Now you are getting it," he said with sarcastic approval. "But you know what—I will tell you. And in fact, you've seen Kuji-in in practice, even if you don't know it. It's the study of nine hand seals—nine syllables that are ways for Ninja to focus themselves and increase their spiritual and mental strength. Everyone is taught the syllables and the hand seals, and each one represents a different aspect of a Ninja's powers." He raised a sardonic brow. "But no one has spoken to you of it, have they?"

I frowned. "No. Why should they?"

"Why shouldn't they is the question you should ask—and the answer is, it's because they are using it against you."

"Don't be ridiculous," I scoffed.

"Certain people are skilled at different aspects of the Kuji-in. Rin actually takes her name from the first syllable. It means strength and power. And Hitomi? Her *minding* skill makes great use of Hyo, the channeling of energy that she uses in her disguises and to hide her presence."

"What does any of that have to do with me?"

"Just listen. Have you wondered why Akemi is so good at the obstacle course? It's because she is skilled at Kai, the premonition of danger. The warning signals in her head give her nearly perfect timing."

"So Akemi is a cheat. Am I supposed to be shocked?"

"It's far more pervasive than that. Advanced practitioners attain great powers, abilities that let them heal themselves and others, even control time. Even young Sho is recognized as a master. His specialty is Jin, the power of reading thoughts."

He raised his hands and began to run through hand signals, like the one I'd seen Ken use earlier, and others that I hadn't seen before. I frowned, disbelieving, until one triggered a memory.

I remembered . . .

Me, feeling slightly dizzy and uncomfortable on Sho's stage, while he sat at meditation, with his hands folded just like that—fingers interlocked, and tucked inside. "Wait. What is that? What was that about Jin?"

A knowing look spread across Reik's face. "Ah, they set the sneak on you, did they? Jin is the power that allows a Ninja to read the thoughts of others. And no one is better at it than Sho. He often does his little monkey trick at the general's behest."

I didn't want to believe him. But I remember how I felt—sick and uncomfortable and like there were too many people too close . . . And I remembered Rin's reserve, the careful, flat way that she watched me.

The anger burst inside of me, urged on by a sour, acidic wave of betrayal. I spun on my heel and began to stalk in the opposite direction. Shivering, I

pulled my jacket tighter. Either it was growing colder
or I'd just been hit with the chill of my own naïveté.

"Wait! Where are you going?"

"You made your point," I shot back. "Now let
me be."

"Oh no, that's just the tip of the iceberg. Not
even close to all of it."

I turned and held out my hand. "That's all I
need to hear from you. Leave me alone, Reik."

He trailed to a halt. I marched on; sure I knew
where to find at least a couple of my so-called friends.

I burst into the auditorium and strode down the
center aisle. "Sho!" I shouted. "Hitomi!"

"Back here!" Hitomi's voice echoed from the
back. "In wardrobe!"

I headed backstage. There was no sign of Sho
as I went. When I burst into the room, full of fire,
Hitomi looked up at me from a mat on the floor.

I gasped and fell back.

"Oh, sorry." She waved a hand and the gaping,
bleeding wound at her throat faded away. "Sorry."
She bent down and removed the length of silk that tied
her thighs together. "I'm playing a samurai's wife in
the next production. I get to commit ritual suicide!"

My hand still clutched my chest.

"I thought I'd take a page from your book and
craft an illusionary wound instead of using stage
makeup. What did you think?"

"Never mind that," I answered harshly. "I have
to talk to you. Where's Sho?"

"In the village. He'll be back soon. What is it?
What's wrong?"

I let some of my hurt and bitterness show.
"Kuji-in, Hitomi?"

"Yeah?" Her expression brightened. "Did Ken

explain it? Are you going to begin to study?"

"Ken told me nothing. Reik explained what Kuji-in is—and how you've been using it against me."

"What? That's ridiculous."

"Exactly what I said—until I remembered something. I saw it, Hitomi. I saw Sho using that sign. Jin? I felt him . . . doing *something*."

Her indignation drained away. Behind me the door opened. "Hey! Is someone using my name in vain?" Sho entered, his hands full of fabric.

"Reik told her we've been using Kuji-in against her," Hitomi explained, indignant.

Sho set down his bundles, then turned to face me. "Well, he's right. At least a little."

Something twisted inside of me. I'd wanted him to deny it. "Sho?" I whispered.

"I'm sorry, Mei, but I have to tell you the truth. I don't have any flashy *minding*, but I'm damned skilled at Jin. No—I don't know what Reik told you, but I can't read your thoughts. But if I try, I can sense your emotions, your dominant traits. It's reading your character more than anything else. And sometimes, Rin asks me to sort of . . . check someone out."

I spun around, knocking a chair aside as I crossed to the opposite side of the room. "Why would she ask you to do that? What? Does she think I'm some kind of psychopath?"

"I think that's exactly what she was worried about, but she knows now that you are good," Sho said staunchly.

The door opened again and Ken entered. "I thought you might come here—" He caught a glimpse of my angry face, at Sho's level of calmness and Hitomi's distress. "What is it?"

Hitomi quickly explained.

"Good?" I demanded of Sho. "What does that

mean precisely? That I won't murder you all while you sleep?"

Ken stepped forward. "Rin was determined to be cautious with you, Mei. I have not always agreed with her, but even I admit, she has reasons which make sense to her."

"Like what?" Of all people, Ken had known me the best. And he hadn't taken up for me?

"She worried that your experiences out there might have . . . affected you."

"They did!" I snarled.

"Yes. They made you smart and careful and strong. But not desperate or manipulative or frightened, as she feared."

I refused to be mollified.

"You remember that you and I speculated that your father kept you away from Ryu because he didn't trust someone here?"

"Yes, well, it's beginning to feel like he was right."

"Rin brought up the opposite point. That perhaps he kept you apart because you might be dangerous to us."

I snapped my mouth shut. Then I snorted. "Well, I guess that leaves us at a stand off, now, doesn't it?"

"Listen. We've all known Rin a long time. We know she's wrong. She knows she was wrong now. But we knew she felt she had to be careful—because of some mistakes that she's made in the past."

"What mistakes?" I demanded.

"Akemi," Hitomi said harshly.

"What about her?"

Ken sighed. "Rin took a special interest in Akemi and in her training. She thought she had . . . potential." He faltered to a stop.

"Because of her eyes," I said flatly.

"The attention had the wrong effect," Sho said.

"That—and her mother's extreme snobbery," Hitomi added.

"Between the two, Akemi is nearly spoiled," Ken said. "She'll never be of much use, I'm afraid."

"And will I be of use?" Was that all they wanted—all of them? The thought hurt. Far worse than I would have expected.

But it was as if Ken was following my thoughts now. "No, Mei. It's not like that."

"I wish I could believe you. You don't know how hard this is for me," I whispered.

"I have an idea," he said.

"I just want to go back," I moaned. "Back to this morning, when you were all my friends."

"We were and we are," Hitomi cried. "Nothing has changed."

But Sho stood suddenly. "You can," he said. "You can know for sure. Hitomi told me about your spells. How you are practicing small magics. If you can do that, you can train in Kuji-in."

"But Sho," Hitomi protested. "Some people don't pick it up right away. It can take a lifetime—"

"She picked up everything she's tried quickly, didn't she?" He shot them both a significant look.

"Shards!" I knew that look meant something. "Stop. Just stop." I dug my fingertips into my tightly pulled hair. "There's more, isn't there? More that I don't know. More that you haven't told me."

They all looked at each other, then at me. As one, they nodded.

Ken opened his mouth.

"No. No more. I'm sorry. This sounds insulting, I know, but you've hit every trigger, every alarm, every distrustful instinct that has ruled me over the last years—and kept me alive. It's all I can do right now not to just get up and walk right out of Ryu altogether."

"No!" Ken protested. "It's not safe—"

"Stop. I want to believe you. Maybe more than anything, and that's why I have to be careful. So don't tell me anymore. I don't want to hear any more until I know who to believe." I looked at Sho. "I want to try."

"Okay. Let's go somewhere quiet for a bit. You have to be calm for this to work."

I snorted.

"Take all the time you need," Hitomi encouraged me. "We'll be here when you are ready."

Pinching my lips together, I followed Sho out.

Chapter Twenty-Two

Sho was a good teacher. I calmed considerably as he talked me through all nine syllables and demonstrated the nine hand seals. He was patient and earnest—and seemed to genuinely want to make up for his part in my anger.

As I calmed, I began to see things more clearly. I was able to widen my vision and see past the hurt and anger. He was correcting my finger placement in one of the signs when I stopped and placed a hand over his. "I'm sorry. I couldn't help my reaction. It's all bound up in everything that's happened to me. But I understand why you did it—it's for the same reasons—all the things that you and your village have gone through. I just needed to quiet down enough to see it from your perspective."

"Good. I hate to say it, but I would probably do it again. But I am sorry it distressed you so badly."

I sighed. "We all have to be careful." My shoulders hunched as I looked at my hands. "Maybe I shouldn't do this, after all."

"No. You should. It might be important that we know if you can. And—you might feel better." He grinned up at me. "Besides, I owe you one."

I breathed deeply, trying to marshal my courage.

"Okay. Get comfortable on the mat. Legs crossed. There. Fingertips inside, like I showed you? Good. Close your eyes. Just listen to me for a while and let your mind clear."

I let myself slip into meditation mode. It wasn't my greatest strength. But Sho's voice was soothing as he told me how he believed it was going to be simple for me. Told me to breathe and just hear the music of my breath moving in and out.

"Hitomi spoke to you of your life force. Of the lines of energy that connect us all. Yours are all through you, all about you. Can you see them?"

"Yes."

"Now, stretch a little further. Can you see mine?"

I reached out. Everything was a blur, bright and in motion. But I did as my father had taught me and gradually, as I grew used to the chaos, the lines of energy running everywhere began to adjust themselves into an image that made sense. Looking around, I saw that there was a bright spot nearby. "Are you blue?"

He chuckled. "Maybe. It's my aura that you must be seeing. You have to look past it. Further in."

I hesitated.

"It's okay. Just give it a try."

I breathed deep and mentally moved closer. But all I could see was a gorgeous swirl of varied blues, with an occasional maroon or deep red swirl.

"That's a deep blood red thread there, Sho." I tried to keep my tone light. "Are you harboring violent thoughts?"

I heard him suck in a breath and his aura wavered violently for a moment. But then he sighed. "You'll see for yourself soon enough, if we are successful. You see the colors. Can you get any sense of emotion or character?"

I concentrated . . . but nothing changed. "I don't think so."

"Okay. Hold out your arm. I'm going to try taking your hand."

He did and as his fingers closed around mine I felt a jerk, a tug inside of me. Abruptly I was sucked into a whorl of swirling blue, moving fast to the beat of a pulsing heart. I gasped and pulled my hand away and sat back.

"Whoops. That *was* close. Sorry. But now I know how to guide you." He took my hand, lightly this time. "Try from right where you are. Just look, a little at a time."

I did as he said—and the difference was profound. More than just colors, I realized that I could see so much of him. The real Sho. Emotion and determination and fear and caring—everything that makes a person. His love of the theater blazed inside him, and pride in his work. His grief for his parents was there. And his ironclad determination to fight back against the evil that had destroyed them. I could see the genuine affection he felt for his friends—and the respect he felt for me. There was something else there too. Worry? And hope.

"You're beautiful," I said, pulling away.

I startled a laugh from him. "So are you. And I should know. Now, keep your eyes closed. We don't have to bring Ken and Hitomi closer. You should be able to read them from here. Extend your senses. Can you find them?"

I tried. "Hitomi's pink!" I said, caught by surprise.

"And you are a million glorious shades of green, but that's just the surface. Go on, but not too close," he reminded me.

I hovered right where I was. A half hour ago, this was all that I'd wanted. One look and I would know. But now, I wasn't sure I could do it. It was a line that I shouldn't need to cross.

"I don't think I want to," I told Sho.

"You don't have to, of course. We know you can. And that's something."

"I've trusted my own instincts for a long time. I'll trust them now. And I have to learn to trust someone else, sometime."

"We all do," he said quietly.

I couldn't resist a peek at Ken before I left. His aura was a beautiful swirl of silver and gold. Small bolts of blue and red flashed fleetingly on the surface before disappearing again. I let out a long, appreciative breath.

"Ken? I know," Sho said. "He's pretty impressive. Inside and out."

I drew back into myself and opened my eyes.

Sho had done the same. He was staring back at me. "Are you worried about what you'd see there?" He smiled gently. "I'm afraid it doesn't take a mastery of Jin to know that Ken feels something for you."

I sucked in a breath.

"I've been friends with him for a long time. Long enough to know that there is a ball of seriously gooey mush on the inside of that spectacular armor. And you've got off to a great start, here, but I will ask you to please treat him gently."

"Will you ask him to do the same?"

"Going a little mushy yourself?" he asked hopefully.

"More like liquid with fear. Who does he have feelings for? Me? Or the girl he dreamed of finding all those years? The one from his bedtime fairy tales?"

Sho grinned. "I suggest you find out the old fashioned way."

With a flourish, Sho opened the door to where the others waited. "Well, with only a little help, she's proved as good at Kuji-in as she's been with everything else she'd tried. Though she decided to only test herself on me."

"That's very generous of you, Mei," Hitomi said, her eyes wide.

"But you should do what you have to do—"

Ken began.

"No." I interrupted him. "I'm not good at everything, no matter what Sho says. For sure, I've never been good around people. But maybe this will be a start."

I walked in and took a seat at one of the dressing tables, turning the chair around so that I did not have to look at my reflection. "I can't believe I'm asking this." I rubbed my temples with my fingers. "But what is it? You said there was more. What don't I know?"

Ken and Hitomi looked at each other as if debating who would go first.

"Wait!" I said suddenly. I looked from one to the other. "Does any of this happen to be *good* news?"

Hitomi pursed her lips. "Well, yes. At least, I think you might think so."

My shoulders slumped in relief. "Well, bless all the pretty green kappa." I smiled at Ken. "Or at least the ones with chi rings. Tell me the good news first!"

Hitomi opened her mouth, but Ken stood, sending his chair scooting back. "No. I want to tell her. Show her."

She pouted.

"Let them go," Sho said. "Alone."

I paused. "Is the other news . . . really bad?"

Sho looked serious. "Bad?" He shrugged. "It's weighty."

I shuddered and moved towards the door. "Then good news first, definitely."

"Wait!" Hitomi chased after me. She gripped my elbows and glared at Ken. "I'm going to tell her this much at least—and I don't want any lip about it."

Her face softened as she looked back at me. "I know it sort of freaks you out, the whole bedtime story thing. But there's another you should know of."

I groaned and Ken made a sound of protest.

"Hush," she snapped at him. "Listen, Mei. The stories tell of a girl born to Ryu who will be gifted in the Kuji-in seals of Zen and Zai."

"Zen. Understanding, right? And Zai?" I thought back to all that Sho had just taught me. "The one about control of the elements of Nature?"

"Yes. And I think you are the girl in the story."

"Me?" I snorted. "I don't even have any *minding*. It's Ken who has a measure of elemental control. What he does with wind—"

"Yes, but I've noticed some things. We all have."

"We've all been in the Temple gardens," Sho said. "Have you noticed that the section behind Tak and Noff's house is more green and full of new growth than the rest?"

I laughed. "No, but that sort of thing happens all the time. It likely gets more sun or has better access to an underground water source." I shrugged. "It's just Nature."

Hitomi looked exasperated. "The flowers that you turned blue? I sit on those rocks and feed the koi all the time. I've been taking my little brothers and sisters there for years. Those flowers have never bloomed before."

"They probably just reached the right maturity level."

"I've been by there several times without you in the last few days, experimenting. Mei—they only bloom when you are with me."

I blinked.

"The tree in the Temple, Rialka's tree, it's grown healthier since you arrived," Ken said. "Did you hear everyone talking this morning? It has buds on it. As if it might bloom. It never has before, Mei. Not in hundreds of years."

"It can't be because of me," I whispered. But I was remembering what Reik had said about the vine at the smithy.

"I noticed it even before we arrived in Ryu. Remember Oba's bamboo? And the grass where you sit is always greener than the rest. I saw that in the park in Greensboro. Even the trees bent and swayed behind you as you ran, trying to help you escape from the Tengu."

"I don't know about control of Nature, but it looks to me as if Nature is pleased with you...and is trying to please you in return," Hitomi said.

My mind raced. I'd always felt better, surrounded by green. It was one of the reasons I struggled, hiding in the cities. Maybe it's why I chose Raleigh, where there were trees planted strategically in the parking lots and even in the highway medians. Where there were still so many lovely yards and gardens and small wild spots to be found. But could they be right? "You're all serious about this?"

They all clamored together, trying to convince me.

I was trying to come to grips with the idea. "I might someday be a master at Kuji-in? Like Sho?" Strangely, the more I thought about it, the better I felt. I might not be able to *mind*, but I could fight. And if I might now also be able to—

I stopped. My mouth dropped. I started to bounce on my toes. "Oh! Oh! Oh!" I grabbed Hitomi? "Don't you see what this means?" I spun around, piercing them all with my happiness. "If I study and train and become a master at Zai—I could learn to *control the elements of nature*!"

"Yes?" Hitomi said it, but they were all looking

at me blankly.

My voice lowered to a whisper. I was almost afraid to speak the words out loud. "I could defeat the wind demon!"

Hitomi's mouth dropped open too. Ken looked stupefied. Sho cheered.

"I never even thought of that!" Hitomi said.

"Yes! Yes! Thank you! I've waited so long. I've never had a hope of a clue before—and now this! This really *is* good news! Thank you!"

Hitomi looked sheepish. "Actually, we didn't even think that *was* the good news." She looked at Ken. "Did we?"

I could almost see the synapses firing in his brain. He knew. He knew what this meant to me. He would already be trying to come up with ways to bring Fuma Jinnae down. "Well, no. I can't believe I didn't follow that thought through. I was so focused on the other . . ."

"Wait. There's more? More *good* news?" Maybe this was my reward for having made the right choice about using Jin.

"Uh, yeah. If you still want to . . ." He motioned toward the door.

I flushed in pleasure and anticipation. "Yes!"

My heart sang as we walked back through the village and set out, heading north. "The smithy is this way, right?"

"Yes, although we won't be going quite that far."

We walked on, each lost in our own thoughts, both probably thinking of what this new development might mean.

Freedom. The word echoed all through me. I would finally have the means to defeat Fuma Jinnae once and for all. No more hiding and worrying. No more waiting for my life to begin. I would be *free*!

I pulled my jacket a little tighter. "It's grown so cold," I shivered. "And look—snow flakes! If I was able to control the elements," I told Ken, "you can be sure that I would not be bringing snow this late in the season."

"It is unusual," he agreed. "I hope it doesn't hurt the crops."

He stopped in front of a smallish building. It looked like one of the craftsmen's workshops I'd seen with General Rin. "What is it?" I asked. It looked dusty and run down, as if it had been deserted for a while.

"Go in and see," Ken said. "But you should know that Rin forbade any of us to show it to you. She doesn't want you to know about it yet." In the fading light, he looked a little shamefaced. "And I agreed with her."

Questions arose, but he opened the door and I held them back and entered instead.

It was too dim in here to see anything but bulky shapes. I felt around until I found a light panel. I waved it on—and gazed around in wonder.

It was a workshop, set up splendidly for the making of washi. My heart tripped a little. It was so like the one I'd long dreamed of. There were two big tubs where the screens would be dipped and swished in the fiber solution. A sunken cauldron for boiling of the pulp and a long water channel for picking out impurities. Multiple sized mallets. A press. The boards needed for drying the paper in the sun. Everything one could want for making washi by the traditional methods.

"It's wonderful!" I ran my hands along the planking where the pulp would be flattened. Struck, I turned to him. "My mother? Did she work here?"

"I think she set it all up." Ken looked miserable. "She was to start up a paper guild here, when she and your father settled here permanently."

"But I don't understand?" Just being in here filled me with joy. "Why hide it?"

"Rin was keeping it back, to use as a final weapon, a temptation to keep you here, if she needed to convince you to stay. She thought you would be hard pressed to resist the idea of staying on to take up your mother's work."

She would have been right. But now I'd learned the lesson of thinking things through to their logical conclusions. "And if she didn't want me to stay, then I wouldn't be tempted." I didn't hide my bitterness.

He nodded, his face hard.

But the rest of his confession was hitting me now—and hurting my heart. Disappointment rode me hard—and the sudden worry that I'd been a fool. "And you went along with her? Why"

Everything about his expression changed. He looked suddenly fierce, and yet also . . . caring. "I didn't want you to be confused."

I drew a deep breath and decided to just be brave about it all. "I thought . . . that is, I was under the impression that you might actually want me to stay."

"You know I do." A flash of something that looked like yearning showed behind his eyes, before he banished it. "I don't know what I'm doing here, Mei. I'm trying to be smart about it—about us. And when I can't be smart, then I try to think of what's best for you."

"Me?" It came out a squeak. I was suddenly reminded of Reik. *Don't help me*, he'd said. I wanted to shout the opposite. *Help me. Think of me. Want me.*

"I do listen, you know. And I see—although not as well as you do. But I do know one thing. You need to defeat that demon before you commit to anything—or anyone."

He'd surprised me. The simple truth of it rang like the stroke of a gong. I felt a rush of gratitude and a rising tide of joy. He did listen—and he understood. He'd put my needs ahead of his own wants. I felt . . . cared for. Seen. Cherished. Maybe that was a normal thing in other peoples' worlds. An everyday occurrence. But it wasn't in mine.

I took a step towards him. It was all there again. I wanted him to kiss me. I wanted to launch myself at him and kiss him madly—just to get the awkward first step over with. But he was right. We should be smart.

But I had to show my gratitude and appreciation somehow. So I grabbed his hand instead. "Come on. This time I have something to show you."

Chapter Twenty-Three

I pushed open the Temple doors. "Tell me, do you ever feel anything at the tree—Rialka's tree?"

He shrugged. "I feel the usual things, I suppose. Gratitude that she was willing to sacrifice herself to thwart Inaba. Respect. A little awe, I suppose, to think that part of her spirit lives on inside of it."

That wasn't what I'd meant. "Yes, but—"

The words died away as we entered the center chamber. We both stumbled to a halt.

It was beautiful.

A thousand soft, pink blossoms covered the tree, reached for the sky, tumbled down along the branches. The feeling of warmth and welcome settled over me like a balm.

"Do you feel that?" I whispered.

"I *see* that. It's stunning." I felt frustrated that he couldn't experience the same wonderful effect. He looked happy and worried at the same time. "And I know what it means."

"Why does it mean anything? Other than the fact that Rialka is growing stronger?"

"More than that, Mei. She is growing stronger, because of you. You are the one we've waited for. It is you. You are Rialka's child."

"I think we all are her children."

He turned and took me by the arms. "I wasn't sure if I could tell you tonight, Mei. But you need to hear the rest of what you don't know. Rialka's trying to tell you, herself. She's sending you a message."

"She's sending me a welcome. And it's lovely." I didn't want him to ruin it.

"It's more than that. And Hitomi is right. You are the girl in our stories. But there is more to it than just Kuji-in and Zai. Each generation has a girl who is close to Rialka, you know that, right?

"Yes."

"Well, each one has learned a little more about the girl in the story. How we'll know her."

"Wait," I pleaded. "It's been such a roller coaster of a day. I don't know if I want to hear anymore."

"I think you have to."

"But I'm ending it on such a high, with the hope of learning what I need to know to be free, and the workshop and . . . you. I'm not sure I want to hear whatever 'heavy' news awaits me. It will drag me down from this lovely feeling."

He hesitated. I saw the conflict in his face.

We both jumped when the Temple doors slammed open. Pounding footsteps sounded. A blast of cold air came in—and Reik came with it.

"Oh, goodness. It must really be coming down out there now." His hair and shoulders were covered with snow.

"What is it?" Ken asked at once.

"Playtime is over." Reik was talking to me. "It's time to go." He shot forward and grasped my wrist. "We're leaving. Now."

"What?" I shook away from him. "You're talking crazy."

"They are *here*," he almost shouted. "We leave now, or you are done!"

"Who's here?" Ken demanded.

"We have no time! The Council knows the tree has bloomed. Rin has called it. She's named Mei as Rialka's Child. The *one*. Akemi had hysterics. And none of that matters—because it's snowing! It's not coming down because of a passing cold front, you fool. It's falling because the wards are down! They are here!"

I took a step back, away from both of them. "Wait. The wards are down? Where's Boru?"

Reik didn't answer. But his face gave the answer I didn't want to hear.

I looked between them both. "Alright. Tell me. What's going on? What does all of this mean?"

"You *baka*!" Reik rounded on Ken, branding him with the Japanese word for a fool. "You *still* haven't told her? Great gods and little monsters—you are an idiot!"

"Tell me!" I ordered.

Reik eyed me with a cold, measuring stare. "They've decided it's you. The one in their little nursery rhyme.

The Girl With the Stars in Her Eyes
The One for Whom Nature Strives
The Girl who can See Past All the Lies

They've picked you, Mei. You get to be the one to rescue Ryu! And if that's not enough, once you've saved the village, you get to save the world, too." He let out a bark of laughter. "Except, you're not their first pick, are you? They thought it was Akemi." He laughed again. "I knew they were wrong about that one years ago. She was never going to help anyone but herself."

I swallowed. "Akemi thought she was special? You all thought she was?" My heart sank. No wonder she'd hated me on sight. "And then I showed up."

"I know," Reik continued. "It's ridiculous. But it's okay. I know it's not you, either. So let's just go. Let's get out of here before she—" He stopped and swallowed. "Before they throw you at Inaba anyway."

I turned to Ken. "That's what you meant? Rialka's child? The One with the Stars in Her Eyes?"

He nodded.

"Is that why you wanted me to come to Ryu? Why you wanted to bring me here? Why everyone welcomed me and Rin wanted me checked out." My shoulders drooped. "Why Akemi didn't like me! She thought it was her—that I was stealing it away."

"Yes, yes!" Reik was nearly exploding with impatience. "The foolish girl has lorded it over the village for years—and now she's gone to confront the enemies at the gate—just to prove it *is* her." He pleaded with me. "Don't you see? She's bought you some time with her stupidity. Now let's put it to use and get *out* of here!"

I ignored him. Both of them. I turned away, walked back to stand on the edge of the moat, to drink in the beauty of Rialka's tree. I closed my eyes. I was at a crossroads and I knew it. The scent of cherry blossoms filled the air around me, but that little blue flower hovered in my mind. I was that flower. All the forces of my past had shaped me, molded me to fit this moment—but I knew it had to be my choice.

I explored a tangent. Why did Reik know so surely that it wasn't me? That I was not the one Ryu was waiting for? What was it that he'd recited? *Stars in her eyes. For whom Nature strives. Sees past all the lies?*

The lies. If I didn't see past the lies, then I wasn't the one. Is that what he'd meant? What lies had I failed to see past?

Just like that, the universe shifted. I'd been collecting puzzle pieces my whole life and in that instant they shuffled and clicked and fitted together—and the great, grand, gloriously dangerous and wonderful picture formed before me.

I spun around and tilted my head. I couldn't hear anything. No hue and cry. No alarm raised. No one rushing about or preparing for battle.

"Who is out there, Reik? Into whose arms did you send Akemi rushing? Who is the 'she' that has you so spooked?" I tried to keep my voice neutral, my expression kind. "It's your mother, isn't it? She's *yokai*."

He blanched.

I spoke to Ken. "My father was right. There was someone in Ryu who couldn't be trusted." I waved a hand. "It's been him all along."

Ken shook his head.

Reik deflated. All of his passion and bravado slid away. "How—"

"I know. I saw past the lies. I understand."

I suddenly realized that I'd felt myself slipping down this path since I got to Ryu. All along, I'd been bracing myself to resist. But now I knew that I didn't have to. The choice was mine.

"I'm sorry, Reik, but you're going to have to face the truth. Our paths are not a destiny laid down on us by anyone or anything else. We can't blame others for this spot we find ourselves in. It's a series of events and choices. Decisions that we made. And now we have to make the most important ones of all."

I suffered a brief, stabbing moment of pain, that I had not had the chance to learn more that might help in what was to come, but still, with Ken worrying for me and Ryu hoping for me, and Rialka's approval warming me—it was an easy decision to make.

Chapter Twenty-Four

"Where's Akemi?" I asked Reik. "Where are they?"

He still hadn't recovered. He just stared.

"I'm not asking you to come with me, Reik. Just tell me where they are."

"The second gate," he whispered.

I stopped to take his hand. "Thank you. Please, wake Rin. Warn the people before you go." I squeezed him. "Good luck."

Ken was by my side as I stepped out onto the gallery. I could see the snow coming down thickly now.

"I don't even know where the second gate is," I realized.

"Come on." He cupped my face in both of his hands, watching me with wonder and pride and fierce protectiveness. "I'll show you. You're not doing this alone."

We ran past the orchards, to the wilder forest beyond. This gate was more elaborate than the one I'd passed through when I arrived. It boasted two tiers of tiled roofing and was stained in rich ebony and mahogany tones. At the edge of the forest, a flagstone surface led up to it, then a path passed through the gate and onto a carved stone staircase that climbed to the top of a mountain crag.

Standing in the protective cover of the trees, I scanned the area. Snow had gathered on the branches, but the ground had been too warm for it to survive long there. Nothing moved except the mist that ebbed and flowed about the mountain pass and ebbed as low as the roof of the gate.

"Come out, little one." The rich voice purred like a great, self-satisfied cat. "The time for hiding is long past."

From the mist at the top of the gate, she materialized. A beautiful woman, who's dark hair hung far down past her seated position. She smiled down at us with blue lips set in a milky pale face. "Let us finish this at last. Everyone awaits you."

I stepped out onto the flagstones, Ken following quickly. Like a snowflake herself, she floated down from her perch, her hair and her beautifully embroidered kimono billowing gracefully about her.

"The wards *are* down," Ken whispered. "She's Yuki-onna, the snow woman. Don't let her too close or she'll drain your chi."

"Whispering in company?" she said to Ken. "I thought the children of Ryu were taught better." She turned her attention to me. "Such a little thing to cause so much trouble."

"So everyone says," I sighed. Her hair continued to float, trailing in the currents of the air about her. It triggered a memory—the snow globe that Reik had held at the Dragon's Eye. It had been her image inside.

"Where's Akemi?" I asked.

"The other one? She is an imposter, is she not? She does not have the look of Rialka—not like you. Her eyes are different. And try as I might, I can detect only the slightest scent of power on her." She leaned toward me and breathed deeply. Ken yanked me back.

Yoki-onna laughed. "I smell it on you, though. Such a curious mix. And my son's scent too." She straightened. "Where is Reik?"

"Where's Akemi?" I repeated.

She flipped a hand over her shoulder. "Awaiting us. Inaba will be pleased indeed, when I return with you both."

"I'm sorry, but I'm not interested in pleasing

Inaba."

She moved like lightning. I barely saw the movement as she reached out to grab for my wrist. But I was fast too. I flipped backwards in a single back handspring—just beyond her reach.

She inclined her head, impressed. "Very nice. But you see, not many of us are interested in pleasing Inaba—yet we are compelled to do so. As you soon will be."

I ignored the jibe. "Where's Boru?"

"The witch?" She sucked in a satisfied breath. "Now she put up a credible fight, but I drained her in the end." Her expression fell. "It's so tiresome, having to replenish both blood and chi. But this is a new age and I was not consulted before the changes were made—and the side effects have been interesting." She snapped her fingers and one of her languishing strands of hair shot out to wind around Ken's neck. "I gained this little trick along with the witch's blood. I think I'll find it so useful."

The hair wrapped tighter and Ken began to choke. I ducked another lock, as it aimed for me, and came up with my boot knife, slicing through the one attacking Ken as I stood.

Two more shot out at me. I turned to run as Ken clawed the hair away. Yuki-onna moved after me, not hurrying, letting her writhing hair extend her reach.

I jumped as one swiped at my feet, then I changed direction and ran for a maple with a low hanging branch. I grabbed on and used my momentum to swing me around and up into the tree. It was a trick I'd performed a thousand times with my father. As the chasing strand passed below me, I reached out and sliced through, cutting that one's reach by several feet.

Ken was free now. As I leaped down and

danced away, he sent out little swirls of air to misdirect and harass the pursuing locks.

She snarled in frustration, unable to handle us both. Allowing the majority of her floating strands to merely drift, she concentrated on chasing me and controlling just the few in front. She blocked Ken's view of them with her back, decreasing the effectiveness of his whirlwinds.

I ducked through the trees, slicing at any that got close, but I was hard put to fend off four at a time.

Eyeing the gate, I jumped across the flagstones and around a pillar. I significantly shortened another strand as it followed me, and I came around and encountered it stretched out on the other side.

Abruptly, I recalled my newfound skill—and what Ken had said about the trees trying to help me escape Tengu. I sent out a silent plea, inviting help—and yes, I felt it as the trees answered, drawing on me to allow them to dart and intercept the flowing locks of hair at their will.

But the real advantage came when I jumped beyond the gate onto the stairs and discovered a Moonseed vine growing on the hillside. I asked for its help—and within seconds it had sent up tendril after tendril, tying up and entangling nearly every moving strand of the Snow Woman's hair.

"Enough!" Yoki-onna suddenly rose in the air, pulling relentlessly until vines and branches snapped. She lost more than a few strands of her own hair and she looked disheveled and furious as she took up her previous perch on the highest roof. Ken shot a blast of air at her, unsettling her balance and she let out a shout of frustration.

Then her eyes flashed bright blue and Ken abruptly stopped. "Let's do this the old fashioned way," she growled.

She beckoned with a finger. In a daze, Ken began to move toward her.

I tried to block him, but he pushed past. I called his name. I stripped a handful of snow from a branch and threw it at him, to no effect. I tripped him and he merely climbed to his feet and continued, single-mindedly responding to her call.

"I'd heard you were partial to this one, though I could scarcely believe it." She smirked. "Well, he's mine now."

He'd reached the bottom of the gate. Yuki-onna made a gesture and he rose right up into the air until he hovered right before her.

"Stop!" I shouted.

She leaned in. Her mouth opened and she breathed deeply. "Ah, delicious. There's more to this one than you would suspect, is there not?" She leaned in again.

"Let him go!"

She arched a brow at me. "Are you offering yourself in exchange?"

"No!"

I jumped, startled. The answer had not come from me. Reik pushed through the surrounding trees and strode onto the flagstones. "No, Mother, she is not."

"Is this how you greet me, Reik?" she asked with disapproval.

He stopped in the middle of the stone surface. "Hello, Mother."

"Darling." She glanced behind her. "Glad as I am to see you, you really must be going. This place will be flattened in a matter of hours."

He stared at the mess we'd made of her once gleaming hair. "How did you get past the wards, Mother?"

She sniffed. "Well, since you continued to be unable to provide me with a token from the witch, I took a page from these pathetic Ninja." She smiled. "Just like in ancient times, I acquired a dragon's scale. It did the trick."

I thought he went a little paler. "Where did you get a dragon's scale?"

"Don't you worry, I came out ahead in that battle too. Although a mother dragon is quite the fiercest of foes."

"You might have been killed," he said, aggrieved.

"I had my orders. And I have them now, too. Nor am I the only one. Run along, darling." She tilted her head. "Unless you planned on leaving with me?"

He stared at her hair again. "You promised me that Boru would not be harmed."

"I'm sorry, but she *would* fight me. She had to be dealt with."

Reik's eyes closed. "I earned the boon you granted me—and protecting Boru was the prize. You failed, Mother, which means that you still owe me. I demand a replacement."

"Yes, yes. But not now—"

He pointed. At me. "Her."

The Yoki-onna's beautiful eyes grew almost sorrowful. "It won't signify, darling. She will be Inaba's before the day is out."

"But not by your hand," he insisted.

She huffed. "And if I agree, will you leave this place so that you will not get caught up in the destruction?"

'Yes." He glanced at me. "I'm heading north, to search for Yeti."

The *yokai's* hard angles softened for a moment. "You are sweet. I forget sometimes how human you are." She sighed. "Very well. I will suffer Inaba's displeasure, but I will grant you your replacement."

She rose in the air, away from the gate and backward, dropping Ken as she went. I cried out, but he struck the hillside and rolled easily.

Yuki-onna dipped down into a copse near the top of the crag and came out with Akemi in her arms. The girl moaned and rolled her head as they lifted into the air again.

"She's alive," I whispered.

"Yes, but you will not be. Not for long." She shifted the direction of her gaze. "Do hurry away, Reik. None of you will like what is coming next."

She rose higher still, above the crest of the mountain and popped away into the ether, taking Akemi with her.

Cursing, I ran to help Ken to his feet. My insides were curdled, held in terror by the creature's last words. I very much feared that I knew who was coming next.

Ken was coming around, getting his senses back. Reik was blank-faced and still.

"You have to go, both of you," I urged. "Go, warn the village. Get them out. You've seen what this demon can do," I said to Ken. "If he's let loose here, there will be nothing left."

"We have to try to stop him," Ken said, thickly.

Panic was racing along my nerves, but I pushed it away. There was no time. "I'm not ready," I said, despairing. "Maybe if I'd had time to train. But flowers and branches and vines are not going to be a help this time."

I stopped talking. My stomach heaved. There it was. That distinctive, sickly smell.

"Go." It came out on a sob. "Maybe this was how it was meant to be all along. Maybe this is how I save Ryu. I'll stay out of his clutches for as long as I can, but if I give myself up, then maybe he'll leave with me straightaway. You can get everybody out before he—or something else—comes back."

Ken's eyes widened. He stared over her shoulder. "Mei."

I whirled, already knowing what I'd see. The first swirling tendril, creeping down the carved stairs.

I turned away. "Please, go," I whispered. Neither of them moved to listen to me. I ached a little, wishing I was more like them, tall and strong and in command of elemental *minding* that would be a help in nearly every situation—except for this one.

I paused.

Their elemental *minding*. Wind. And Ice.

The memory of Hitomi talking about Zai merged with image of Rin discussing her scientist friend's theories. *Control of the elements. Cold downdrafts. Warm updrafts.*

"Wait," I whispered. "Maybe we can do this."

Chapter Twenty-Five

"What? What can we do?" Ken asked immediately.

I looked over my shoulder. I watched, my insides frozen, as more tendrils spilled over the top of the crag. Turning back, I looked first Ken, then Reik in the eye.

"Can you stay? I'll need you both."

Ken nodded immediately.

"Reik?"

"Yeah." He shot me a loaded look. "I *choose* to stay."

"Thank you."

My shoulders hunched. Almost involuntarily, I turned on my heel. He was there, Fuma Jinnae, his form floating just above the edge of the crag.

He hovered there a moment, his robes flowing and his white eyes shining through the veil beneath his conical hat. He didn't move. But after a moment, his deep, rumbling laughter rolled down to fill the valley.

I couldn't help it. I stepped back until I was even with the two boys. I felt a little better, with them flanking me.

"Can you two combine your *minding*? We'll need a steady stream of air and a blast of the finest ice you can manufacture—merged into one. One stream of really cold air. Can you do it?"

"I don't know," Ken admitted. "I don't think anyone has ever tried."

"Try. Try it now, with just a tiny stream. Quickly." I turned. "Here, so I'm blocking and he can't see."

They tried it. But their streams kept crossing through one another.

"Adjust your positions, so that you're aiming at

the same thing, along the same line. Hurry."

But the air and the ice just kept slipping and sliding over each other.

The demon was descending the stairs. My gut clenched.

"We have to try. We have one shot at this. I'll try to combine them. Ken on the right and Reik on the left." I clutched them both. "You'll have to trust me, to give over a measure of control. At least, I think that's what will happen." I groaned. "I have no idea if this is going to work. If it doesn't, both of you run."

Another glance behind me and I realized the demon was heading for the same perch on the roofed gate that Yuki-onna had left. What was it about these stupid *yokai*, always having to have every advantage? Like he wasn't heart-attack-inducing scary already?

Without waiting for an answer, I turned to face my enemy. I couldn't see his face, but I could feel the triumph coming off of him in waves. Hear his delight as he started to laugh again.

He raised his arms. From each sleeve snaked out two twisting columns of air. They all reached for me.

"Now."

Ken and Reik did just as I asked. The two columns shot out on either side of me. I breathed deep and reached out with my mind, feeling the power of both elements, and the incredible control that both boys were holding over them. Gently, I added my own mental hold on each column. Ken adjusted quickly. Reik offered up a bit more resistance.

Fuma Jinnae's tentacles of air reached me. They closed about me, one on each limb.

I ignored the terror. It tried to shut my brain down, but I refused. I invited the blasting ice and air to combine their powers, gave them a mental picture of them working together to defeat the demon. They began to merge, but it was just the thinnest line of overlap. Someone or something was resisting. Or maybe I was too tired, too depleted from lending my energy to the plants and vines before. I just didn't have the power or knowledge needed.

I let out a shriek as I was lifted in the air. I pushed away the memories trying to surface and just concentrated on making the merge happen.

It didn't progress any further. This wasn't going to work.

I would not fail. I closed my eyes against my enemy's delight. I could not fail! I'd come too far and I could not risk Ken and Reik and everyone in Ryu. I opened my mind, my heart. I sent out a plea. *Help us. Please.*

The demon's laughter stopped. His glowing eyes widened in anticipation.

But something had heard me. Something huge and terrifying and wonderful. Something that rushed into the glen, filling the air, making the earth bulge, sending a burning through my airways and a roaring through my ears. My eyes opened up almost against my will and in the rocky soil of the mountain above me, I saw another set open up and look back at me.

I think I passed out, but only for a second. I snapped back awake as a single shining surge of power shot from the top of the crag into the air.

Fuma Jinnae felt it. He faltered and glanced back, but the bolt disappeared quickly. I hung in his grasp, helpless while he searched the sky and the glen. Then the demon turned back and refocused on me. The rumbling chuckle started again, rolling like thunder.

I was pulled spread eagle in the air. I closed my eyes again, against the end.

But something tickled the edge of my consciousness. A figure moved. I could see it, shining and tinged slightly blue, moving toward me. And then on the other side, another one. Transparent and wispy, with bronzed edges.

I opened my eyes again and they disappeared.

Then I felt it. On either side of me. Someone—something *else*—took hold of the two columns of blasting air and ice.

I could only see them with my eyes shut. A figure made of water, with a tear drop shaped protrusion rising from the midst of her brow. Her eyes were black and silver speckling decorated her form. And on the other side, a figure made of moving wind, more geometric than human in form, with an endless cycle of air dancing in restless patterns, and a young man's reckless grin giving me hope.

They laid gentle hands over my own loosening hold on the blasting columns and pushed them into one solid beam.

"You did it!" Ken shouted. "They've combined!"

There was no time to contradict him. "Aim for the left shoulder," I gasped.

Together we all strained to change the direction of the powerful surge. It moved slowly until we succeeded in aiming the blast of super cooled air right up the demon's sleeve.

Nothing happened.

Then Fuma Jinnae stopped laughing.

Abruptly the two columns erupting from the left sleeve dissipated.

I jerked in the air as my right side fell, and I was left hanging from the holds on my left arm and leg. "The right! Now the right!" I shouted.

It was easier this time, as if the air and the ice

had gotten the hang of it and liked the first taste of success. Our column of cooled air slid right up the right sleeve.

"It's working!" Ken said on a laugh. "Science and magic?"

The last two columns petered out.

The demon roared his anger.

I fell to the ground, fighting to maintain my hold. "Don't stop," I yelled. "Go for the cushion of air at his feet!"

I didn't think we were going to make it. I was tiring. My hold was slipping.

Then the demon started to sink.

The two ethereal forms showed bright in the real world for the briefest of moments, and then winked out.

The column fell apart, and then both ice and wind petered out.

I jumped to my feet, fumbling with my pocket. "Nobody move," I shouted. "This one is mine!"

My enemy stood before me, robbed of his elemental power, but still a dangerous, vengeful spirit.

But I had a weapon for that.

I pulled out my *seihoukei.*

"Go to hell," I shouted at him. Then in Japanese, I said the words to trigger the spell. "You are banished." I threw the thing. It traveled true and struck him straight in the heart.

He shrieked his defiance and roared his anger the entire time it took for the blackness to engulf him. I reveled in it. Smirked my triumph at him as, in the end, he popped out of existence just as the Tengu had. Something small dropped to the earth where he'd been.

I stumbled as Ken and Reik came up beside me.

"I cannot believe that just happened," Reik said.

"Did you see something there, just for a

moment? Two somethings?" Ken asked.

"Thank you. Thank you," I said to them both.

And then I collapsed at their feet.

Epilogue

I awoke in my bed, back at Tak and Noff's. Hitomi was dozing in a chair beside my bed. She snapped awake when she heard me stir.

"The demon?" I croaked as I sat straight up. My mouth was desert-dry.

"Gone." She poured me a glass of water from a carafe. "And he won't be back for a very long time." She glanced over my head and I looked up to see a little bird staring back at me. "Go and tell them she's awake," Hitomi ordered. With a little chirp of affirmation and a shake of its tail, it flew off.

"I was afraid it was a dream," I rasped. I lay back—then jerked upright again. "Akemi?"

She shook her head. "The Council says she's likely in JanFran, being held by Inaba."

I sat up, swinging my legs over the side.

"But Mei?" Hitomi squeezed my hand. "Boru is alive."

My shoulders slumped. Tears formed at the corners of my eyes. "I'm so glad." I looked up. "Where is she?"

"In her home. She'll rest easier there."

"I have to see her." I glanced askance at her. "Something happened out there that I don't understand."

"She'll want to see you, too."

"I'm leaving, Hitomi." I braced myself for the argument. "I'm going after Akemi."

"I know." She reached down and pulled a backpack from under the bed. "I'm going with you." She rolled her eyes. "They can keep their scout trials."

"No, you're not."

"Yes, she is." Ken appeared in the doorway, yawning. His old pack was strapped to his back, too.

"Keep it down or you'll wake the rest of them."

Sho slipped in beside him. "The Council's still at it. You should hear them. They are planning your life down to the nanosecond. Full scale training, hours of sleep, even your diet." He made a face.

I shook my head. "I made my decision. I know what I am. But they cannot order me."

"Order us," Sho corrected. He pulled another pack from the hall. "I'm going too—and I'm getting my chance to fight back. We're in this together."

I teared up again, just looking around at them. Just weeks ago I would have panicked at the mere thought. I was probably being stupid. It was going to be dangerous. But I was so glad to have them.

I stood and began pulling my hair back into a ponytail—and I grinned when Ken pulled the elastic from his wrist and did the same.

"I like your hair down," I said, "but I have missed seeing you do that."

He smiled back at me. "I like your hair down too."

"Eww. Stop it, both of you," Sho ordered. He checked his watch. "We'll have to slip out while they are still arguing. Once they reach a consensus, I don't think they plan to even let you sleep until morning."

"Let them plan what they like," said Ken.

"Let's go," I said. "We're going to do this our way."

Author's Note:

Thank you for reading *Eye of the Ninja!* I
sincerely hope you enjoyed it.

Would you like to know when my next book is
released? Sign up for my newsletter at my website:

http://www.dmmarlowe.com

You can also connect with me on:

On Facebook

On Twitter

or at

http://www.RedDoorReads.com

And don't miss the second book in the Eye of
the Ninja Chronicles:

Obsidian's Eye

Coming in December 2015

About the Author

D.M. Marlowe lives in North Carolina with her family and two cats. When she is not spoiling them all, she is probably writing. Failing that, she's likely lost in movie or a book, on a long walk, gardening, or hanging with her friends.

In her other life, she is a USA Today Bestselling Author of Regency Historical Romance for adults. You can find her other incarnation at www.DebMarlowe.com

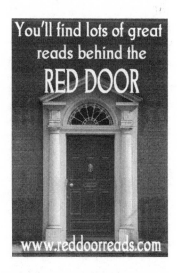

Made in the USA
Charleston, SC
20 November 2015